NORTHERN HEIST

Also by Richard O'Rawe

Blanketmen: An Untold Story of the H-Block Hunger Strike

Afterlives: The Hunger Strike and the Secret Offer that Changed Irish History

In the Name of the Son: The Gerry Conlon Story

A RUCTIONS O'HARE NOVEL

NORTHERN HEIST

RICHARD O'RAWE

MELVILLE HOUSE
BROOKLYN • LONDON

NORTHERN HEIST

First Melville House Printing: February 2021
Originally published in the UK by Merrion Press

Melville House Publishing
46 John Street
Brooklyn, NY 11201

and

Melville House UK
Suite 2000
16/18 Woodford Road
London E7 0HA

mhpbooks.com
@melvillehouse

ISBN: 978-1-61219-964-1
ISBN: 978-1-61219-904-7 (eBook)

Library of Congress Control Number: 2021930413

Printed in the United States of America
10 9 8 7 6 5 4 3 2 1

A catalog record for this book is available from the Library of Congress

NORTHERN HEIST

ONE

They say lazyboneitis is in the blood. It isn't in James 'Ructions' O'Hare's blood. Not when it comes to robbing banks.

At RJ's gym, on Belfast's Boucher Road, Ructions watches his childhood friend, Billy Kelly, set down dumbbells on the weight bench and inspect his bulging biceps. He likes what he sees.

A female fitness trainer yells at her aerobics class, exhorting the masochistic faithful to spill even more sweat. A middle-aged Arnold Schwarzenegger lookalike, in a tight pair of latex shorts, with clenched fists in black fingerless gloves, strolls across the floor. Mini-Arnold's eyes inspect the pot-bellied and the over-the-hillers. Chesney Hawkes' 'The One and Only' blasts over the loudspeakers as Mini-Arnold grins at himself laciviously in a floor-to-ceiling mirror. He sees Billy, winks and strolls over towards the pull-up bar. Billy, the pocket-sized champion weightlifter, opens his bottle of water and puts it to his lips.

Ructions – forty-five years old, blond hair, full lips, thin Roman nose and athletic build – lies on the bench, breathes deeply and prepares to start his set of bench-curls with the dumbbells. After only five bench-curls, Billy's upside-down face appears above him.

'One hundred and fifty large? Before the move? That's what you said. You're going to give me—'

Ructions sets down the dumbbells, sits up and wags his finger. 'Ah, ah, ha, Billy.'

'Let me get this right ...'

'Uh-huh?'

'You're going to give me one hundred and fifty—'

'I'm not *giving* you anything, Billy.'

'Now,' Billy says, 'your client—'

'Uh-huh?'

'Who we both know well—'

'We know a lot of people well, and any of them could be the person to *whom* you are referring.'

Billy ignores Ructions' provocations. 'Let's call this person to *whom* I am referring Robin Hood.'

Ructions feigns surprise. 'You've guessed my client's name.'

'So, Robin Hood is going to give me ...' Billy looks about, making sure he will not be overheard, 'one hundred and fifty thousand pounds *before* the job is done?'

'Yes.'

Billy's foxy eyes try to read Ructions' face. 'Nice bait.'

Ructions does not disguise his ire. 'Nice bait? Nice fucking bait? Are you serious?'

'There's a catch,' Billy says, pointing to Ructions' chest. 'C'mon, amigo. This is your best mate you're talking to. What is it?'

Ructions puts his arms on Billy's shoulder. 'You and me – we joined the Immaculata Boxing Club together, didn't we?'

'We sure did.'

'And I taught you how to swim in the Falls Baths, didn't I?'

'No,' Billy says. 'I taught you.'

Ructions is reminded that Billy will be a controversialist to the day he dies. 'Take my word for it, Bill, there is no catch. Once the money is in your hands, it's yours. So, if the move goes ahead, you get paid the big bucks. If, at the last minute, it gets called off, you still get paid the big bucks. If your boys get knocked off by the cops, they eventually come out of the nick to the big bucks.'

Billy strokes his black moustache. 'I see.'

'And remember this – you're the boss man. You pay your employees what *you* think they're worth.' Gone is the frivolity as Ructions whispers in Billy's ear. 'Billy, believe me, it doesn't get much better than this.'

'Robin's no philanthropist.'

'I never said he was.'

'So, for him to claw back his money – and get the wages he's used to – this thing has to work.'

'Bingo.'

'Ructions O'Hare,' Billy says, beaming, 'you must be one hundred and ten per cent.'

'Aren't I always?'

'I'm in. You knew that anyway. You knew that before you came to me.' Billy inspects his biceps in the mirror and sings, 'I am the one and only ...' He falls silent for a few seconds and then turns to Ructions. 'You fellas must be expecting a heavy haul.'

'I'm an optimist, Billy. I always expect a good result.' Ructions had anticipated that Billy's greed would kick in sooner or later, and he is not disappointed.

'Can we say two hundred, Ructions? Our pal, Robin, he can do that, can't he?'

'No.'

'That's it?'

'That's it.'

Billy nods. 'Be thankful for small mercies, eh?'

'Small mercies can be plenty costly.'

'Yeah. Well, as I say, I'm in.' Billy lifts his towel to go, and then stops. 'Oh, I forgot to ask – how many players do I need?'

'Five max, maybe less – if you'd a mind to do the prep work yourself and go no-frills.'

'Hey! You're looking at "No-Frills Kelly".'

'And one more thing.'

'Yeah?'

'I might need you to do some overtime. I probably won't, but if I do, I'll look after you.'

'Time-and-a-half?'

'Double-time.'

'I'm your man.'

Seamus McCann is a man who thinks the world of himself. Lanky and thin, and with a sombre disposition, this former commander of the South Down IRA Brigade looks more like a door-to-door Mormon missionary than someone who has spent the best part of his life plotting to kill British soldiers and police.

The dark mornings are upon them, and Seamus and Ructions are the only people on Bright Castle golf course, outside Downpatrick.

Ructions puts on his golf glove, takes out his driver and turns his attention to the first fairway. 'Is there any point in hitting a ball?'

'It'll lift soon,' Seamus says, his head tilting backwards as he scans the mist for signs of a break in the weather.

Ructions inhales the dewy crispness in the air as Seamus slowly pulls back his driver and drills the ball into the lifting mist. 'Straight up the middle.'

'You think so?'

'I know so. I haven't missed this fairway in ten years.'

Ructions pushes his tee into the ground and sets a golf ball on top of it. He takes some practice swings and focuses: arms straight, eye on the ball and a sharp strike. His ball flies straight into the trees to the right.

'A decent effort,' Seamus says, 'but you didn't aim for the fairway. You'll find your ball easy enough.'

The two men pull their golf trolleys up the fairway.

'Do you ever miss it, Seamus? The IRA … the struggle?'

'Nah. It'd run its course. Too many people died for too little, Ructions, and too much time was spent in jail. Like, I've done twelve solid years.'

'Yeah, you told me that last time.'

'Did I? There y'are now. You were saying?'

'Saying what?'

'About big money.'

'Oh, right. My client—'

'Panzer O'Hare—'

Ructions gives Seamus the undertaker's stare: measured and stern. 'My uncle is not the client.'

Seamus studies Ructions with bemused eyes. *Are you trying to read my thoughts, Ructions? You are, you fucking reprobate.*

Seamus cannot turn back the tide of a smile. Neither can Ructions. Both men have worked together before, and each knows that Panzer is the client, but for Ructions to acknowledge it would be unprofessional. Seamus puts up his hands. 'Sorry about that.'

Ructions nods his acceptance of the apology. They walk towards the trees. 'My client is committed to investing a large sum of money in a team that would be prepared to hold some people for twenty-four hours – thirty-six max.'

'Yes?'

'The money would be paid up front.'

'Before the move?'

'Yes.'

'So all they've to do is to hold people till the job is over? Nothing else?'

'That's it.'

'And the money, it'd be …'

'Made available twenty-four hours before the job commences.'

Seamus points towards the trees. 'Your ball is in there.'

The two men go into the trees to search for Ructions' ball. Ructions finds it and takes a club out of his golf bag.

Seamus walks up the fairway. His thoughts are like dodgem cars crashing into one another. *We get paid before the move? But no percentage of the take? Old Panzer must be expecting some turn. Demand a percentage of the take. Hold on there, Seamus, ye boy ye. Ructions will walk if you do that. Maybe he won't. He'll get another team. He will. He won't. He will.*

Ructions chips his ball out of the trees. The mist has lifted, as Seamus had predicted. His ball is in the middle of the fairway, as he had also predicted. He takes out his five wood and drives the ball to the edge of the green.

'Nice shot,' Ructions says. 'You should make your par.' Ructions hits his ball up the centre of the fairway. They amble on.

'If a man was to express an interest in this job,' Seamus says haughtily, 'what, ahh, what sort of wages might he expect to take home, like?'

'One hundred and fifty large.'

Seamus' arching eyebrows tell Ructions everything he needs to know. Realising immediately that he has made a serious faux pas, Seamus tries to sound non-committal. 'Not bad. How many men?'

'That'd be up to the controller, but it's straightforward enough. I'd say three – four at the very most. And it'd be up to the controller how much he pays his workers. As long as the job gets done, that's none of my business.'

'I see.' Seamus stops and turns to Ructions. 'And how much money is there in the job?'

'That's none of *your* business.'

Seamus can't shackle the greedy voice in his head: *ask for a percentage of the take*. 'Ah, but it *is* my business. I'd like to think there'd be a percentage—'

'Shh!' Ructions says, as he zips up the top of his golf bag and unclips the button on his glove. 'Be seeing you, Seamus.' Ructions puts out his hand.

Astonished at the sudden turn of events, Seamus automatically takes Ructions' hand, but his grip is weak.

'This conversation,' Ructions says, 'never happened, okay?'

Seamus looks like a man who has pulled his house apart and still cannot find his winning lottery ticket. 'Wow, Ructions, wow! We can talk about this, can't we?'

Ructions looks at his watch. 'I need to go. I've to be up the road for half-eleven.'

Seamus has no idea where 'up the road' might be, and he cares even less. Sensing that his stock is dwindling away, he decides to play the man-to-man card, chuckling and holding up his hands appealingly. 'Come on now, Ructions, you're not gonna blame me for having a rattle, are you?'

'You declared your hand,' Ructions says, 'and I've moved on. That's it.'

Seamus smiles and points a golf club at Ructions. 'You'd have done exactly the same thing. Admit it.'

If Seamus finds the situation amusing, Ructions doesn't. He rolls his head from one side to the other, as if evaluating his options.

'I got greedy,' Seamus says. 'It won't happen again.'

'No more shit talk.'

'Gotcha, buddy.'

No, I've got you, Seamybo – and by the cobblers too. 'Okay. Now, if I *was* to give you this job, I'd expect the same protocols as before.'

'I know – no forensic traces left behind, everything on a need-to-know basis.'

'I'd want a clean, professional operation.'

'Isn't it always?'

'As always, you're the only one on your side who knows who I am, and I'm the only one on my side who knows who you are. We keep it that way – just you and me. We watch each other's backs.'

'Ructions, I'm the only person alive who knows the names of the volunteers who stiffed fourteen Brits and cops. I know how to keep my trap shut.'

'I know you do, but what has to be said has to be said, and just when we're on the subject of—'

'You don't have to—'

'Listen to me—'

'I'm telling you—'

'Fuckin' listen to me!' Ructions snaps. *You're not an IRA commander now, Seamybo. I give the orders, and you take them.* 'My client would be really pissed off if the IRA turned up at his door—'

'That won't happen,' Seamus says icily.

'It'd better not.'

One shallow breath later, and Seamus' irritation finds its voice. Are you threatening me?'

'I don't do threats. I state the position on behalf of my client.'

'Don't talk to me like I'm a little boy.'

'I'd never do that.'

'It sounded very like it.'

'If it did, then I apologise.'

Seamus swallows hard. 'Okay. The IRA won't find out about this from my end. You've my word of honour on that.'

Ructions puts on his glove again, unzips his golf bag and takes out a club. 'I'll finish this hole,' he says. As he readies himself to take his shot, he turns to Seamus. 'One last thing before we get down to the nitty-gritty ...'

'What?'

'No regrets.'

'I'm not with you.'

Ructions lets almost thirty seconds pass. 'It's simple: I don't want you getting your greedy head on again after the job. I don't want you whinging in my ear that you want more dough. The deal we do now is the only deal there is or will be. Are you with me?'

Seamus is aggrieved, almost to the point of distraction. 'Are you trying to make an asshole out of me altogether?'

'No. I'm stating—'

'The position on behalf of your client. I know. I heard you the last time.'

Ructions puts out his hand again. 'Do we have a deal?'

Seamus takes Ructions' hand and this time his grip is firm. 'We have a deal.'

TWO

Finbarr O'Hare's face is as pallid as wet bonding plaster and his eyes are as black as the devil's tongue. His father, Johnny 'Panzer' O'Hare, and Gerard 'Geek' O'Reilly – red-haired, red-faced and red-necked – watch Finbarr as he emerges from the farmhouse, which is affectionately known as the 'Big House'. The 22-year-old strides purposefully across the farmyard towards the middle barn. Panzer rubs the grey stubble on his chin. *There's something on that gobshite's mind, something nasty.* Panzer's suspicions are compounded when Finbarr lifts a pitchfork from the side of the barn and disappears through the barn door. 'Go see what he's up to,' Panzer says to Geek.

In the middle barn, two mechanics, Rudy and 'Apple', are looking under the hood of a lorry. Another mechanic is down in the pit, working on the underside of a black Nissan car. Three piles of new tyres are stacked neatly in a corner. In another corner, fifty used car batteries and new exhaust parts fill the elevated shelving. A radio blasts out the latest hits from an oil-stained bench. A bare-breasted woman smoking a large cigar looks down from a calendar.

Finbarr walks over to the two mechanics and, holding the pitchfork in both hands, thrusts it into Apple's left thigh. There is a scream of unsolicited agony as Apple turns around, the spanner in his hand poised to strike back. Finbarr puts the pitchfork to Apple's neck, one hand flat against the base of the tool and the other holding the shaft from above. Apple drops the spanner.

Geek charges into the barn. 'What the fuck's going on here?'

'Don't ever call me a bastard again, or I swear,' Finbarr says with a wicked grin on his face, 'I'll leave your windpipe so full of holes, people will think it's a cheese grater.'

'I didn't—'

'Shut your fuckin' grease-trap!' Finbarr growls, his hands gripping the pitchfork even tighter.

'Finbarr,' Geek shouts, 'put it down and get out! Go on, get out ta fuck.'

Finbarr backs off, the pitchfork still pointed at Apple.

'Rudy, bring Apple over to the Big House and patch him up.'

'You've got off light,' Finbarr says as he reaches the barn door. 'Next time ...'

'Out, Finbarr,' Geek orders. 'Now!'

Finbarr leaves.

Apple puts his hand on his thigh, and when he brings it up again, it's coated in blood. 'The bastard stuck me in the leg! I'll—'

'You'll thank your lucky stars he didn't stick you in the windpipe,' Geek says.

'Are you going to let him away with this?' Apple says in a hysterical voice.

'I'm going to report it to the boss.'

'Is that it? You're going to tell Daddy his son was a bold boy? Is that all you're going to do?'

'What else do you want me to do? Shoot him? Maybe I should tell Panzer O'Hare you want his son shot?'

Apple screws up his face and turns to Rudy. 'Fuck this. Take me to the hospital.'

Rudy looks at Geek, who nods his approval.

Ructions pulls up into the O'Hare farmyard, switches off the ignition and stares at the bronze statue of his grandfather on his horse, Phantom. The plaque on the plinth simply reads: THE DEVIL. Ructions had hardly known his legendary horse-dealing ancestor, but he has a vivid memory from his own sixth birthday, of standing outside the large gateway to the family's stables in Yewtree Street, off Belfast's Falls Road, and of holding his Granny Mary's hand.

He still recalls the detestable fawn overcoat that covered his knees, the woolly ski mask that roasted his ears and the hearty pong of horse manure. In his granny's other hand was a small white pipe, which she sometimes wedged into the right side of her toothless mouth. From beneath her black shawl, whiffs of white hair stuck out, while dough-coloured skin scarcely covered jutting cheek and jaw bones. 'Keep your eyes peeled, James,' Granny Mary had said, sucking on the pipe. 'The Devil and his disciples will be coming soon.' Bewildered, the young lad looked all around. On the far side of the stables' entrance, the yellow streetlight seemed to flare up before becoming smothered in the early morning fog.

Even now, decades later, Ructions can hear the clip-clop of hoofs on the cobblestones as three horsemen emerged from the fog at the entrance to the stables. In the middle had been The Devil, hunched and riding bareback on his palomino gelding, Phantom. On each side of him were his sons, Johnny and Bobbie. Bobbie, Ructions' father, was leaning forward, stroking his horse's ear.

Ructions can still remember how he had shuddered at the sight of The Devil on horseback. The lapels of his grandfather's ankle-length brown overcoat had been pulled up to meet his black, crumpled hat. The only visible facial feature was his eyes, which, in the child's vivid imagination, seemed to be glowing red. The Devil glanced down at Granny Mary, touched his hat with his riding crop, and steered Phantom to the left, breaking into a trot in the direction of Raglan Street. Granny Mary saluted her husband by raising her pipe, a lipless smile spreading on her sallow face. To this day, Ructions could recollect how he burned with envy as twelve of The Devil's disciples followed their principal down the street on their way to the docks, where the animals would be shipped to England for sale.

The sound of an approaching engine catches Ructions' attention. Panzer, with Geek alongside him, drives around the side of the Big House in his four-seater golf buggy, a golf bag set in the back of the vehicle.

Stopping some way from Ructions, Panzer turns to Geek, 'And how is Apple?'

'It's not much more than a scratch,' Geek says. 'He'll survive.'

'I know Apple. He'll remember this. I should talk to him.'

'You should talk to Finbarr.'

'Sure.'

'I mean it, boss. The lad has a shotgun temper.'

'I hear you. Now, how's he coming along otherwise?'

'You asked me a year ago to prepare him to take over the hands-on side of the business ...'

'Uh-huh?'

'Well, he's almost there.'

'Almost?'

'Almost,' Geek says. 'Besides his short fuse—'

'Yes?'

'He can be a bit chilled out, you know?'

'Okayyy.'

Geek chops the air with his hand. 'Don't get me wrong, he has only to be told something once and he gets it. Like, this kid is ... he's laser-sharp. For example, your bar isn't making money—'

'It hasn't for years.'

'Finbarr has an idea to turn that around.'

'He has?'

'Yeah. He thinks you should lease it out at a reasonable rate and do a deal with the lessee on the profits from the gaming machines. That way, instead of losing dough, the bar makes you a few quid, and you still own the licence and the property.'

Panzer tilts his head thoughtfully and strokes his ear. 'That's not bad, not bad at all.'

'If, if you were of a mind to lease it out,' Geek says, 'I'd like a rattle at it. I've been in business before.'

'I know. If I remember right, your taxi business was flying until—'

'Until that cunt Tiny Murdoch decided to close me down.'

'Remind me again.'

'He sent the 'RA to warn me to close down my taxi depot and when I didn't, he had it burnt.'

'And then he broke your leg?'

'Yes. The cunt. With a breeze block.' Unconsciously, Geek reaches down to rub his right leg.

'When was that?' Panzer asks.

Geek responds immediately. 'Six years ago – 12 October 1998.'

Panzer raises his left eyebrow. 'If I were you, I'd be careful about calling Murdoch a cunt. You're right, he is a cunt, but he's an IRA cunt, and that makes him dangerous.'

'The fucker had my leg smashed with a breeze block – for nothing.'

'I know he did,' Panzer says, his voice trailing off. 'Now, back to Finbarr.'

Geek is not ready to return to the subject of Finbarr. He must make sure that the idea of him leasing Panzer's pub is firmly fixed in his boss's head. 'You'll keep me in mind, though, if you do decide to lease the pub?'

'Sure,' Panzer says. 'So ... Finbarr.'

Geek runs his tongue around his parched lips. 'He can be off-piste, if you get my meaning.'

'Will he be able to run this place?' Panzer asks pointedly.

'He's not quite there yet but yes – yes, he will.'

Geek glances suspiciously at Panzer. 'Is there something you're not telling me, boss? Why's it suddenly so important that Finbarr gets involved?'

'You've had him for a year now, so it's hardly sudden. Look, he's turning out to be a pain in the ass, if you must know,' Panzer says, barely able to disguise his exasperation. 'He needs the discipline of responsibility.'

'Don't all kids? I'll take him down to Dublin with me next week, shall I?'

'Good idea. But make it clear to him that he's there only as an observer. These druggies are dangerous hombres.'

'Tell me about it,' Geek says, walking away. He turns back. 'This Dublin thing ...'

'What about it?'

'Are we getting into the drugs business, permanently, like?'

'No. This is a one-off.'

'Good. I don't like drugs.'

Seeing Geek move away, Ructions approaches Panzer and gets into the passenger seat of the golf buggy. Not for the first time his attention is drawn to his uncle's startling weight loss. *What's going on with you, Panzer? What are you not telling me? You're looking more like The Devil every day. Has his errant spirit transferred to you?* 'It's a good day for mountaineering,' Ructions says.

'I need to catch a dog trial first,' Panzer says, driving over behind the stables to his dog track.

The oval-shaped, sandy track is 660 yards in circumference, but the trial distance is only 525 yards – the length of an average greyhound race. Private greyhound trials have always been a nice earner for Panzer; his discretion is celebrated, and owners throughout Ireland know that whatever times their dog records, it never leaves his track.

Panzer speaks to a middle-aged man in a duffle coat. He has a hugely impressive Salvador Dali moustache and a lanky teenage sidekick. Ructions takes out a fifty-pence piece and twiddles it from one finger to the next. Down at the starting stalls, the handlers put two yelping dogs into the traps. One handler speaks into a two-way radio. The artificial hare is released. The stall doors open as the hare flashes past, and the dogs bolt after it. As the leading dog blazes past the finishing post, Panzer and the man with the Dali moustache click their stopwatches simultaneously, while the teenager goes after the greyhounds. After a while, Panzer looks down and scuffs the ground. Ructions has seen this routine before; it's anti-up time. No one gets ripped off, but Panzer always comes out of these things richer than when he went in.

A fat rat disappears behind the back of the stables and scurries along the wall into the nearby field. 'I'm gonna have to do something about these rats,' Panzer says as he gets into the driving seat of the golf buggy.

The drive across Hannahstown to the Black Mountain is interrupted only by occasional greetings from walkers and joggers, most of whom know Panzer as 'The King of Hannahstown' – a title bestowed upon him by an over-zealous press. They pull up just below the BBC Television mast and alight. Ructions lifts the golf bag and slings it over his shoulder. A pathway of squishy, rubbery mats cuts a corridor across the mountain. It seems to Ructions that the mats, with their hundreds of tiny squares, are losing the battle against the encroaching moss and bogland. Nature is the real king up here. Soon they cross the wooden bridge, veer right, and then carry on to the end of the rubber pathway. They toddle along silently, each man cultivating his own thoughts, until eventually they cut down the mountain and halt before a steep drop.

'My God,' Panzer exclaims, 'will you look at that?' He inhales deeply, his chest expanding and his shoulders rising and falling. 'I've been up here hundreds of times and every time, it just … it just knocks the malt out of me.'

'It never lets you down, that's for sure,' Ructions replies, his eyes straying right to the hazy Mountains of Mourne.

Belfast's two giant shipyard gantry cranes, 'Samson and Goliath', reach up into the ripe late-autumn sky. Two cross-channel ferries pass each other in the shipping lanes of Belfast Lough. A doe rabbit bolts out of the side of the mountain and runs into a bank to their right.

Ructions reaches into the golf bag. 'Five iron, M'Lord?'

'Oh, I don't think so, O'Hare,' Panzer says fancifully. 'I rather think I want distance today. Perhaps the driver?'

'An excellent choice, M'Lord.'

Both men put their tees in the ground and set their golf balls on top of them. Ructions' practice swings have the fluidity of one who knows what he's doing.

'So, nephew, our insider,' Panzer says, 'do you trust him? I mean, do you really trust him to—'

'He's a she,' Ructions says, 'and yeah, she's sound.' Ructions draws back slowly and drives the ball so far that it disappears beneath the curvature of the mountain.

'Not bad,' Panzer says, standing over his ball. He steps away and sits down on a large stone. 'So tell me about her?'

'Her name's Eleanor Proctor—'

'A Prod?'

'No, she's a Catholic who married a Prod. You would've known her old man … Tommy O'Driscoll.'

'"The Fair Man"?'

'One and the same.'

'I knew Tommy well. He was the best councillor ever to sit on Belfast City Council. Did me a few turns with planning applications, he did.' Panzer addresses his golf ball, then turns back to Ructions. 'What's she like, this Eleanor?'

'She's feisty.'

'What way feisty?'

'She knows her own mind; she'll not be led.'

'Not even by you?'

Ructions hesitates as he tries to find the right words. 'She's a strong woman.'

'You never answered my question.'

'She's helping us because she wants to.'

'Ah, but why does she want to?' Panzer asks. 'That's what I want to know. What's in it for her?'

'Me.'

'You?'

'Me.'

Panzer kicks the ground below him, just like he had done before he settled up with the greyhound owner with the Dali moustache.

Come on, Panzer. Spit it out – whatever it is.

'You're wondering what's going through my mind, aren't you?' Panzer says.

Ructions shrugs.

'I'll tell you. I'm asking myself if my right arm has fallen for the mark.'

'Don't be ridiculous.'

'Don't be ridiculous? I'll be as ridiculous as I fucking well want to be.'

Ructions zips up his golf bag, an act not unnoticed by Panzer. 'Shall we head back?' Ructions says.

Panzer stands directly in front of Ructions. 'You don't think I've a right to ask hard questions?'

'Sure you have, and I've no problem answering them. But suggesting I've fallen for the mark—' Ructions points his finger. 'That's way out of order. I deserve better than that from you and you know it.'

Panzer puts his hands on Ructions' shoulders and looks into his eyes. 'Ructions, son, this is serious shit, and I don't mind admitting I get the jitters every time I think of this job. I can't remember myself ever being so edgy.'

'So am I. But it'll be all right, boss. Believe me, it'll be sweet.'

Panzer sighs deeply. 'I honestly hope so – for both our sakes.'

'You've my word on it, it'll be fine.'

'Your word is good enough for me.' Panzer waves his hand dismissively. 'Your turn.'

Ructions unzips his golf bag, takes out a ball and hits it down the mountain.

'So tell me, how did Eleanor meet the Prod?'

'Eleanor met Frank Proctor at Queen's University. They were both on the Students' Executive Management Committee and they hit it off. She graduated in sociology and politics and he in economics. She became a social worker, and he's a banker.'

'Does she know about Maria?'

'Yep.'

'She can't be too happy about her being around.'

'She isn't, but I've promised I'll drop her.'

'I'll leave that end of things to you. You've a flair for handling the women,' Panzer says, addressing his ball again. 'That Maria comes from good stock. Her father, Mickey McArdle, dabbled in the greyhounds for a while. Good man. Helped me out on a few occasions when I needed to … well, smoothed some wrinkles.'

'What type of wrinkles?'

'The less said the better, Ructions. Let's just say, he's top-drawer. Mickey's a real family man, so end things well with his daughter. Now, what'll Eleanor be like in the cop shop?'

'I've sat her down and talked her through it. She'll do. Besides, she's the last person the cops will suspect.'

'So the last shall be first – Matthew 20:16,' Panzer says sternly. 'Ructions, make no mistake about it, *nobody – but fuckin' nobody* – will be beyond suspicion after this little set-to.'

Ructions nods. 'You're right.'

'I hope *you're* right.'

'I know I am.'

Close by, barking dogs distract Panzer at the top of his backswing. This results in his golf ball slicing to the left. Panzer turns to Ructions. 'Fuckin' mongrels,' he says in disgust. 'Who else knows about this?'

Ructions clamps his lips shut in case his thoughts tumble out. *Who else would know about it, Panzer? I've been working on this robbery for over two years – on my own. Know why I've worked on my own, Panzer? Because I won't fuckin' tout on myself to the cops.* 'You, me and Eleanor,' Ructions says cordially.

'We'll need somewhere to dump the loot after the job.'

'I've a camel's hump sorted.' Ructions whispers into Panzer's ear, telling him the location of the dump.

'I like it.'

Ructions can sense a dangerous scepticism in Panzer's tone. It's as if Panzer has yet to be convinced of the robbery's bona fides. He reckons that a spot of flattery and a pledge of allegiance might ease the situation. 'Boss, I want to be clear about something: this is your job, not mine. If you want to pull it, that's fine with me.'

'It's *our* job,' Panzer says, grinning. He pats Ructions affectionately on the cheeks. 'You're a thoroughbred, kiddo, a fuckin' thoroughbred.' Panzer embraces Ructions. 'It's you and me, Ructions, all the way. Fifty-fifty – that's it.'

'There's one good thing …'

'Only one?'

'The cops will think the wrap-the-green-flag-around-me boys are behind it.'

Panzer hesitates before replying. 'That'll hold up, but it's difficult to say for how long. Remember this – irrespective of what the cops think, the IRA will *know* they didn't do it and if they find out that we *did* do it, they'll have Tiny Murdoch up looking for his fifty per cent tax.'

'Aye. Like we'd give it to them too! Fuckers!' Ructions replies with a sneer.

'The Provos can be a right pain in the dick when they want to be,' Panzer says, grim-faced. 'We can't afford one loose word. No outsiders.'

Ructions coughs delicately. 'Boss, don't take this the wrong way—'

'I know what you're going to say.'

'I'd prefer if—'

'If Finbarr is shut out.'

Ructions winces. 'Does he know about the job?'

Panzer lies. 'No, he doesn't. And if he did, would it matter?'

Ructions pretends to clean the face of his golf club with a cloth in order to avoid Panzer's stare. 'I think it would.'

'Why? Why would it matter if I were to tell my son about the job? He's a smart kid.'

'I know that, but he's unpredictable and we can't afford unpredictability.'

'I don't accept this unpredictability bullshit,' Panzer says. 'You've a bee in your bonnet about Finbarr.'

'I wouldn't say that.'

'I would.'

Ructions decides that, on this occasion, silence is better than confrontation.

Panzer sets a ball on top of a tee and lies again. 'My son doesn't know anything about the job and he won't find out from me.' He sweeps the horizon in front of him with his driver, addresses his ball and smashes it down the mountainside. 'That's more like it,' he says.

The vital concession secured, Ructions knows to move on. 'I swear to God,' he says, 'I've had sleepless nights going over the people I'd pick to do this heist. Who'd cover our backs if there's a shoot-out? Who'd be blabbermouths in the cop shop? Who'd have the wit to keep their traps shut after the job, when the money's in their pockets and the IRA starts beating the bush for answers? Never mind Finbarr. I don't think we should involve *any* of our own boys in this.'

'Not even Geek?'

'Not even him.' Ructions grimaces and, for emphasis, taps the air in front of him with his clenched fist. 'What Geek and the rest of the boys don't know, they can't tell – even if they're taken away and tortured by the paramilitaries – which is very possible.'

'There's a lot of sense in that.'

'Panzer, I've put the deal to the farmers and they've accepted the terms – subject to your final approval, that is.'

'Why doesn't that surprise me? You know, Ructions, my hands are so far into my pockets here, I can count the goosebumps on my balls.'

'I don't doubt it for a second. But the return will be phenomenal. We should be looking at tens of millions. Not only that, but what we don't want is for the farmers to come away from this feeling like they've been cut up.'

'If that's the way it has to be. Who are the farmers?'

'We've used them before: Kelly and McCann.'

'Good choices.'

A police helicopter approaches and hovers about one hundred yards in front of them. A plain-clothes police photographer leans out of the helicopter and takes photographs of the two gangsters. Ructions puts down a golf ball and aims it at the helicopter. He misses. Both men turn their backs and bare their backsides. When they pull up their trousers and turn around, the police photographer gives them the one-finger salute.

THREE

A pink stretch limousine, with music blaring from in-car speakers, pulls up outside Robinson's bar in Belfast's city centre. A window comes smoothly down and a vortex of smoke spirals into the air.

A chauffeur opens the limousine door and helps a young lady in a white dress and wedding veil out of the vehicle. Tucked under her arm, the bride-to-be has a blow-up male doll with an enormous penis. Behind her, fourteen scary 'schoolgirls' in stilettos and loud make-up emerge from the limousine, their ages ranging from seventeen to sixty-four. The women form a conga line and sing and slither towards the doors of the bar, passing by Finbarr O'Hare, three bouncers and at least twenty smoking revellers.

Well-juiced and well-groomed in a blue Armani suit, a grinning Finbarr joins the end of the conga line, which penetrates the packed bar as a passage is made to an elevated, reserved area in a far corner. The schoolgirls take their seats. Some pull out make-up bags. Others look to see who they know in the bar. Finbarr stands around awkwardly.

'Amm ...' he says, 'can I get you ladies a drink?'

Aggie, a blonde, spiky-haired, fifty-something, in a navy miniskirt and white open-necked shirt with loose tie, examines Finbarr and then smiles. 'Oh, you little honey.' She raises her voice. 'Girls, this charming young man wants to buy us a drink.'

'I'll have a gin and tonic, Aggie.'

'Make that two.'

'Brandy and ginger ale.'

'Sit down, handsome,' Aggie says. Finbarr sits down and Aggie grabs and squeezes his cheeks. 'Couldn't you just eat him?'

'You *will* be eating him before the night's out,' one of the girls screams. Squeals of exuberance follow.

Someone says, 'Yvonne, call a waiter.'

'What's your name, lovey?' Aggie asks.

'Finbarr.'

'Finbarr? No way! You're too good-looking to be a Catholic.' Aggie puts her hand at the back of Finbarr's neck, pulls him into her and kisses him, her tongue finding his. He breaks off. 'Wow!' she says. 'This little taig kisses like a Prod!'

Finbarr spots his scruffy friend Peteris and gets up to leave. Aggie grabs his arm. 'Where are you going, gorgeous?'

Finbarr smiles deferentially. 'I've an emergency, missus. I've got to skite. Sorry.'

'But what about our drink? You said you were going to buy us a drink.'

'Some other time, yeah?'

'Some other time, my arse. You said—'

'Piss off, cockaholic!'

'What did you just say there?'

'Hey, you, Pea-dick,' another 'schoolgirl' shouts, 'don't you dare talk to a lady like that.'

Finbarr knows that their wrath is about to descend upon him and he makes for the exit post-haste. Following him is Peteris – black-haired and black-hearted – a Latvian pimp and human trafficker. He whispers in Finbarr's ear as they leave the bar.

Surprisingly, given Peteris' dark persona, his apartment is clean and pleasantly decorated. Finbarr's eyes focus on the five neat lines of cocaine that are laid out on the glass coffee table.

'Help yourself,' Peteris says.

Finbarr snorts a line. His head jerks as he absorbs the hit. 'String 'em up, Sheriff!' he says.

'Is good?' Peteris says.

'Very tasty, Pete. Now where's the chick?'

'In here.' Peteris leads Finbarr into a dimly lit bedroom where a frail, blonde-haired girl, no more than twelve years of age, lies naked on a double bed. 'Fresh tenderloin of beef, my friend,' Peteris says, running his hand up the girl's leg. 'Only shipped in yesterday. Sweet? I not have her myself yet.'

'What've you given her?'

'Rohypnol.'

'What's that?'

'It drug-rape pill. She no remember who fuck her when she wake up.'

'What's her name?'

'Galina.'

With the back of his fingers, Finbarr brushes aside some strands of the girl's blonde hair. 'How much?'

'She virgin.'

'How much?'

'For stranger, two hundred. For you, only one hundred.'

'Fifty.'

'Eighty.'

Finbarr removes three twenty-pound notes from his wallet and, without taking his greedy eyes off Galina, dangles them between his fingers. Peteris glibly takes the notes.

When Finbarr steps out the door of Peteris' apartment, he feels nothing: no remorse, no self-loathing, no guilt. Rohypnol, he thinks – that's a name worth remembering. What was the girl's name? He cannot remember.

Eyes bulbous, drenched in sweat and gasping for air, Ructions springs upright in bed. Maria McArdle puts her arms around him. 'It's all right. It's all right, Ructions. It's a nightmare. Nothing else.' Ructions falls back. Maria goes to the chest of drawers, takes out fresh pyjamas and throws them at him. 'Here, put these on.'

Ructions removes his pyjama top and lies bare-chested on the bed.

'Are you okay?' Maria asks. 'Do you want to talk?'

Ructions waves his hand dismissively.

Maria turns, intending to give Ructions a dirty look, but walks to the window and looks across Belfast harbour. Ructions has told her about the glory days when dozens of cargo ships were moored along the quay. Now, there are only two lifeless cross-channel ferries. She watches a little pilot boat lead a cruise liner up the channel, and she wants to shout, 'Hey! People of the liner. Go back. Turn around. Why are you coming to Suffocation City?' *Fuck! I need to get out of Belfast, out of Northern Ireland.* Jealously, she watches an early-morning plane from George Best city airport endeavouring to gain height. She knows it's not going to Buenos Aires or Los Angeles, but at this stage she'd settle for Malaga.

'Come back to bed, love.'

Maria moves away from the window and throws herself on the bed. She sighs. *Oh, Sweet Jesus, she's having another of those 'Fuck this' moments. I can do without it, kiddo.* It strikes Ructions just how beautiful she is, with her flawless skin, slim body, and natural blonde hair which he twirls affectionately with his finger. He's well aware she's been sighing a lot recently. *Our relationship is on life support and I know why: Eleanor Proctor. I have fallen for the mark, despite what I said to Panzer.*

He remembers better times. It was Kelly's Cellars, in Belfast city centre, and The Dead Handsomes were playing. The place was so crowded there was barely room to lift your drink. Terry Sharpe, the charismatic lead singer, made his way down from the stage during the break and had a drink with Ructions and his two friends. Ructions stood aside at the bar as Maria squeezed through. Terry knew Maria and introduced her to Ructions. The attraction was instant. She had repeated his nickname aloud a few times and told him she didn't know why but 'Ructions' seemed appropriate. At the end of the night, she instantly accepted his offer of Indian food. Both knew they would end up in bed together.

The physical attraction and white-hot sex never waned. But sex, no matter how good, isn't enough to sustain a long-term relationship, especially when a substantial age gap exists. Ructions was well aware that Maria was unsettled: there were clubs, gigs and protests to attend; there were elephants, orangutans and rainforests to save; and there was her dream – South America – to explore. Ructions was just a bank robber. It was a bonus that she was well versed in the art of 'ask no questions', her father being a major green-diesel launderer on the Armagh–Louth border. She couldn't care less what he did for a living; above board or under, it was of no concern to her.

'I don't want to live in Belfast any longer, Ructions. It's oppressive, it's so fucking claustrophobic. When are we leaving?'

Ructions leans over and lifts up a packet of cigarettes. It's empty. He gets out of bed, takes an unopened packet from his coat and gives a cigarette to Maria.

'You're tired of me.' Maria smiles. 'Admit it. You are, aren't you?'

Fucked if I'm getting into this juvenile shit again. 'No.'

'No?' Maria says. 'Is that the best you can come with?'

'What do you want me to come up with? That everything's hunky-dory? Is that what you want to hear, Maria? I can say whatever you want, or I can tell you I know crap when I hear it. Woman accuses man of what she herself feels. 'You're tired of me. Admit it.'

'I can't do this, Ructions.' Maria starts putting on her clothes.

'Where are you going?' Ructions asks.

'Out.'

FOUR

Ructions removes his yellow hard hat and rubs his hair as if to shake out dandruff. *How the hell do workmen wear this crown of thorns from morning to night? And this hi-vis jacket … it's like a second-hand shroud.*

Panzer doesn't seem to have a problem with his disguise. He adjusts the mirror of the open-back jeep and squints intently at the street behind him. A small dry wheeze is followed by a prolonged bout of coughing. 'I'm … out of puff,' he rasps.

Ructions stares. *Sounds to me like you're out of time.*

Panzer recovers. 'What happened between Eleanor and what's his name?'

'You mean her husband? Frank?'

'Yeah, him.'

'She caught Frank banging his secretary.'

'That wouldn't have helped.'

'No.'

There is a mischievous grin on Panzer's face. 'She must be some ride, all the same.'

Ructions sighs. 'She's not a ride.'

Panzer sniggers. 'You're riding her, but it's only business, isn't it?'

Ructions does not respond.

Panzer's mood changes. 'Are you sure she'll be sound if the cops lean on her?'

'She'll hold up.'

Ructions' mobile phone rings. He looks at the number. It's Maria. He turns it off.

'You can't be certain,' Panzer says.

'Certain about what?'

'About the bold Eleanor holding up.'

'I'm telling you, she'll be fine.'

'You say that, but it isn't going in here.' Panzer taps his temple.

'She has to be tight.'

'Why's that?'

'Because she's supplied me with a full rundown of the security system, the rotas, the security guards, the staff levels and the exact amount of money that's in the bank. If that doesn't make her a player—'

'Jesus Aloysius Christ! Will you shake your fucking head, man,' Panzer says dismissively. Clicking his fingers, he adds, 'The cops wouldn't give two fucks about any of that.' He starts coughing again. 'To get to us,' he catches phlegm in his handkerchief, 'they'd dig up Marlon Brando to make her an offer she couldn't refuse.'

Ructions is alarmed at Panzer's deterioration. 'Good God, boss, you look like a corpse that's been sent back amongst the living on weekend parole! Are you all right?'

'Thanks. That's cheered me up.'

'I didn't mean—'

Panzer points a finger. 'Nothing you're saying makes Her Ladyship any less of a potential problem.'

'But how? What would she tell them? I'm the only person she knows. It'll be her word against mine.'

Panzer taps the steering wheel with a pen. 'And a jury would take your word against hers, would they? They'd think you a more upright citizen than the deputy bank manager's wife, would they?' Panzer opens the glove compartment and throws in the pen. 'If she fingers you, she fingers us.'

'She won't finger anybody.'

'Why not? What makes you so sure?'

'You don't want to get it, do you?'

'I fucking do want to get it. Fuck! I want to get it big time, but you're not convincing me.'

Ructions runs his hand across his forehead. From experience he knows that the pistons in Panzer's mind can sometimes turn very slowly. 'She's not on the bank's payroll, so why should she come up on the cops' radar?'

Panzer is still dubious. *She's on your radar, Romeo, because you're letting your dick rule your brain.* Panzer rolls down the window and pretends to adjust the side mirror. He turns his face away from Ructions because he knows his protégé will not like his next proposal. 'When this job is put to bed—'

Ructions has a good idea what's coming next. 'Uh-huh?'

'Why don't we ...?'

'What?'

'You know.'

'No, I don't.'

'Course you do.'

'Clip her? You want her clipped?'

Panzer turns towards Ructions. 'Yeah, I do. Fuck her!' he rasps. 'She's a loose end and we don't do loose ends. Have you forgotten the golden rule? Have you?'

Be calm, don't let him rile you. 'How do we know she hasn't a diary somewhere?' Ructions says. 'Or a recording of her handing me over the bank details? How do you know she's not watching *us* right now – maybe even filming us?' For a split second Ructions thinks he sees alarm in Panzer's eyes. 'Listen, Panzer, my judgement has always been good, hasn't it? I've *never*, in all the years we've been together, screwed up.' Ructions puts up one finger. 'Not once.'

'I can't argue with that.'

'I'm not going to screw up on this one either. If I even get a whimper that she's going to give us grief, I'll put her to sleep myself. I will. No fuckin' sweat. But I'm telling you, she's up for this job.'

Panzer stares at Ructions, lips pursed. He doesn't say it, but he's thinking it: *You'd better be right, my friend*. But now it's time for a change of tack; now it's time to throw the dog a bone. 'Look, kid,' Panzer says smiling, 'I'm your greatest fan and you're my Uri Geller.' Panzer pretends to punch Ructions in the stomach. 'You're the Magic Man. Now, tell me again, how much was in the bank last week?'

'Give or take a few hundred grand.'

Panzer cannot suppress a smile. 'Listen to you, give or take a few hundred grand.'

'Forty-one million in sterling, seven million in euro and two million in foreign currencies, mostly US dollars. Of the sterling, only twenty-eight was usable, the rest was coin and new print. I reckon we should be in a position to harvest about thirty to thirty-five million.'

'Harvest, Ructions? Is that what we do? Harvest bank money?' Panzer has a vision of a field of green money plants, with fifty-pound notes flapping like leaves in the wind. 'Still, why not? The O'Hares: money farmers. I like it. You and Eleanor can't have any contact for at least a couple of years and—'

'She's okay with that.'

'You've told her?'

'Yes.'

'And you believe her?'

'Yes.' *You're still not certain, are you, Panzer? You'd just love to put a bullet in the back of her head and remove even the sniff of a problem, wouldn't you? No, I take that back; you'd love* me *to put a bullet in the back of her head for you. Isn't that the way of it?*

'Heads up,' Ructions says.

Eleanor Proctor – five feet seven inches, thirty-two years old, curvy, with long auburn hair and a spring in her step – walks out of her home carrying a gym bag.

'She's a stunner, amigo, I'll give you that. How long have you been banging her?'

Eleanor gets into her red Volvo and drives off.

'Amm, about a year? I've been chasing her properly since May 2003, but she played hard to get.'

'The old Ructions charm didn't work right away, then?'

'It took a while, but Ructions always gets his woman.'

Panzer laughs. 'How did it start?'

'I set her up.'

'Why doesn't that surprise me?' Panzer says.

'It was at the Bruce Springsteen concert in the RDS stadium in Dublin,' Ructions says. 'She was chatting to her friend, Stacy, outside the venue. I knew who she was, who her husband was. The only reason I was there was because *she* was there. So, I gave a kid a few quid to snatch her bag. I pretended to give chase and got the bag back. She was very grateful.'

'Extremely grateful,' Panzer says.

'In the end,' Ructions says.

The Proctors' garage door opens, and Frank Proctor drives out in a silver Saab.

'I'll catch you later,' Ructions says, getting out of the passenger door.

Panzer lifts the stopwatch on the dashboard, turns the ignition key and leans over to Ructions. 'Make sure you do. We need to talk this thing through some more.'

Ructions gets into his car and drives off, taking to the back streets to get to the gym before Eleanor.

The gym is usually quiet at eight o'clock in the morning. As Ructions waits for Eleanor to arrive, snippets of his conversation with Panzer rampage through his mind like a terrified elephant in a shopping centre. *'Look, kid, I'm your greatest fan ...' Yeah, you're my greatest fan, Panzer – as long as I'm making you cartloads of money. What was it you said? 'You're the Magic Man.' Too fuckin' right, I'm the Magic Man.*

Eleanor's car enters the car park and pulls up alongside Ructions. On the far side of the car park, in the back of a yellow Volkswagen van, a small freckled man with strands of white hair brushed across his pate to conceal his baldness zooms in his video camera on the couple. 'Mr James O'Hare is getting out of his car and is walking towards the car of Mrs Eleanor Proctor.'

Ructions gets into Eleanor's car. They kiss. Eleanor instantly feels the electricity. Ructions offers Eleanor a cigarette. She shakes her head, wipes away a strand of hair from her face. 'I look a mess,' she says defensively.

Ructions toys with her silver earrings, then traces a finger along her breast. 'Actually, you look extremely fuckable.'

'More fuckable than Sweet Maria?'

'Infinitely more fuckable.'

Eleanor shakes her head. 'I want you to get rid of her,' she says.

'She'll be gone soon.'

'When?'

'Very soon. She's already picked up that things are different between us. It's over bar the sighing and sulking.'

'It'd better be. I mean it, James. I'm not going to be yours or anybody else's mistress.'

'Trust me, El.'

'I do.'

Eleanor feels a lessening of the tension in her stomach. She nibbles his ear while pulling down his trouser zip. 'Besides robbing banks, is that all you ever think of?' she says huskily.

'In case you haven't noticed, love, that's your hand on my joystick.'

'Is it? Bad hand.'

A car pulls up close to them and a man and woman carrying gym bags get out. Eleanor takes her hand away and Ructions pulls up his zip. 'Are you okay?' he asks.

'Yes, I'm fine.'

'That doesn't sound very convincing. What's wrong? Out with it.'

'It's you.'

'Me?'

'Yeah, you. James, I'd better not be just a recreational fuck with a bank rota.'

'Hey, that's—'

'Tell the truth. Am I only a way for you to find out what's happening in the bank?'

Ructions shows genuine surprise and pulls back his head to get a better look at Eleanor. 'Can we rewind this tape? I must have missed the first act.'

'You're avoiding the question.'

Ructions looks at Eleanor. *Holy fuck! What do I say?* He folds his arms and turns to her. 'You know what? We should make a clean break now.'

Eleanor reaches across Ructions and opens the car door on his side. 'Away you go then,' she says dispassionately.

Away you go then? Ructions had not expected this reaction from Eleanor. He closes the door. 'Would it be that easy for you?'

'Easy? It'd be the hardest thing I've ever done. But if you want to break up, there's nothing much left to say.'

Fucking tough wee woman this. Ructions puts his arm around Eleanor's neck and presses his forehead to hers. 'Breaking up with you is the last thing in the world I want to happen. And you're not a recreational fuck.' Ructions frowns. 'El, where did that come from?'

Eleanor pulls back, her eyes searching Ructions' face. 'I've fallen in love with you, James.' She points a finger at him. 'But you don't own me. Nobody owns me. And I don't give in to threats. I said I'd help you to rob this bank and I will. But I'm doing so with my eyes wide open.'

'I'd never—'

'Let me finish,' Eleanor says. 'At the start you were just a bit of fun, and I was flattered by the attention you paid me, but things have moved on from then. I've moved on. You've helped me feel alive again. I said I've fallen in love with you and I have. If you don't feel the same way about me—'

Ructions leans over, draws Eleanor to him and kisses her. There is no hiding the passion as his tongue searches out hers. When they pull back, Ructions stares at Eleanor, his face inches from hers. 'You want me to say—'

'I want you to be honest with me. Nothing else.'

He plants another kiss on her lips, a light kiss, a kiss so intimate that it sweeps away all Eleanor's nagging doubts.

Ructions breaks off. 'I love you.' He flops back in his seat. 'Holy Christ! Did I just tell you I loved you?'

'Yes, you did,' Eleanor says jubilantly, her eyes dancing. 'You did – and you meant it!'

Ructions closes his eyes. *Good God! What am I doing? Am I only churning out the words to keep this woman sweet because I can't empty the National Bank of Ireland without her help? Or do I really love her? Do I? Yeah, I fucking do! Christ! Ructions O'Hare, how the fuck did you ever get yourself into this mess?*

Eleanor reaches for her handbag, takes out her make-up bag and reapplies lipstick. Her lips don't need a fresh coat, but she has to be doing something. She puts away the bag. 'Why don't we get out of here, James? Start afresh. Go to London, wherever. I've got money. We can—'

Ructions puts his finger to her lips. 'After,' he murmurs. 'When this is over, we can go wherever we want.'

Eleanor's eyes search his face. 'Do you mean that?'

'Every word of it.'

'Do you know what? I believe you.'

'Mr O'Hare has got out of Mrs Proctor's car and returned to his own car,' the man with the video camera says. His phone rings. 'Oh, hello,' he says, still recording. 'Don't worry on that score; they haven't spotted me.' As Ructions drives off, he shuts down the recorder and concentrates on the phone call. 'There's no doubt, Tiny; the evidence is overwhelming.'

'What is the purpose of your visit to Ireland, sir?' the Irish customs official asks as he examines Serge Mercier's passport.

'To see if your golf courses are as good as they say they are, Monsieur. Are they?'

'Oh, certainly,' the customs official says, handing Serge back his passport. 'Where do you hope to play?'

'My friend tells me, er … Port … Portmarnook?'

'Portmarnock, sir.'

'Portmarnook—'

'No, sir, Portmarn … ock.'

'Portmarn … ock.'

'That's it.'

'Pardonnez-moi.'

'That's okay, sir. It's a fabulous course. You'll enjoy it. The fourteenth and fifteenth holes are amongst the best in the world.'

'How nice.'

'Enjoy your visit, sir.'

FIVE

Ructions and Panzer sit in the hot-food section of a service station on the Belfast–Dublin motorway, their heads almost touching. Panzer kicks Ructions under the table as he looks over Ructions' shoulder.

'Who is it?' Ructions asks.

'Tiny Murdoch, Colm Coleman and two heavies.'

'What are they doing?'

'For fuck sake,' Panzer says, 'they've seen us. They're coming down.'

Robert 'Tiny' Murdoch is six feet six inches tall and has the build of a professional wrestler. He is also a member of the Provisional IRA's general headquarters staff. With the signing of the Good Friday Agreement in 1998, the IRA has disavowed armed struggle as a means of achieving its aim of uniting Ireland. This convinces some political commentators that the Provisional IRA has been neutered, but Ructions, Panzer and the criminal underclass know differently.

Murdoch sits down next to Panzer, while Coleman slips in beside Ructions. The two heavies take seats at a nearby table.

A middle-aged lady, with tied-back greying hair and glasses, enters the eating area and slides into a seat several tables away from the heavies. She opens her handbag and takes out her purse, but not before she presses a button which activates a pinhead surveillance camera in the side of her handbag.

'What about youse, lads?' Tiny Murdoch says, as his huge JCB fingers scoop up some of Panzer's fries.

'Sound, Tiny,' Panzer says, looking relaxed. 'Help yourself to those fries, why don't you? I hear they're very good.'

'That's very civilised of you, Panzer,' Murdoch replies as he gathers up the rest of the fries before pulling Panzer's tray towards him. 'Jesus, Panzer, you haven't half lost the weight.'

'I'm cutting down on the fast food, Tiny,' Panzer says.

Murdoch guffaws. 'A good idea.'

When Colm Coleman reaches towards Ructions' fries, Ructions' lean hand and long fingers grab his wrist. Coleman tries to pull away, but Ructions' grip is too strong.

'I told you, Colm, didn't I?' Murdoch says. 'Look at him. A fuckin' Rottweiler. He'd put a bullet in the back of your head for a main course and one in mine for dessert.'

Ructions releases Coleman's wrist. 'Be my guest,' he says, gesturing with his hand.

'Be your guest?' Coleman says insolently, rubbing his wrist. 'You'll be lucky if you don't end up being *my* guest.'

Words from the grave echo in Ructions' brain, advice from The Devil: *Never let your enemies see your anger.*

Barely able to speak after shoving Panzer's cheeseburger into his mouth, Murdoch mumbles, 'Have youse any moves on?'

'Nah,' Panzer replies. 'I'm telling you, Tiny, I've never seen it so tight. Have *you* ever seen it this tight?'

Murdoch finishes off Panzer's cheeseburger and wipes his mouth with a paper serviette. 'I enjoyed that.' He belches. 'What was that?'

'I said, there's nothing on.'

'It's hard to get a turn these days, I'll give you that. Hard times, Colm.'

'Desperate times, Tiny.' Coleman looks at Ructions' cheeseburger and then at Murdoch. 'Would you recommend that?'

'Ten out of ten.'

'What about you, Ructions? Would you recommend it?'

'I hear they do a good cheeseburger here.'

Coleman laughs heartily. The infection spreads to Murdoch, Panzer and Ructions. 'That was funny,' Coleman says. 'Wasn't that funny, Tiny?'

'He's a funny guy is our Ructions – a regular Charlie Chaplin,' Murdoch says.

The hilarity subsides. Coleman lifts Ructions' cheeseburger and takes a bite. Unlike Murdoch, Coleman chews slowly. 'Oh, boy, this is juicy.' He holds Ructions' cheeseburger up to Murdoch. 'We should get into this, Tiny. This is exceptional.'

Murdoch stabs his finger into Ructions' chest. 'This boyo's a hard bastard to kill. Three times we went for him.'

'Why's he still breathing, then?' Coleman asks.

'Because he cleared his slate.'

'How? What did he do?'

'It was during the ceasefire. Talks were at a ...' Murdoch waves his hand, 'delicate stage and we had to hold back. So the bullet-dodger here clipped a bad boy for us.'

Ructions looks out the window. Murdoch puts his hand on the top of Ructions' head and turns his face around. 'I said ... you're a goddam killer.'

Ructions yawns, making no attempt to disguise his irritation.

'Goddam killer in motorway services,' Murdoch says loudly, pointing to Ructions. 'Read all about it.'

'So, Ructions,' Coleman says, 'what's on the pot? What are you and old Panzer cooking up?'

Colm, if I'd the governor of the Bank of England in the trunk of my car, you'd be the last person on earth to hear about it. Ructions shrugs and waves his hands in resignation.

Murdoch studies Panzer's face. 'Would you tell me if you'd a job on, Panzer? I don't think you would.'

Panzer knows that if he says he would let Murdoch know of any move, it would be a blatant lie, so he opts for the truth. 'You're right, I wouldn't. Why should I, Tiny? So you could take the food off my plate?'

'I wouldn't do that.'

Panzer looks at his empty plate and grins. 'Of course you wouldn't.'

Murdoch whispers in Panzer's ear, 'You don't begrudge me a burger, do you?'

'Of course not.'

'I fuckin' hope not. Now, you can deny it all you want, but I know you two pulled off that million quid cigarette move at Balcoo in January—'

'Ahh, Jesus, Tiny!' Panzer exclaims. 'Now that's out of order. You boys did that.'

'Em, I don't think so. We got the blame for it – as we always do – but you and the bullet-dodger here,' Panzer nods to Ructions, 'did it.'

'You're up the left on that one, Tiny.'

Murdoch takes the plastic top off Panzer's Coke, puts the cup to his mouth and swallows its contents. 'Colm?'

'Yes, Tiny?'

'Did we get any tax out of the Balcoo move?'

'Not a washer.'

'Imagine not paying your taxes, eh? You know, people get sent to jail for that.'

'People have been put down holes for that,' Coleman chips in.

'We didn't do it, Tiny,' Panzer says. 'I swear.'

Murdoch touches Panzer's arm. 'I'm going to let that one go because, well, I like you, Panzer. You did us a turn or two back in the day.' He points to Ructions again. 'But I don't like him.' Murdoch puts two of his fingers to his temple. 'You'd love to nut me, wouldn't you?'

Ructions looks nonchalant and does not reply.

'See, Colm? See?' Murdoch says, a look of contrived consternation on his face. 'The little shite hasn't even the decency to deny it.' Murdoch continues to stare at Ructions, still waiting for a denial that will not be forthcoming. He turns to Panzer, 'If I hear—'

'There'll be nothing to hear,' Panzer interjects.

'Belt up when I'm talking.' Murdoch pauses to see if Panzer will defy him. 'If I hear you've a job on and we don't get our tax, I'll be paying you a visit. Got it?'

'Sure.'

Murdoch's attention returns to Ructions. Both men try to outstare the other. Murdoch breaks first. He looks out the window before returning his gaze to Ructions. 'Colm, were we tailed?'

'I don't think so.'

Murdoch looks about to see if there are any close-circuit cameras in the building. There are. One of the heavies, reading the signs, puts his hand in his waistband as if to pull out a gun.

Ructions' eyes concentrate on Murdoch's nose. *I'll lockjaw on to that big fuckin' beak before your pups whack me, asshole.*

Two uniformed policemen enter the shopping area. Murdoch shakes his head and the heavy withdraws his hand.

Tapping Ructions' cheeks, Murdoch smiles. 'Panzer, bring your Rottweiler to heel, or I will.' Murdoch gets up and walks away. He turns, rubs his belly, and says, 'Oh, and thanks for that snack. It hit the spot.'

Ructions' eyes follow Murdoch and his comrades as they get into their car. It pulls around past the window and stops. Murdoch stares out the passenger-side window at Ructions before waving on the driver.

'You shouldn't annoy him,' Panzer says. 'It's not good business.'

'He's easily annoyed. I never opened my mouth.'

'You could've been more diplomatic.'

'You mean I should've grovelled to him?'

Panzer winces. 'Ructions, we've got to—'

Ructions' face looks like a red-hot boil that is about to burst. 'I don't crawl to the likes of that bastard, Panzer. And when we're on the subject – fuck him – and fuck his tax. Who the fuck does he think he is to tax us? I'd—'

'All right! I hear you!' Panzer snaps. Ructions retreats behind his wall of silence again. 'Look, Ructions,' Panzer says in a more even tone, 'I'm gonna be out the guts of a quarter of a mill before this thing kicks off …' Panzer holds up one finger. 'Before one single pound coin comes back. So I need you to be with me one hundred per cent. If you're not, then fuck off now before I lay out the money.'

Ructions feels genuine contrition. 'I'm with you all the way, Panzer. Count on me.'

Panzer grabs Ructions' cheeks in the palm of his hands and pulls his face close to his. 'Son, if we have to shovel shit, we shovel shit together – not because we fear the IRA – but because it's good tactics.'

Once more Ructions opts for silence; he wouldn't know how to shovel shit.

'But you are right about one thing.'

'I am?'

'Yeah. We're paying tax to nobody. Fuck them all, the greedy bastards.'

Ructions smiles. 'I'm starving. Fancy a hamburger?'

SIX

In Dublin, Finbarr sits on the wooden window ledge, gazing out at a long back garden that is surrounded on all sides by fir trees. Ennio Morricone's 'Gabriel's Oboe' from *The Mission* plays on the radio. 'Benzo' Mullins leans against a furry animal skin that adorns the back of a cream sofa. His feet are resting on a matching pouffe. The drug dealer's eyes are closed and his right hand waves an invisible baton. Beside Benzo is Ian 'Twenty Bellies' McClure, rubbing his Uzi sub-machine gun with a cloth.

Finbarr speculates whether a cut-throat razor had been used to give Benzo his 'Glasgow smile'. He reckons that the scars at the corners of his mouth are each about an inch long. Involuntarily, he strokes the sides of his own mouth with his thumb and index finger.

Geek O'Reilly does not take drugs, but he knows that Finbarr has a nose for coke, so he invites him to sample the goods. Finbarr comes over to the glass coffee table, bends down and, using a rolled-up ten-euro note as a funnel, snorts a line of coke. He throws back his head.

'Well?' Geek asks.

The innocuous grin on Finbarr's face soon turns into a full-blown smile. 'It's good stuff.'

Benzo stands up, walks towards Geek, puts one hand on his shoulder and points a finger at the kitchen. 'That mule is carrying an awful lot of Charlie. Now, tell me you're going to look after her, coz the minute she walks out of here, she and Charlie are your responsibility.'

'It's all sorted,' Geek says.

'How are they getting up to Belfast?'

'That's my concern.'

Benzo makes an appealing face. 'Indulge me.'

'Like I said, how Charlie reaches Belfast is my concern.'

Benzo nods. Twenty Bellies, sub-machine gun in hand, stands up. 'That's okay, but terms still have to be agreed.'

'Of course,' Geek says.

'You get a month's credit.'

'No problem.'

'Ahh!'

Geek remains unmoved by Benzo's outburst. 'What's wrong?' he asks soberly.

'I hate those fuckin' words! Every cunt that tells me there'll be no problem ends up being the fuckin' problem.'

'Hey!' Geek snaps, 'I'm no cunt.'

'I didn't mean it like—'

'When you call me a cunt, you call my boss a cunt, and he takes exception to being called a cunt.'

Benzo nods slowly. 'No disrespect intended, Geek. You're no cunt, and neither is my good friend Panzer—'

'What a strange name,' Geek says with a glint in his eye. 'I can't say I know anyone by that name.'

Unruffled by the sudden spike in tension, Benzo strokes the scar at the right side of his mouth. 'You've got your ways of doing things and I've got mine, and business is business. I want my two hundred large by this time next month. No excuses, no sob stories. I really don't give an elephant's fart if your boss is down the bury hole and you're lying on top of him. I want my poke. And if the gear's caught, I still get my poke.'

'Are you finished?' Geek says.

Benzo whispers in Geek's ear. 'The General had a saying: "familiarity is the slippery slope to bad judgement". This way, nobody can say they didn't know the score if one of the boys has to blow them away.'

'My boss has a saying,' Geek says. '"Don't make threats – but keep promises".'

Finbarr is open-mouthed, his eyes shifting from Geek to Benzo and back. He hears a swaggering voice inside his head: *Cheeky bastard! One of your boys will blow who away? Me? My old man? Ructions? And what are we going to be doing, eh? Blowing bubbles out our arses?*

Benzo has said his piece and decides against making things worse. 'Your boss is a man of honour, Geek, a man I respect.'

'That he is. Finbarr, go see to the mule.'

'Sure.' Finbarr goes into the bathroom where Beatrice, a friend of Peteris, is strapping a cocaine belt around her midriff.

'It heavy,' Beatrice says, as she adjusts the cocaine belt for comfort.

'Get it right, Bee,' Finbarr says. 'Take your time.' Beatrice puts on her dress and coat. Finbarr inspects her. Nothing looks amiss. 'Stay here.' He goes back to the living room. 'That's us ready for the road.'

'Stall,' Benzo says. He takes out his mobile and dials a woman who is scouting the area in a car, looking for signs of a police presence.

'Anything?'

'Nothing.'

'No cops,' Benzo says, offering his hand to Geek, 'and no hard feelings?'

'None. As you say, business is business.'

'Give your boss my best, will ya?'

'Will do.'

'And tell him it's a pleasure to do business with him. Yeah?'

'Sure. Finbarr, you and the mule leave first.'

Panzer and Ructions are sharing a table along with some French supporters in the front garden of The Bath Pub beside the Lansdowne Road Stadium in Dublin. Directly below them is a white bath that has been converted into a flowerbed. Standing behind them on the tiled walkway to the bar entrance is a host of Irish supporters singing the Irish national anthem.

An earthy, rumbustious voice emerges from amongst the passing rugby fans. 'Ructions! Ructions!'

Ructions stretches his neck to see who is calling his name. Serge approaches, bedecked in a French scarf and a welcoming smile. Ructions holds out his arms to Serge and they hug.

'Bonjour, mon ami,' Serge says, glowing with delight.

'Bonjour, Serge.' Ructions holds him at arm's length. 'Vous avez l'air très bien.'

'Merci, Ructions.'

'Really, I can't get over it. You're looking twenty years younger.'

'I've discovered Botox, my Irish friend,' Serge chuckles as he turns to give Ructions a side profile.

A group of Irish supporters approach and one puts his arm around Serge's neck. Both Serge and Ructions join the Irish supporters in singing 'Amhrán na bhFiann'. Ructions leads a swelling chorus of Gaelic goodwill. 'Come on, Ireland!'

A bonding, a spiritual union from Serge, 'Vive l'Irlande!'

'Vive la France!' Ructions shouts.

A French supporter bumps into Panzer, who is approaching with two pints of Guinness. Miraculously, none of the Guinness is spilled. The two apologise to each other. Panzer, his face alight, hands one of the pints of Guinness to Serge. 'Thought you might need this, old-timer.'

Serge has to look twice before he recognises Panzer. His dramatic weight loss and grey pallor shocks him, but he quickly recovers and smiles widely at his old friend. 'Ha!' Serge says. 'Old-timer, indeed! You're older than me!' Serge takes the pint from Panzer and sips it gingerly.

'You've hardly wet your whistle there, Frenchie!' Panzer cries. 'Take a decent slug.'

Serge drinks the whole pint. A white foam moustache adorns his upper lip. 'C'est magnifique, Irish,' Serge says, thumping the pint glass down on a table. Panzer and he throw their arms around each other and warmly embrace.

Walking into the stadium, Panzer gets a phone call and drops behind Ructions and Serge. After a few seconds, Serge stops to tie his shoelace. He looks up at Ructions. 'Can I ask you, Ructions,' he says, 'how much do you expect to lift?'

'It's difficult to say. At a rough guess,' Ructions purses his lips, 'I'd say anything from thirty to fifty.'

Serge stands up, clearly taken aback. 'Million?'

Ructions nods.

'Mon Dieu!'

'Can you handle it?'

Serge hesitates before replying. 'Yes, yes, I can. But understand this – money of that quantity will be extremely expensive to clean.'

'How expensive?'

'I don't know yet, but it could go to fifty or even sixty per cent.'

Ructions stands with his hands on his hips, hanging on Serge's every word and mannerism. 'Jesus, that's rough. Wow!' Ructions puts his hands in the back pockets of his jeans. 'I'm gonna come right out with it, Serge, I wasn't expecting that.'

'It may not be as much as that or ...' Serge holds up his palm and shrugs, 'it may be more. I simply don't know yet. I admit, I've never had to deal with that amount of money before.' Serge is lost in thought. 'I'll have to make enquiries.'

Panzer comes back. 'We'll talk after the match,' Ructions says.

'Well, you two,' Panzer says, putting his arms around both men's shoulders. 'What's the buzz? Tell me what's a happenin'.'

'Ireland's playing France,' Ructions says. 'Come on, Ireland!'

'Éirinn go brách!' Panzer shouts.

Back at the hotel after the match, Panzer flicks a half-smoked cigar over the hotel balcony railings. It spirals downwards, revolution after revolution, until it lands on the roof of the concrete hotel entrance, bounces and comes to rest. He sits down, lifts his gold cigarette lighter with his thumb and index finger and tumbles it repeatedly. He didn't really understand rugby, but he liked the physicality of it, the die-for-the-cause attitude of the players. His thoughts are interrupted by thumping on his bedroom door.

Panzer peeks out the spyhole, pulls back, squints again at the figure on the other side and rubs his eyes. Whoever it is, he or she is wearing a black, ankle-length leather overcoat and a large black hat and is facing away from the door. Then Finbarr turns around. Panzer opens the door and Finbarr walks into the room. 'Sweet Jesus!' Panzer exclaims, coming behind his son, 'I thought for a minute there, Old Nick himself had come to put me to the scythe.'

'Nope,' Finbarr says. 'It's just me.' He makes for the minibar, takes out a small bottle of whiskey and puts it to his mouth. 'That other thing's sorted,' he says casually as he empties the whiskey down his throat.

Panzer turns up the volume on the television, motions Finbarr out to the balcony, closes the glass doors behind him and sits at the table. Finbarr fidgets. 'So, Charles is away, then?' Panzer asks.

Finbarr nods.

'Where's Geek?'

'With Charles.'

'I thought you were going back to Belfast with him?'

'No, I'm meeting up with a few mates for a drink.'

'Okay.'

A glass door slides open in the next room and Ructions steps out on to his balcony.

Finbarr raises his hat. 'Hello, Ructions.'

Ructions sniggers. 'Like the outfit. Creepy.'

'So everybody keeps telling me.'

'What time is our table booked for?' Panzer asks.

'Eight o'clock,' Ructions says and heads back inside to take a shower.

Panzer stands up and puts his hands on the balcony railing. Without turning around, he says, 'Remind me, when Benzo gets his two hundred large, how much do we come away with clean?'

'Three hundred.'

'And you're certain you can move the stuff?'

'That won't be an issue. I know people who'll break our arms for it. Dad, when we're on the subject of goods, I think we can move at least another container of cigs a week, maybe even two. I know people who work in Dundalk harbour and they'll turn a blind eye for the right money.'

'Interesting,' Panzer says.

'And sooner or later, the IRA are going to get out of the fuel-laundering business altogether.'

'What makes you think that?'

'The politics of the peace process will demand it. And once they go, they'll leave behind a very lucrative diesel-laundering market. We should grab that market; we should start looking for sites where we can launder our own diesel and develop our own client base.'

'Your mind has been at full throttle, hasn't it?'

'Not really. It's just—'

'What makes you think the Provos are just going to walk away from a multi-million-pound annual turnover?'

'They've no choice if they want to become politically relevant.'

'You know, in the broad political sweep of things you'd be right, but some Provos might be persuaded to go into the fuel-laundering business for themselves; some might, like you, see an opportunity.'

'I think there'd be enough room for everybody.'

'Now …' Panzer wags his finger, 'that is a dangerous concept. Sooner or later, one man always gets greedy and convinces himself he doesn't need competition and then … well, then the guns usually come out and bodies are found lying face down in the streets.'

'Surely that possibility could apply to any business.'

'That's not strictly correct, but in our marketplace, in the underworld, it's always a possibility.' Panzer puts his hand on Finbarr's shoulder. 'Son, you'll be taking over from me soon and you should be looking for legitimate business opportunities … the property market, for example; it's exploding at the minute.'

'Sure,' Finbarr says.

Panzer cannot help but frown at his son's apparent disinterest.

Finbarr clears his throat. 'Something has been puzzling me, Dad.'

'Oh dear,' Panzer says in a resigned tone. 'What is it?'

'Why did you do this drugs deal with Benzo? I thought you hated the drug business.'

Panzer chooses his words carefully. 'I do, but I'm going to be laying out a lot of money for that bank job I told you about. You know ... the one with Ructions.'

'Okay.'

'This way I take the risk out of the equation. It's an insurance policy against a potential loss. A one-off.'

'I see.'

'I've told you before, but I'm going to say it again – don't ever let him know I took you into my confidence on that job. He doesn't like you.'

'He's a jealous asshole. He can't abide me getting the farm and business and him not.'

Serge, Panzer and Ructions are seated in the hotel restaurant. A waiter brings a bottle of dessert wine and presents the label to Serge. 'The 1996 Château d'Yquem Sauternes Premier Cru Supérieur, monsieur,' the waiter says.

Serge nods and sniffs the cork. 'An exceptional bouquet,' he says.

The waiter pours the wine and leaves the table.

'The pork was excellent, non?' Serge says.

'Very nice,' Ructions says.

Serge lifts his glass and swirls the wine. 'If I may say so, gentlemen, this is an ambitious project.'

'It'll work, Serge. I know it will,' Ructions says.

Serge's silence testifies to his reservations. 'And you, Johnny ... are you confident?'

Panzer pauses before answering. 'I'm optimistic, put it like that.'

'In my view,' Serge says, 'optimism is overrated.'

'Perhaps, but I've gone through this with Ructions and I can't find fault in it. We'll need a bit of luck, but then you always need the rub of the green, don't you? It's more than worth the risk.'

'I hope so,' Serge says.

'Ructions has never let me down yet,' Panzer says.

Serge sips his wine. 'I know that, but this thing is bordering on extraterrestrial. Nothing like it has been undertaken before.'

'We know that,' Panzer says.

'You'll not be able to launder the money in Ireland or Britain.'

'That's why we're paying for this rather expensive dinner, monsieur,' Ructions says glibly.

Serge bows his head gracefully and looks at Ructions in a manner that is decidedly puzzled. 'Merci beaucoup.' He exchanges glances with Panzer, then turns his attention back to Ructions. 'Would it be unkind of me to play the devil's advocate?'

'I expected nothing less.'

'Let us make a giant leap of faith and assume that all goes according to plan and the merchandise is in your possession.'

'Okay,' Ructions says.

'And let us assume you can resist the attention of the authorities—'

'Yes?'

'You still have the problem of transferring the merchandise out of the country. I should think air travel, given its traceability, would be out of the question. Do you agree?'

'Yes.'

'How, then, do you intend to move the merchandise?'

Ructions makes a wave motion with his hand.

'Yes,' Serge says. 'That makes sense. The police – I do not think it will be long before they find out who did this.'

'Possibly,' Ructions says, 'but it doesn't necessarily follow.'

'The police would be aware that few, shall we say, parties, are capable of achieving a positive result in this matter. They will go through a process of elimination and arrive at the right conclusions, don't you think?'

'The actual enterprise has been subdivided amongst different groups of people who don't know one another,' Panzer says.

'That's as may be, but the central figures – the planners – they swim in a very small pool.'

'The paramilitaries will be blamed for it,' Ructions says.

'Undoubtedly – at the start.' Serge drinks some wine and looks past Panzer in concentration. 'Is it not the case that the police and intelligence services have infiltrated the paramilitaries?'

'To a point,' Ructions says, 'but not completely. There are paramilitaries who don't work for the cops or for MI5.'

Serge stares at the wine bottle. 'That doesn't help, does it? All that tells me is that the paramilitaries who aren't working for the police don't know their friends from their enemies. Hmm ... Can I ask who your people are, or is that—'

'No, it's a fair question,' Panzer answers. 'Actually, they're ex-IRA. Retired revolutionaries. In business for themselves now. Very security conscious. Very forensically aware. We've used them before and there's been no comeback.'

'Only two of them know that we ...' Ructions points to Panzer and himself, 'are behind it, and they don't know of one another's involvement.'

'And it's in their own interests to keep their heads down,' Panzer adds.

Serge seems to be counting on his fingers. 'I like that. I think, perhaps, it would be unwise of me to pose any more questions. I will not ask when this thing is happening, but you appreciate that I have arrangements to make. I will need an approximation, if that is okay?'

'It'll be very soon,' Ructions says. 'I'll let you know when the time is right.'

'There's nothing else to be said, then, is there?' Serge raises his glass. 'To good business.'

SEVEN

Finbarr comes out of a nightclub in Dublin's bustling Temple Bar district. Revellers pack the cobblestoned streets. Traditional Irish music drifts out from the Temple Bar pub, which is surrounded with noisy drinkers. Strong odours of tobacco and grass infuse the cold December air. A man in an elf outfit sups his pint of Guinness while watching four men and three women brawling at the entrance to the pub. The elf finishes his pint and puts down the empty glass on a drinks barrel. He carefully takes off his jaunty hat and pointy elf ears and puts them in his pocket. He breathes deeply and charges into the middle of the melee, only to emerge a few minutes later with a bloody nose. One of the brawlers appears from the pack and raises his fist to punch the elf. Someone shouts, 'It's Elfie! They're beating up the elf!' More people join the fight. A well-fed cloud explodes and a blizzard of hailstones ping off the heads and faces of the scrappers. As quickly as it had started, the fight ends, as the antagonists scatter to find cover. Finbarr remarks to himself that the Irish don't like getting wet during a good fight. He stands in a doorway until the hailstones abate, then walks to a car park. He gets into the car park's elevator and presses the fourth-floor button. Two men, one in his twenties and the other in his forties, rush in just as the door is closing.

Finbarr gets out of the elevator and makes his way to his car. Once inside, he turns on the radio. Bob Dylan's 'Knockin' on Heaven's Door' bursts into life. Finbarr looks around and sees that no one is about. He dips a cocaine spoon into a small plastic moneybag, snorts some cocaine, shakes his head and runs a finger across his nose. His passenger-side door opens suddenly and the older man from the elevator gets in. He is a stocky man in a blue suit, with gelled grey hair tied at the back in a small ponytail. The man produces a hand gun and sticks it in Finbarr's ribs.

'What the—?'

'Fuck up,' the man growls in an earthy Dublin accent. He reaches over, grabs the car keys and says, 'Do you know who I am, Finbarr? Yes or no.'

'No.'

'I'm from the Provisional IRA and you're under arrest. Don't speak unless I tell you to and you'll be fine.' His tone is calm. He takes out a pair of sunglasses and hands them to Finbarr. 'Here. Put these on.'

Finbarr puts on the glasses and finds that the inside of the lenses is covered in black tape. The man searches Finbarr for weapons. 'You're doing good, young man. Now, open your door and get out.' As Finbarr steps out of the car, the younger of the two men who had been in the elevator takes him by the arm, puts him into the back of a second car and gets in beside him. The older man gets into the driver's seat and drives off.

A large photo of Murdoch, Coleman and the two heavies in a car adorns the big screen in Inspector Gerry Rowlands' office at police headquarters, Belfast. Also on the screen is an image of Murdoch, Coleman, Panzer and Ructions at the table in the roadside service station on the Belfast–Dublin motorway.

Four senior police officers and a note-taker sit around a circular table. Christened 'Poxy' by his colleagues because of his pock-marked face, Inspector Rowlands is a jobber, a reliable man: one who has the wit to recognise his limitations. He stands beside the screen with a large stick. His secretary knocks on the door and enters the room with tea and biscuits. She puts the tray on the table and leaves.

Unlike Rowlands, Chief Superintendent Daniel Clarke does have ambition – container-loads of it: he wants to be Chief Constable of the Police Service of Northern Ireland. Bald, chubby-cheeked and frog-eyed, Clarke is hardly a public relations' dream.

Yet, vainly, he considers himself to be good-looking. He reaches over, pops two sugar lumps in his cup and stirs his tea. His eyes never leave the screen. 'Murdoch's on the IRA's GHQ staff now, isn't he?' he says.

'Yes, sir,' Rowlands says. 'Has been for over a year now.'

Clarke lifts his cup to his lips but holds it there. 'And he's conferring with two known bank robbers. Why?'

'It's hard to say, sir. MI5 seems to think that this was a chance meeting. I believe there's merit in that assessment.' Rowlands runs the recording back to the part where Murdoch and Coleman join Panzer and Ructions. 'As we can see here, Murdoch has just sat down at the table when he grabs handfuls of Panzer O'Hare's chips and then wolfs downs his burger. Those are unfriendly acts. A bully boy is throwing his weight about.'

'The look on Panzer's face confirms that,' a female officer adds.

'It certainly appears that Panzer's uncomfortable around these people,' Clarke says.

Rowlands runs the recording to where Ructions grabs Colm Coleman's wrist when he tries to eat his fries. 'This is James "Ructions" O'Hare, sir, Panzer's nephew.'

'Yes,' Clarke says. 'He's really put out, isn't he?' The clip runs on. 'He doesn't say much, does he?'

'His body language says everything,' another officer comments. 'He evidently doesn't like Murdoch or Coleman and he's not afraid to show it.'

'We think Ructions was the brains behind the Balcoo cigarette robbery in January and the Ballymena Ulster Bank robbery in April,' Rowlands says.

'I wonder,' Clarke ponders, 'if Panzer neglected to pay his IRA taxes for those jobs? Could that be the reason for the hostility?'

'I wouldn't be surprised if it was, sir,' Rowlands says. 'We don't know whether he paid or not, but certainly, if he didn't, I suspect it would be an issue.'

Clarke stirs his tea. 'Hmm. Ballymena was a tiger-kidnapping, wasn't it?'

'Yes, sir. They held the manager's wife and two children hostage overnight and forced him to bring them the contents of the safe the next day.'

'And how much did they get away with?'

'Eight hundred thousand in unmarked notes, sir.'

Clarke taps his chin. 'So, we have master bank robbers conferring with master terrorists. Yes.' Clarke waves his hand. 'And MI5 think this meeting is coincidental, Gerry?'

'Yes, sir,' Rowlands says. 'Murdoch doesn't rob banks.'

'The Provisional IRA does. And, anyway, neither do master bank robbers – they get mugs to rob them for them.'

'Quite so, sir.'

'Why is there no audio with this recording?' Clarke asks. 'I hope our friends in MI5 aren't holding out on us again.'

'I asked Controller about the absence of audio, sir, and he said there was interference.'

'Do you believe him?' Clarke asks.

Rowlands shrugs.

'It's stuffy in here,' Clarke says, opening a window. He puts his head out and looks up the side of the building. He turns around. 'Colm Coleman – he's been with the Provos, how long?'

'About eight years now, sir.'

'He seems to have had something of a meteoric rise in the ranks, hasn't he?'

'Yes, sir,' Rowlands says. 'His forte, if you could call it that, is bank robbery. We estimate Coleman was involved in at least ten major robberies with the Frankie Downey gang, before Downey went to live in Spain. With Downey out of the way, Murdoch saw an opportunity, recruited Coleman and now he uses him as his tax collector.'

'Colm Coleman ... the IRA's tax collector?' Clarke says. 'It's a small world, isn't it?'

'Actually, I think recruiting Coleman was a pretty clever play on Murdoch's behalf,' Rowlands says.

'Oh, I agree,' Clarke says. 'Pity we can't recruit Murdoch. Now that *would* be a coup.'

'C3 is of the opinion that he'll do more good where he is. Apparently, he's one hundred per cent behind the Provos' peace strategy.'

'And presumably Coleman would've been invaluable to Murdoch because he knew all the ODCs and their methodology?'

'Exactly, sir.'

Clarke walks up to the screen and wheels around. 'Gentlemen, this is a formidable gathering.' He turns to Rowlands. 'Anything else, Gerry?'

'No, sir.'

'Keep me informed.'

It is 1.55 a.m. Panzer's Land Rover dips and rises on the uneven ground of the disused quarry. He stops and his vehicle lights shine on a grey Toyota. He leans forward. Two faces look up from the steamed-up, back-seat passenger window. Panzer keeps his lights on the Toyota. A young man and a woman with dishevelled hair stagger out of the back, adjusting their clothing. The man squints and holds his hand up to shield his eyes from Panzer's headlights. He takes a step towards the headlights, thinks twice and joins the woman in the Toyota. They drive away.

Panzer turns off his engine. He is used to the darkness of the countryside, but this blackness is impenetrable. Lowering his window, he listens. Nothing. *You're out there. I know it. I can feel your eyes on me.* A car comes up behind him. Its lights are turned off and the driver's side door opens. A figure gets out. Panzer exhales.

Tiny Murdoch gets into the passenger side of the Land Rover. Panzer looks straight ahead. 'Are you all right?' Murdoch asks.

Panzer is in no mood for conviviality. 'What is it, Tiny? Why did you drag me out of bed at this time of night?'

Murdoch ignores Panzer's brusqueness. 'I'm thinking of buying a Land Rover. Would you recommend it?'

'They're ... very durable.'

'Very durable. I'll remember that.' Murdoch holds out his hand. 'Phone.'

Panzer hands over his phone.

Murdoch pats Panzer down. 'Now, let's get into my car.'

'Why?' Panzer asks.

'Coz this car could be wired.'

'It isn't.'

'Says you.'

'It isn't. And anyway, how do we know your car isn't wired?'

'Coz it's not my car.' Murdoch gets out.

As Panzer approaches the car that isn't Murdoch's, a man in a camouflage jacket with night-vision goggles emerges out of the darkness. Murdoch and the man speak in whispered Irish before the latter disappears as quickly as he appeared.

As they sit in silence in the car that isn't Murdoch's, Panzer's mind absorbs the situation. *Ghosters in camouflage jackets ... night-vison glasses ... conversations in Irish ... who the fuck do you think is out there, Tiny? The Viet-fucking-Cong? The Taliban? You're a fucking drama queen, boyo. Bringing me to this godforsaken hole in the ground in the middle of the night*. 'What's on your mind, Tiny?'

'Barry ...' Murdoch glances behind him.

Panzer had not seen anyone in the back of the car when he got in and he is taken aback when a clean-shaven young man with rimmed glasses leans forward and hands over an open laptop to Murdoch. Murdoch points to the laptop.

On screen, Finbarr is naked and tied to a chair in the corner of a room. Besides having a black eye, there are welt marks on his body. His teeth chatter as he stares at the camera. A person wearing a ski mask holds a gun to Finbarr's temple. 'You're a fucking paedophile cunt, aren't you?' the person shouts. Finbarr nods. 'Fucking say it!'

'I'm a fucking paedophile cunt.'

Murdoch closes the laptop. 'We picked him up in Dublin.'

'What for?' Panzer says defiantly. 'What's he done on the IRA?'

Murdoch glances at the car's clock. He turns his head to look out the side window. 'Your son's an animal, Panzer.'

Panzer cranks his neck and coughs nervously. *This is bad, this is really bad*. 'Any confession he made has been beaten out of him and you know it. Look at him. He's been tortured.'

'He's part of a paedophile ring we've been investigating for months.'

'That's bollocks!' Panzer says. 'I don't believe you, not for a fucking second.'

'Doesn't matter to me one way or the other whether you believe me or not. We have him and we know what he's done and what he's capable of.'

'He's my son.'

Murdoch turns abruptly. 'And what's that got to do with it?'

'You've no right to harm him.'

'*I've* no right to harm him? Are you serious, fuckhead?' Murdoch points an accusing finger at Panzer. 'We know about your pervert son. We know he has an associate, a Latvian called ... What's his name, Barry?'

'Peteris Edgars,' Barry says.

'Edgars and your son, amongst others, have been raping children, kids as young as eight.'

'If he has broken the law then—'

Murdoch pulls a gun out of his waistband and jabs it into Panzer's neck. Panzer winces. 'Don't you dare come over all sanctimonious with me, you lowlife shithead! I am the fucking law! The 'RA's the fucking law!'

'Okay! Okay, Tiny,' Panzer says through pursed lips. 'No harm meant. I'm just ...' Panzer rubs his ribs and grimaces. 'I'm a father who's worried about his son, that's all.'

Murdoch sticks the nozzle of the gun in Panzer's nostril, forcing back his head. 'Don't ever, ever try to get clever with me again.'

'Yes. No. I won't. No worries, no worries.'

Murdoch has spent a lifetime honing his responses to certain situations. He knows it is always a matter of control and that when you have a gun stuck up someone's nose, you are in control. He puts the gun back in his waistband.

In a voice that is barely audible in case Murdoch perceives it to be offensive, Panzer says, 'Are you going to hurt him?'

Now that Panzer has psychologically collapsed, Murdoch softens. 'The thing is, Panzer, as we speak …'

'Uh-huh?'

'He's in a car with two members of the nutting squad.'

'No!'

'And they're taking him to a quiet spot on the border—'

'No, Tiny! Not that!'

'The Army Council has made its decision, Panzer. For what it's worth, I voted against it.'

'But you can change it, Tiny! You can stop it, can't you?'

'Panzer,' Murdoch puts his hand on top of Panzer's knee, 'I wish I could. Like, I don't forget: when the Libyan shipments came in, you pulled me out of a hole.'

Panzer joins his hands together, just like he would if he were praying. 'I held a tonne of armaments and explosives for you, for four months, Tiny. Four months. When your back was to the wall and you needed help, I pulled you out.'

'I know, I know.' Murdoch puts his hand to his mouth, as if to throw a fire blanket over his words. 'I shouldn't have come up here. I knew it would be a mistake.'

'Why?'

Murdoch exhales. 'I'm sorry, Panzer.' Murdoch looks forlorn. 'I'm charged with paying you the courtesy of telling you that your son Finbarr is about to be shot dead. I don't have to but I'm doing it because you helped the boys in the past.'

They're gonna shoot my Finbarr dead! Panzer can see it in his head: a car with its lights out, the passenger-side door open; the driver behind the wheel, looking on; Finbarr, hands tied behind his back, kneeling on wet grass at the side of a remote country road. He can see the gunman putting the barrel of a gun to the back of his head and firing the fatal shot. He can see Finbarr collapsing forward, face down: dead.

Panzer's fingers tap a secret code on his temples. He fidgets and shakes and then looks directly at Murdoch. His upper lip quivers. 'Umm, Tiny … we can fix this, can't we?' His extended index finger seems like it is on a tightly wound spring as it points to Tiny and then himself. 'You and me, we're fixers; we can fix it.'

'I'd like to help you, old-timer, but—'

'Money. I've got money. How much do you want?'

'It's not that simple.' Murdoch looks at the clock in the car. 'Even if we did do a deal, it might be too late.'

'What would it take?'

Murdoch strokes the underside of his chin, ponderously. He looks at Panzer and holds his gaze. 'I don't know … you've no idea what you're asking me.'

'I know, I know, I know.' Panzer exhales slowly.

'I could get into serious shit for interfering with an A/C decision,' Murdoch says. 'Like, it's not as if this is some kid who stole a car.'

'Please, Tiny. Please. You can put this right. What will it take?'

Murdoch drops his head onto his chest. He lifts it again, as if he has come to a decision. 'What will it take? Everything, Panzer. Absolutely everything.'

EIGHT

They say The Devil O'Hare was a miser. They say he laid every single brick that went into the construction of the Big House back in 1953, and that he 'stroked' the plasterers, electricians and painters by giving them only half the agreed fee for the job. They say he bought all the building material on the black market. 'They' had the good wit to say nothing until he was dead.

Three months before construction had finished, The Devil and his wife, Mary, were sitting on the veranda of the old stone house, drinking Irish coffees. Mary had told her husband that she did not want apple trees planted on their land. When he asked why not, she had replied, 'No apple trees, no temptation; no temptation, no serpent; no serpent, no sin.'

Emptying her pipe, Mary proclaimed that she wanted the farm called 'The Garden of Eden'. So that was that. In matters of religion and the hereafter, The Devil had accepted that his wife knew more about the convoluted mind of God and the ponderous ways of heaven and hell than the Pope in Rome.

Ructions pulls into the yard and gets out of his car. The outside of the Big House, with white pebble-dashed walls and a featureless double-door entrance, is unimpressive. Behind the front doors is a solid-steel security door that is locked into place at night with heavy drop bars. There is a similar contraption behind all the windows. Yet the character of Mary O'Hare still stalks this house in the form of the mosaic floor in the hall, which has, as its centrepiece, the image of the Archangel Michael, his wings outstretched, a sword in his hand and his foot on Lucifer's head.

And, in the uprights of the Italian marble fireplaces that grace the four reception rooms, are angels blowing trumpets, heralding the majesty of God. However, despite Mary's manifestations of piety, God is not in this house.

Panzer is in this house. He is in the kitchen mixing meal and tinned dog food in two steel bowls for his Alsatians, Popeye and Bluto, whose ears are pricked as they frenetically circle the backyard, homing in on Panzer's every movement.

Something has been playing on Ructions' mind and he decides to blurt it out. 'Are you ill, boss? I can't get over the weight you've lost recently.'

'So it seems. This is the second time you've mentioned it.' Panzer sighs. 'Has it occurred to you that the doctors have told me to cut back on fatty foods to lower my cholesterol? I do have a dodgy ticker, in case you've forgotten.'

'Oh, right,' Ructions says, reaching for the kettle to make the tea.

'Sorry, I didn't mean to be snappy,' Panzer says. Setting down his mixing knife, he adopts a southpaw stance and jabs Ructions' cheek with the tip of his fingers. 'I can still handle a whippersnapper like you! Come on, champ, let's rumble.' Panzer throws another jab, but Ructions slips under it and delivers a fingertip blow to Panzer's nose. Unfazed, Panzer circles Ructions. 'So, how was Eleanor?'

'Educational.'

'Educational?' Panzer stops and cocks his head. 'As in the business sense?'

'Jesus! Get your mind out of the sewer!'

Panzer smiles and asks, 'Are we all set?'

'Yip.'

Panzer stops sparring and brings the two generously filled bowls out to the dogs in the yard. While the Alsatians devour their grub, Ructions emerges with two mugs of tea. The two retire to the tool shed and sit down beside a small workbench.

'Jesus, it's Baltic out here,' Ructions says, grateful for the hot tea in his hands. 'So, we're ready to go on Monday morning. There'll be forty-four million pounds ready for harvesting.'

Instinctively, Panzer whistles.

Ructions continues, 'The two keyholders we've been waiting on are both working that day. On top of that, the bank is updating its security the next day. At the minute, the keyholders carry master keys that give them access to all areas. On Tuesday, those master keys are being withdrawn. The long and short of it is this – it's Monday or never.'

Panzer tries to envisage that amount of money in one place but finds it impossible. He can feel an excitement that he has never known before. 'Is Eleanor sure about this?' he says calmly.

'Yes.'

'No chance of a set-up?'

Ructions regards Panzer's continuous questioning of Eleanor's trustworthiness as personally undermining, but he presumes that his vigilant and provocative attitude has more to do with letting him know who is boss than with questioning his judgement. 'None,' Ructions answers. 'This is it.'

'Everything and everyone is in place and ready?'

'All I have to do is to give the thumbs up – sorry – all *you* have to do is to give the thumbs up.'

Panzer holds out his hand and the two men shake. Despite the animosity that sometimes surfaces between them, each respects and depends on the other.

Suddenly Finbarr enters the shed. He is sporting a shiner. Ignoring Ructions, he looks at the ground and quietly says, 'Dad, is there anything I can help you with?'

'After I finish here,' Panzer says, 'I'd like you to ...' Panzer doubles-up and clutches his chest, his face turning plum red. He reaches shakily into his waistcoat pocket and fumbles with a box of tablets. Ructions races to the kitchen and fills a glass of water, while Finbarr puts two tablets on Panzer's tongue. Ructions returns and Panzer gulps the water quickly.

'Deep breaths,' Ructions says. 'That's it.'

Finbarr says, 'Take your time, Dad. Deep breaths.' He rubs his father's back as Panzer's breathing begins to return to normal. His lips form a narrow O, allowing a steady stream of breath to escape.

'It's my own fault,' Panzer says, his speech laboured. 'I should've taken them a couple of hours ago. I was so wrapped up in paperwork – I fuckin' hate paperwork.'

'You know, boss,' Ructions says with more than a hint of joviality, 'death wouldn't become you.'

'Don't I know it?' Panzer touches Finbarr's arm. 'Son, I'm okay now.'

'Are you sure, Dad? Can I get you—?'

'I'm fine. Give us a few minutes, will ya?'

'Sure. Whatever you say.' Just as Finbarr reaches the shed door he turns around and winks to Ructions with his good eye.

As soon as the door shuts, Ructions says, 'He's a cocky little fucker.'

'He's young,' Panzer says, waving his hand dismissively, 'that's all. In case you've forgotten, you were a cocky little fucker yourself when you were his age.'

Ructions puts his hand on Panzer's shoulder. 'Are you really okay?'

Panzer nods. 'It was nothing.' As if expunging a virus, Panzer's shoulders and chest heave. 'I need to stand up.' Panzer grips the workbench and pushes himself up, while Ructions holds him under his arms. He walks slowly out of the shed and hovers around the bottom of the garden. Ructions is right behind him.

'You know, Ructions, I've waited my whole life for this one. My whole life and now it's here.' He nips his bottom lip between his teeth. 'What happens afterwards?'

'Let's worry about that when the time comes.'

'I'm going to have to tell Finbarr about the job.'

Are you fuck! 'We have an agreement,' Ructions says.

'I know but—'

'I don't want him told.'

'But what if something happens to me?'

'Nothing will happen to you.'

'You don't know that. What if it does? What if I'm dead? Will you—'

'Wow! Slow down, Panzer. Do you know something I don't?'

'I'm just covering loose ends, that's all. Have I your word Finbarr will get my cut?'

'I don't want to talk about this.'

Panzer turns to face Ructions. 'But I do.'

You don't even know he's a paedophile, do you, Panzer? Should I tell you? Would it make any difference if I did? I doubt it. 'I'm dealing with you, Panzer, and you'll not be going anywhere between now and next week. After the move, you can take your half of the money and give it to anyone you want.'

'Will you make sure that Finbarr gets my full share of the money from the job if I'm not about? Yes or no?'

'Yes, I will. But he can't know about the move beforehand. Yes or no?'

Panzer nods. 'Okay.'

They walk towards the kitchen, where the older man twists the top off a bottle of Merlot and pours two glasses.

'To us. To you and me. We've got this, haven't we?'

'We sure have.'

They touch glasses and sip the wine.

'Listen up, Panzer. This is the third time you've had a close shave with the tablets. You're playing fast and loose with your life. It has to stop.'

Panzer starts blinking, a sign that Ructions has come to equate with agitation.

'What's up, boss? Come on, spill.'

'Why have you never asked me about my buying your father's half of the farm?'

Ructions feels his face flush. 'It was none of my business.'

'But if my brother hadn't sold out, you and I would be partners,' Panzer says.

'Bobbie was thinking about Bobbie,' Ructions says. 'Nothing or no one was more important to him than himself.'

'I didn't want to buy him out, Ructions, but I had to. He was threatening to sell his half of the farm to the highest bidder. I couldn't allow it to go outside the family.'

You expect me to salve your conscience, Panzer? Okay. I can do that. 'Look, Panzer, my father did what he did. He was an alcoholic. No guilt.'

'Oh, I don't feel any guilt.'

'Good.'

'I tried to talk him out of it, in fact.'

'Fine.'

'I just thought you should know.'

'Righto.'

Panzer stands up and walks into the yard. The rain has stopped, but it is still cold. He lifts the hosepipe and hoses the dogs' waste towards the drain. The two Alsatians peek out from their kennels. Panzer pats his leg with his free hand and both dogs come to him. He pets them.

Ructions looks out the kitchen window. It strikes him that this is a scene that might have captured the imagination of Rembrandt or Vermeer: the smiling, aged dog-owner with the black, open-necked shirt, red waistcoat, rolled-up sleeves and heavy, stained jeans; stubby fingers caressing the dogs' heads. What would the masters have called such a painting? Something simple: *Man and Dogs*.

Ructions has often wondered why Panzer still feels the urge to carry out robberies. He's already a millionaire. Ructions asked him once, but the reply – 'Because it occupies my mind' – did not seem adequate. Ructions surmises that the thought of retirement equates with old age in Panzer's mind and maybe he is not ready to join the over-the-hillers. It is typical of Panzer to find some chore to do when there is important business to be discussed. It is not that he is incapable of absorbing details, he just feels more in control if he is carrying out a secondary task.

Panzer beckons to Ructions, who joins him in the yard. 'One thing bothers me,' Panzer says, 'If everything turns out rosy—'

'It will.'

Panzer sets down the hose. 'Do you trust Serge with this amount of money?'

'I—'

'How do you know he won't screw us?'

'He's handled big money for us in the past and he's never turned us over.'

'Yeah, but this is different. The money involved. It's super-league stuff. What makes you so sure?'

'It's hard to put my finger on it, but I'd trust him with my life. He's an honourable man.'

Panzer makes no effort to hide his alarm. 'An honourable man? Are you serious? He's a thief – just like us! A bit more upmarket, I grant you, but a thief nonetheless.'

'Then he's an honourable thief.'

'A rare breed.'

'If he cuts us up, I'll kill him myself,' Ructions says.

'Does he know that?'

'It goes without saying.'

Panzer's eyes narrow. 'No, it doesn't. You need to say it. Serge has to know we'll chase him to the ends of the earth and kill him if he dumps on us.'

'He'll not like that.'

'Too bad.'

Ructions' phone rings. It's Seamus McCann. He turns away from Panzer and walks towards the house. 'Yeah?'

'We need to talk. Are you free?'

'Okay. I'm on my way.' Ructions hangs up and turns towards Panzer.

'Everything all right?' Panzer asks, his eyes searching Ructions' face.

What are you looking for, Panzer? A telltale sign of ... what? 'That was Maria.'

Billy Kelly opens the front door of his sister's house in the Markets area of Belfast to let in his former IRA comrade, Ambrose Peoples. Ambrose is a chunky eighteen-stoner with wavy fair hair, sideburns and a chin that reaches the top of his chest. As Ambrose comes into the hall, Billy peeks up and down the street for signs that anything is amiss. Billy and Ambrose proceed upstairs and into a back bedroom where three other gang members are gathered.

The darkened bedroom is illuminated only by a small lamp. The three gang members are sitting and partially lying on the bed. Billy puts on surgical gloves, opens a holdall and hands each gang member a pay-as-you-go mobile phone and a handgun. The gang members immediately check the guns by removing the magazines and ensuring that there are no rounds in the chambers.

'We've done two dry-runs and gone over this a dozen times,' Billy says, 'so I'm not going to flog the thing to death. But before I move on – are there any questions?'

'I suppose there's no point asking who we're working for?' Ambrose asks.

'You're working for me,' Billy replies. 'Any other questions?'

There are none. Billy's attention is drawn to the sound of a car pulling up outside. He steals a look through the drawn venetian blinds. A blue Renault Clio is parked directly in front of the house and the young man in the driving seat is on his mobile, gesticulating with his hand. He seems agitated and this is confirmed when the youth closes his phone, smacks the dashboard with the heel of his hand and storms into Mrs Duffy's next-door house. Confident that nothing is untoward, Billy turns around. 'My number is the only number in your phones. You don't phone anyone except me and you phone me only if there's a problem. That means you don't phone your wife, your girlfriend or your dentist – no one. We're all clear on that?'

Everybody nods.

'And you don't take any calls, except mine. I'll only call if it's really necessary.'

'What if we run into trouble?' Ambrose asks.

'I've seen the target and I don't anticipate any grief. But if he does get stroppy, do what we always do: threaten to shoot his ma. That never fails.'

'True,' Ambrose says.

'We rock 'n' roll at ten o'clock tonight,' Billy says. 'Ambrose, get the cards out.'

'Dealer's choice?' Ambrose says as he takes out a pack of cards from his coat pocket and shuffles them.

'Yes,' Billy says.

'Any limit?'

'A fiver's the limit. I don't want you boys owing me your wages before you've earned them.'

Seamus McCann is stuck behind a tractor on the Belfast road, outside Downpatrick. He revs up the engine and bounces about in his seat as if his posterior is being ripped apart and carted away by legions of soldier ants. Ructions is in the passenger seat.

'For Jesus sake, Ructions, the lads have done four dummy-runs and they've been casing this house for nearly a month. They know the Divers better than the Divers know the Divers.'

Ructions ignores Seamus' protestations. 'Tell me about Liam.'

'Liam Anthony Diver: branch manager; thirty-four; five feet ten; fair, greying hair; drives a silver C-Class Merc; drinks Heineken and red wine – but only in the house – never in the local pub; leaves for work in the National Bank in Belfast every morning at seven o'clock and comes home between seven and half-seven every evening; looks out the curtains before he goes to bed to check if anybody's about—'

'And his missus?'

'Stephanie Carol Diver: five feet four inches; blonde hair, usually up in a bun; likes to wear dark glasses; a looker and a teacher in the local primary school—'

'That's fine,' Ructions says.

'Is it?' Seamus says, his eyes darting from the car's interior rear mirror to its side mirrors. 'Are you sure?'

Ructions fixes his gaze on the road ahead while Seamus snorts like a bull readying itself to charge a matador. The former IRA commander struggles to regain control. Releasing his white-knuckled fists, Seamus tries to generate a smile. What appears is little more than a sneer. 'Do you think I don't know what I'm doing?' Seamus says, yanking the car out and in to see if any vehicles are approaching in the opposite lane.

'What are you on about?' Ructions says. 'I didn't say that.'

'You didn't have to. You reckon I'm going to screw this up, don't you?'

Bewildered, Ructions turns towards Seamus. 'Why would I think that? You've done this before. You've proved yourself. I'm … What's got into you, Seamus?'

Seamus pulls out to overtake the tractor. A white van is immediately in front of them, approaching in the oncoming lane. The van driver angrily blasts his horn. Seamus jerks the steering wheel left, almost losing control of the car as he pulls back in again behind the tractor.

'Fuck me!' Ructions screams. 'Are you trying to get us killed?'

Seamus edges out again to see past the tractor and successfully overtakes.

Ructions' index finger taps his top lip contemplatively. 'So?' Ructions says.

'So what?'

'So when's the last time you got your hole?'

'What the—?'

'Is that what's behind this tantrum?'

Seamus reaches for his tin of orange juice, takes a drink and sighs. 'For your information, I had my hole yesterday.'

'I'm glad to hear it. Now—'

'Look, Ructions. I've been knocking around a long time and I've led men on capers a lot more dangerous than this, and you're undermining me with your constant harping on about detail.'

'You've just made my point, Seamus,' Ructions says. 'You, more than anybody, know the importance of detail. It's the difference between getting collared and not getting collared.'

'I hear you,' Seamus says, and the tension leaves his shoulders.

'Okay,' Ructions says. 'Enough said.'

They reach the ruins of Inch Abbey, a former Benedictine monastery. Ructions has been there on several occasions with Eleanor. It is a hideaway, a sanctuary for two-timers. They get out of the car and walk towards the abbey.

'Let's dander down to the river,' Ructions says.

Viewed from Inch Abbey, the River Quoile looks more like an Arthurian inland lake than a river. Ructions feels in no hurry to talk business. That can wait. *Nurse the baby; give him his dummy teat.* Ructions looks at his tourist guide brochure. 'Says here old Sitric the Viking, King of the Danes, sailed up the Quoile in 1002 and plundered a monastic settlement at Inch.'

'Viking cunt.'

'You don't like outsiders, do you Seamus?'

'You're the exception.'

'Not everyone who didn't join the 'RA is an outsider, Seamus.' Ructions claps him on the back and laughs heartily.

NINE

Everyone would remember where they were at ten o'clock that Sunday night.

Outside the Diver bungalow in Loughshore, County Down, Seamus McCann and another 'policeman' get out of their 'police car'. Tiny Murdoch and Colm Coleman are walking their dogs around Milltown Cemetery. At police headquarters in Belfast, Chief Superintendent Daniel Clarke is handing out Christmas presents to colleagues. Eleanor Proctor is sitting in her friend Stacy's house in the Newtownards Road area of Belfast, pretending to listen to Stacy's prattle but really thinking about running away with Ructions. Maria is packing her bags. Serge Mercier is strolling around the shores of Lake Geneva, considering whether or not he should employ three money launderers instead of his usual two. Panzer sits alone in one of his living rooms, sipping red wine. He is not a drinker, but he likes a good Burgundy. Ructions is outside the Butler household in Riverdale Close, west Belfast.

Meanwhile, inside the Butler household in west Belfast, all is quiet and perfectly normal. Declan Butler's fringe falls over his beefy face and almost brushes the scar across the bridge of his nose – an ill-deserved legacy from a bottle attack outside a Belfast nightclub. The quiet 25-year-old National Bank official is sitting on the sofa in the living room, struggling to keep his eyes open in front of the television and a sleep-inducing fire.

An Aston Villa football supporter, Declan had returned from Villa Park that afternoon, having watched his team lose to Birmingham City 2-1. During the journey home through Belfast, he hadn't noticed the blue Volvo estate car that had been following his taxi, for the simple reason that it had never entered his head that anyone would ever want to follow him. Yet he is one of only nine supervisors at the bank who possess a master key that can override all internal security systems and offer access to every part of the bank, including the vault. The talent scouts in the National Bank recognise that Dylan is a bright spark, a star in the making: someone worth keeping an eye on. Very close at hand are those who also hold Declan in high regard and who too believe that he is worth keeping an eye on.

Declan's father, Alec, sits in his bottle-green leather chair by the fire. His bare feet are planted on the hearth. Every now and then, he pulls them back to let them cool. Portly and with ruddy cheeks, Alec has the air of the contented country gentleman, yet he is inner-city Belfast through and through. He lifts his mug of tea in both hands and sips. The doughnuts on a plate on the arm of his chair look mouth-watering. He takes one and bites into it. His taste buds delight in the sugary hit. Outside, a gale is blowing. Inside, it is sweltering. Upstairs, Alec's wife, Colette, and his daughter, Kate, are cleaning out the spare room. The house is settled.

There is a heavy knock on the front door. Alec looks at Declan. In Ireland, fathers don't answer doors in the wilds of winter when they have big sons to do it for them. Declan knows his place.

In Loughshore, County Down, there is another heavy knock on a door. Stephanie Diver, sitting in the living room, hits the security channel on the television. She opens the front door to two policemen. 'Hello, officer.'

'Good evening, ma'am,' Seamus McCann says.

'Good evening.'

'Are you Mrs Diver?'

'I am.'

'Mrs Stephanie Diver?'

'Yes?'

'Amm ... I'm very sorry, ma'am—'

Stephanie's jaw drops. Her hand reaches for her cheek. 'Oh, my God. It's bad news, isn't it?'

'I'm afraid so. May we come in?'

Stephanie stands aside. 'Please do.'

The two 'policemen' enter the Diver household. As soon as Stephanie closes the front door, McCann grabs her waist with one hand, while his other hand covers her mouth. His colleague takes off his policeman's hat and pulls down a ski mask before drawing his gun. 'If you don't do exactly as I say, I'll kill Liam,' McCann says. 'Do you understand?'

Stephanie, her eyes bulging, nods. McCann pulls down his ski mask and pushes Stephanie into a corner. Wearing a brown bathrobe, Liam comes out into the hall, drying his hair with a towel.

McCann puts a gun to Stephanie's head. 'On your knees, Liam.'

Liam gets down on his knees.

'Life or death?' McCann snaps. 'Quickly! What's it to be?'

'Life,' Liam blurts out. 'Life.'

McCann puts the gun to Liam's temple. 'Life or death, Stephanie?'

'Life.'

'A wise choice.'

The concrete lamp post outside the Butler family's front door looks as if it is being shaken by the hand of an invisible giant. In the ferocious wind, a pair of old tennis shoes swing precariously from an overhead telephone cable. A white plastic bag whirls about in a blustery current. A drip from leaky guttering produces a quick-beat drum-rattle on paving stones. Shadow, the next-door neighbour's mongrel, has been barking all night. It is ladling it down: rain, sleet, occasionally snow. Not a night to be out if you can avoid it. Yet there are some people who do not want to avoid it, and one of them is Billy Kelly. He tugs down on the front of his baseball hat, adjusts his plain-glass, thick spectacles, smooths his white wig and pulls up the collar of his coat. One gang member puts his arm around another's back and they pretend to laugh at an imaginary joke, both doubling up as if they have just shared the greatest gag ever told. It is a ruse they have perfected over time to allay the suspicions of nosey neighbours.

The door opens. Declan gazes at the three faces, none of which are familiar. There is something odd here, he feels, something that's not quite right. It's as if these three people do not want him to remember their peculiarities, as if they are hiding beneath other people's faces. Two wear wigs and false moustaches, and the third has a black beard that looks like it has just been pulled out of a spin dryer. The two mustachios have on baseball caps, while the bearded one sports a trapper hat and haversack. That all three have thick glasses is hardly a coincidence. And are those surgical gloves? Avarice, indulgence and wickedness smile at Declan. He smiles back, though his chubby face is already losing its flushness. 'Can I help you, fellas?' he stammers, even though he has an overwhelming inkling they are there to help themselves.

Billy Kelly opens his coat, takes out a handgun from his waistband and holds it down by his side. 'You certainly can, Dec.'

Declan would remember those chilling words for the rest of his life. Suspicion has done a runner, taking doubt along with it. Still, Declan does not want to believe that this is real. A manufactured, mystified look appears on his face. 'You're joking,' he says jovially, his eyes darting from face to face, seeking out the giveaway grin that would tell him this is a practical joke. Even a smirk would do. A wink of the eye? A tapping finger on a nose? But no. No one is grinning, smirking, winking or tapping.

Billy sticks the gun in Declan's ribs. 'Step back, nice and slowly, and keep your hands by your sides.'

Declan steps back and the three tiger-kidnappers follow him into the hallway. One of the gang closes the front door.

As an avid football supporter, Declan is used to having butterflies in his stomach, but those are the friendly type; these butterflies have teeth like piranhas and appetites like blue whales. 'Lads, can't—?'

'You can do exactly what you're told,' Billy says quietly.

'But—'

'Shut up and listen,' Billy says, grabbing Declan by the bicep and squeezing. 'I'll stiff your whole family if you hit any panic buttons. I'll stiff them if *they* hit any panic buttons. I'll stiff them if you don't co-operate fully with us. Are we on the same channel here?'

'Sure. Completely.'

'Let's meet the Butlers,' Billy says.

Seamus McCann and his crew have already met the Divers. McCann makes a phone call. 'That pup's been sold.'

'Good,' Ructions says. 'I'll be with you soon.' *We're on the road at last. Both houses are successfully breached, and nothing is amiss. You're hitting all the right notes, Ructions lad.* Sitting in a London-style black taxi, fifty yards from the Butler household, Ructions opens the taxi's window. He cannot see any police lurking about but that means nothing, cops are good at making themselves invisible when they don't want to be seen. He listens, open-mouthed, and hears nothing: no helicopter overhead. Popping a stick of chewing gum into his mouth, he hums the last section of Rossini's 'William Tell Overture'. A silver car coming slowly up the street catches his attention. 'Hi ho Silver away,' he murmurs.

Finbarr, inside the silver car, leans over and looks at the door numbers. He drives past the black taxi, slows down at the Butler home, takes a long look at the house and drives on to the end of the street where he pulls in for a quick line of coke. His phone rings. It's Benzo Mullins. He knows that he shouldn't take the call, but nosiness is a drug and Finbarr is partial to drugs. He's pulled in at the top of the street. 'Hello?'

'I've been trying to phone our friend who was down in my neck of the woods with you,' Benzo says.

Geek must be on the beer, or else he can't be bothered talking to Benzo. 'Oh?' Finbarr says.

'He's not answering.'

'That's strange.'

'Is it?' Benzo says suspiciously. 'What's strange about it?'

'Don't ask me.'

'But you just said it's strange, and I *am* asking you.'

'It was just a casual remark. That's all.'

'You see, when you said it was strange, I immediately thought our friend is ignoring me. Well, I would think that, wouldn't I?'

'I guess.'

'So, is it strange or isn't it?'

'I don't know.'

'Give him four,' Benzo says distantly.

'I'm not with you,' Finbarr says. 'Give me four what?'

'I'm not speaking to you,' Benzo says. Obviously conversing with someone beside him, Benzo continues, 'Four will do him. If he needs any more, he knows where we are.' He turns his attention back to Finbarr. 'Is your father thinking of shafting me?'

'Wise up.'

'Did you just tell me to wise up?'

'I didn't mean—'

'I asked you a question: did you just tell me to wise up?'

'I didn't mean to insult you, honest.'

A silence. 'Why isn't our friend taking my calls?'

Coz he's more sense than I fuckin' have. If I'd known that you were going to be like this, you prick, I wouldn't have taken your call either. 'I don't know. Maybe he's left his phone at home.'

'Mmm, that could be it.'

Finbarr can hear Benzo humming a tune in the background. 'I want you to contact him.'

'I can do that.'

'I want you to tell him that few quid is due next Tuesday.'

'Ah, yes. Don't sweat that,' Finbarr says cheerily. 'I've that boxed off, B—'

'No names!'

Finbarr of the Fierce Temper has heard and taken enough. 'Hey, you!' he shouts down the phone. 'You—'

'What about me?'

'Fuck you – that's what about you! I'm Finbarr O'Hare, son of Panzer O'Hare, and don't you fuckin' dare talk to me like that!'

'I don't care if you're Finbarr bin Laden, son of Panzer bin Laden!' Benzo yells back. 'Get my fuckin' money by Tuesday or the Four Horsemen of the Apocalypse are coming to Belfast.'

'Four, Benzo?' Finbarr shrieks. 'Fuckin' Benzo? That's your name, isn't it? Fuckin' Benzo? You're threatening us with only four horsemen? Well, wait till I tell you, dickhead, this is Belfast and this place is coming down with Horsemen of the Apocalypse! We've hundreds of the fuckers! We've—'

Benzo hangs up.

Someone is trying to open the passenger-side door of Finbarr's car. He swivels around. Ructions' face stares in, his breath frosting up the window. Finbarr gapes and stretches in his seat, his head almost touching the top corner of the car. *No, no!*

Ructions tries repeatedly to open the door, but to no avail. When Ructions points to the door lock, Finbarr shakes his head, twiddles his fingers in a farewell motion and drives off.

Ructions watches Finbarr's car disappear. *So, Panzer, you old bastard. You fucking betrayed me. You let your sex-fiend son into our most important secret, despite both of us resolutely agreeing that he wasn't to know about the robbery. Why? Why jeopardise the move and those taking part in it?* He looks around at the upstairs windows of the houses opposite. Nothing. The more Ructions deliberates on Panzer's treachery, the more he sees the father in the son: blood from blood; heart from heart; true reprobate from true reprobate. He casually walks to his own car, taking out his mobile as he goes. Panzer's line is engaged. Not unexpectedly. *No doubt Finbarr has got there before me. How are you gonna explain this one, Panzer? It'll be interesting to hear what you've got to say to me when I do get to speak to you.*

Once inside his car, Ructions phones Panzer again. This time he gets through.

'Hold on a second,' Panzer says, setting down the phone on the arm of his chair. On the other arm, his fingers tap a beat. He feels woozy. *Ructions will be putting in a bill for this folly; he'll see Finbarr's presence at the Butler home, without his knowledge, as a stab in the back. Worse than that, he might reach the conclusion that I'm planning to swindle him out of his share of the loot.* Struggling for breath, Panzer feels as if he has just been keelhauled. His breathing returns to normal as he stares at the phone. Reluctantly, he picks it up. 'Can you come up to me?'

'No.'

'I can explain.'

'I doubt it.'

'Look, we can sort this out.'

Ructions hangs up and shuts his eyelids, just for a minute. An intrusive thought pushes through. *What has happened to honour amongst thieves? It's a wonder the imbecile who came up with that cliché didn't invent a Hippocratic oath for outlaws and bandits.*

His phone rings. It's Maria. 'I'll phone you back in a while,' he says.

'No, you won't,' Maria says.

There is something unsettling in Maria's manner, something that persuades him not to dismiss her out of hand. 'Maria, I'm very busy here. What is it?'

'Goodbye, Ructions.'

TEN

'Pardon?' Ructions says politely, when what he really wants to say is, 'What the fuck?' He hesitates and then says, 'Where are you, Maria?'

'I'm leaving. I've my stuff packed. I'm heading home for a while and then I'm going travelling. South America.'

Ructions doesn't respond.

'Are you still there, Ructions?'

'Yes, I'm still here.'

'It's run its course, Ructions. We both know it.'

'I'm not sure what to say, Maria.'

'Nothing to say. Everything has a sell-by date. We've reached ours. I'm glad we're ending it as friends, though.'

'We'll always be friends, Maria. You'll take care of yourself, won't you? Call me if you need anything or run into any trouble over there. Bail money and the like.'

Maria laughs. 'Thanks, Ructions. Hopefully there'll be no need for that. Same goes for you too. And if you need anything, you let me know. You can contact me through my Dad.'

'Good luck, Maria. Y'know, I think you *will* save the rainforest.'

Maria laughs. 'Bye, Ructions.'

In the Butler household, Declan's sister, Kate, comes into the kitchen holding a vacuum cleaner. She sees her brother having a whispered conversation with three men. There is tension in the room and then there is Billy Kelly with his dazzling, butter-wouldn't-melt-in-his-mouth smile. *These men look like an odd bunch. Why are they wearing hats inside the house? Every one of them has facial hair. That looks like a wig. Why is that fella wearing surgical gloves?*

Declan looks up. 'Give me a couple of minutes, will you, Kate?'

'Come again?'

'Give me a minute, please.'

'What's going on here, Dec?' she asks, leaving the vacuum cleaner aside. Pointing to Billy, she asks, 'Why's he wearing gloves? And why are these people disguised?' Her hand goes to her mouth as it dawns on her that they are there because Declan works for the National Bank and they intend to rob it. 'Get out,' she demands, pointing to the door. 'I'm telling you to get out of our house now or I'm calling the police.'

'Go ahead,' Billy says, handing Kate his phone. 'Go on. Take it. Phone the cops. I'll not stop you.'

Kate stares at the phone, then shakes her head.

'You're sure?' Billy says.

There follows a barely audible grunt from Kate.

Billy inclines his ear to Kate's mouth. 'I didn't hear that?'

'No.'

'Congratulations, Kate.'

'Why? What have I done?'

'You've weighed up the situation and adjusted appropriately.' Billy leans towards Kate conspiratorially, 'You've done very well.'

'Don't patronise me, you—'

Billy simulates shock. 'Dec, she's going to call me names. Can you believe that?'

Declan moves to defuse the friction. 'Don't call him names, Kate. Don't do that.'

Billy presses his hand to his heart in a display of mock indignation. 'I'm not feeling the love from you, Kate. Like, do you really *want* to make me feel unwelcome in this house? If you do, just say the words "I don't want you here" and me and the boys will disappear – with our new buddy Dec. Disappear – that's a big word, Kate. A big word with a big meaning.' Billy looks at his watch. As quickly as it had flourished, the humour in his voice dies. 'Listen, girlie, you can't afford to get angry with me. Not for a fuckin' second. Now go stand in the corner till I tell you to come out.'

Kate goes to the corner.

'Turn around,' Billy orders, his finger twirling. 'Face the wall.'

It is time to go to the next level. 'We're going to take you away for twenty-four hours,' Billy says to Declan.

'Where to?'

Kate turns around. 'Where are you taking my brother?'

'Kate, face the wall.'

Billy turns to Declan. 'Tá tú ag dul go dtí Tír na n-Óg, a mhic.'

Declan recoils at Billy's ability to speak Irish. 'An ceart é sin? Ní raibh mé ann riamh.'

'Sa chás sin, bhainfidh mé sult as,' Billy says.

So, I'm off to The Land of Eternal Youth? Off to the afterlife to live forever? Spirited away by a lowlife who has taken the time to learn the Irish language and Gaelic mythology? Declan is not sure if he should be impressed with Billy's seamless changeover from English to Irish, and his eyes irreverently inspect the intruder from head to toe.

Billy has not missed Declan's derision. 'Are those daggers in your eyes, sonny boy?' he says. 'Tell me you're not being disrespectful, kid, or by Jesus you'll be swallowing teeth in the next few seconds.'

Declan shakes his head. He is perplexed. He had learned Irish at school and at the Gaeltacht in Gweedore, an Irish-speaking area in County Donegal. But where had the tiger-kidnapper learned it? He doesn't know that Billy was born into an Irish-speaking family. Declan knows hoods and criminals, most people do; they are your next-door neighbour's son whom you suspect is plotting to steal your car every time he walks past it, or, God forbid, your next-door neighbour himself, who watches and waits for you to carelessly leave a window open so he can break into your house. But none of the hoods Declan has ever known has taken the trouble to learn Irish – they can hardly speak English, their vocabulary restricted to the same few thousand words. *Who am I dealing with here? Is this an IRA job? Should I ask them? They mightn't like that, and they'd hardly tell me the truth anyway. I reckon they're IRA.* He surveys all three gang members. *Look at them – total confidence; not even as much as a hint of confusion or panic – and their leader – he's lapping up every second of this. They're IRA, Declan. Be very careful.*

Any sign of impertinence evaporates from Declan's face as his spirits plummet. The realisation that these guys are most likely IRA smacks into him with the power of a wrecking ball. He shifts from one foot to the other and then puts his hands in his pockets, only to take them out again. He swallows. *Don't break down. Don't.*

A meltdown is the last thing Billy wants to see; he needs Declan to be frightened, but not so frightened that he becomes incapable of functioning in the required manner. He grabs Declan by the chin and says, 'Hey, stop that snivelling.'

Declan's windpipe bobs like a fishing float in a fast-flowing river.

'Dec, no one *has* to die here,' Billy says. 'Do you hear me?'

Declan nods.

'If you do exactly as you're told, and your family does exactly as they're told, everything will be fine.'

'You'll have no problems with me, mister.'

Billy releases Declan's chin. 'Good man. That's what I needed to hear. It's all down to yourselves,' Billy says, 'but mostly it's down to *you. You* play the game, *you* follow instructions, and we don't need to kill your family. It's simple enough.' Billy pats Declan on the back. 'But if you fuck up, if you try to get clever, they end up in boxes. An dtuigeann tú?'

Declan manages to summon up a weak smile. It's the best he can do. 'Yes, I understand. Don't worry about me. I'll do whatever you tell me.'

'Good. Now, you'll be leaving in ...' Billy looks at his watch, 'ten minutes. I need to speak to your family. Kate ...'

Kate turns around.

'Come here, Kate.'

Feelings of uncertainty and vulnerability take hold of Alec when Declan, the three men and Kate enter the living room. It's as if all the goodness has been drained out of the room by a malignant spirit. While one gang member closes the blinds and stands beside Declan in the middle of the room, another remains at the door. Kate sits on a chair to the side and folds her arms. Declan's mother, Colette, occupies a chair across from her husband.

'Sit down on the sofa, Dec,' Billy orders.

Declan sits on the side of the sofa directly adjacent to his father.

'Not there. That's my seat.'

Declan moves over. Alec and Colette look at each other uneasily as Billy disrespectfully flops himself on the sofa, opposite Alec. He buffs up some cushions and places them behind him. Billy then eases into the cushions, stretches his legs and cups the back of his neck with his hands. He looks at Alec and yawns. He notices that the red light below the Sacred Heart of Jesus picture in the alcove wall has just gone out. Alec notices too. Alec does not need a sign from God to tell him that something is seriously amiss. It is evident from Billy's attitude that he considers himself, not Alec, to be the master of the house.

'Who the hell are you?' Alec asks.

Billy flicks open his coat to reveal a gun in his waistband. 'I'm the big cheese, the guy who puts holes in people.'

Alec looks at the gun. 'If you say so.'

Billy's phone rings. He holds up the phone for Alec to see, puts his finger to his lips and answers it. It is Ructions checking up on how things are going. 'Grand,' Billy says. 'I'll phone you back shortly.' He hangs up.

'I'm scared, Alec,' Colette says, her voice quivering. She begins sobbing softly.

'Colette, love, it will be okay. Don't worry,' Alec says.

'Mum, Dad's right,' Declan says, reaching over to take his mother's hand. 'It's—'

'But, son, they're—'

'Sit,' Billy orders sternly.

Declan looks down coldly at Billy.

'I said, sit.'

Declan obeys.

'Jesus, I hate crying women,' Billy says disparagingly, as he takes a packet of tissues from the inside pocket of his coat and hands them over to Colette. While Colette sniffs into a tissue, Billy says, 'Okay, folks. Here's the deal. If you all do what you're told, we'll sail through this. If you don't, you'll end up with a black bow tied to your front door. End of speech. Have any of you trouble with your hearing?'

Billy looks at each family member individually and they all shake their heads. As if reminding Billy that he is not in control of everything, rain and a vicious gust of wind rattle the window. 'A bitter night,' Billy says. 'Phew. You've no idea what a day I've had, Alec. I'll be glad to see the back of it, I swear.' He yawns again, his mouth a gaping hole. 'So, how's it going, Alec?'

Alec is in no mood for merry banter and does not answer.

'You know,' Billy adds, 'I've been looking forward to meeting you for quite a while now. You appreciate what's going on here, don't you?'

'I know it's sheer folly to be impolite to a gunman.'

Billy smiles. 'Folly ... I like that word. Very well put, if I may say so. Now, about you: Alexander Ciaran Butler, born 12 December 1944; father's name, Alexander Patrick Butler; mother's maiden name, Bernadette Patricia Millar. You married Colette Duffy on Saturday, 17 May 1969. You had your wedding reception in the West Belfast Social Club on the Falls Road. You both lived with Colette's parents before getting your own house in Beechmount Avenue. Like your father, Alec, you were a deep-sea docker until decasualisation in 1970. After being made redundant at the docks, you worked at Corry's timber yard on the Springfield Road until—'

'So *you* know *me*,' Alec says. 'What do I say I called you when I'm being questioned by the police?'

Billy's hand caresses the butt of his gun. 'What makes you think you'll be around to talk to the police?'

Alec puts up an appealing hand. 'Hold on, fella. I wasn't trying to insult you.'

'It sounded like it to me,' Billy says. He runs his tongue around the outside of his teeth. 'What about Mister X? That sounds good, doesn't it?'

Alec nods affirmatively.

'The mysterious, macabre Mister X,' Billy says. 'I like that. It has a bit of the Hitchcock about it, don't you think?'

Alec looks at his son. Their eyes connect, each know intuitively what the other is thinking: *These are dangerous criminals. Whatever happens, let's not wind them up*. 'I want this to be as painless as possible,' Alec says.

'Ditto,' Billy says, putting out his hand to Alec.

Alec hesitates, staring at the hand as if it was covered in warts. Alec's gaze turns to Billy. It is then that he beholds the dark matter in Billy's eyes: the ruthlessness; the potential for unlimited violence. Alec judges that this man would have no hesitation in killing his family, if he thought it necessary. He takes Billy's hand and shakes it.

'A strong handshake, Alec,' Billy says. 'I like that. I said you'd be a reasonable man. I told them all. Everybody's going to come out of this hunky-dory. I can feel it. Can't you feel it, Dec?'

Declan smiles submissively.

Billy slaps Declan's leg. 'For Christ's sake, cheer up, man. Anyone would think you were about to have a root canal.'

Declan wishes that a root canal was the sum of his troubles.

'Kate,' Alec says wryly, 'put on the kettle for our guests. Mister X, what do you like? Biscuits, buns, a few sandwiches?'

'We're okay, thanks,' Billy says. 'We've brought our own cups and tea.'

Alec looks at him. 'Forensics?'

'Something like that. You guys act as if we're not here. Dec, we need to talk.'

Colette Butler gets up from her chair and touches Billy's arm as he leads Declan from the room. 'You're not going to hurt my son, are you? You don't look like a murderer.'

Billy rubs the top of Colette's head and smiles. She turns to her son and wags her finger in his face. 'Declan, you do what these gentlemen tell you. Do you hear me? This is about money – but it's not *your* money.'

'Words of wisdom, Colette,' Billy says. 'Words of wisdom.'

ELEVEN

Bank manager Liam Diver knows himself well enough to accept that he is not cut out to be a hero. He is, however, an intelligent man, one who has considered the possibility that, some day, tiger-kidnappers might invade his home. Should such a catastrophe occur, his wife Stephanie and he had decided that they would fully co-operate with their captors. Translated into hard reality, that means he is now tied up on a mattress in a bedroom of his home with a hooded gunman standing over him. What feeds the hurricane in Liam's stomach is the coarse way in which his captors have been treating Stephanie. One of the gang has already slapped her face three times. Liam would like to have shouted to the thug to leave her alone, to threaten to track him down when this was all over, to promise that he would cut out his tongue; but his own tongue is immobilised, and anyway, he's a bank manager, and bank managers are not cut out to be heroes.

Stephanie Diver is rocking on a sofa in the living room, her hands clasped tightly on her lap. Seamus McCann pulls out a boiler suit from a duffle bag and hands it to her. 'Put this on.'

Stephanie stares blankly at McCann.

'Did you hear me?'

Stephanie's mouth opens and closes as she looks straight ahead.

'I said, put on this fuckin' boiler suit,' McCann demands, stabbing the top of her head with his finger, 'or I'll put it on for you.'

Stephanie's eyes blink incessantly and she inhales deeply, giving the impression that she is awakening from a trance. She turns slowly to McCann, takes the boiler suit and puts it on over her clothes. It is a loose fit.

McCann goes into the bedroom, sits down on the mattress beside Liam and sniffs him. Liam instinctively pulls back his head. *You absolute shit – you're treating us like animals and you're enjoying it.*

McCann lets out a whistle. 'I can smell it. Yip, it's there. And it's good. It's very good. That fear will keep Steph alive, Liam. I don't often do this, but I'm going to give you a piece of advice, a one-off break: keep that fear if you want to see Steph at the end of this. Otherwise …' McCann puts two fingers to his temple, 'we'll execute her.'

Liam holds his breath, fearful that breathing might be interpreted as a sign of rebellion, as an excuse to execute.

'Now, so you know the score, we're going to take Steph away till this is all over.'

Liam's eyes bulge. 'Please take me. Don't take Stephanie.'

McCann grabs Liam by the hair and pulls back his head. 'And there's me thinking you'd a titter of wit. Seems I've overestimated you.'

'I—'

'Tell me,' McCann says, 'what would be the sense in us taking you away as a hostage and letting Steph go? She doesn't work in the bank; she can't bring us our money. Only *you* can do that.'

Liam tries unsuccessfully to pull his hair free from McCann's grasp.

'Hey, hey, hey!' McCann says, his grip tightening on Liam's hair. 'What the fuck's got into you?'

'I'll co-operate. Totally. Just, just don't hurt my wife. Don't take her away.'

'I'm curious. What did you expect was going to happen? You didn't seriously think we were going to let you go to the bank and wait about here with Steph so you could set the cops on us? That would be real fuckin' smart, wouldn't it?'

'I'm sorry,' Liam says, more in the hope that remorsefulness will mitigate in his favour than with conviction.

McCann slaps Liam's cheek with his free hand. 'Pay attention. If you want to walk into the bank tomorrow morning and tell the cops all about us,' McCann waves his hand in a carefree manner, 'go right ahead. But remember two things: one, we'll not be here when they show up, and, two, we'll execute Steph if we get a sniff of any cop involvement. Now, I'd have assumed a brainbox like yourself, a clever bastard, would see the world as it is, not as you'd like to see it.' McCann cranks his neck as if it has only just been greased. 'Liamy, you're our man in Havana, see? Our man on the inside. Get used to it, comrade.' McCann smoothes down Liam's hair and leaves the room.

In the living room, McCann takes aside his 'fellow policeman' and, holding his hand across his mouth, quietly orders him to phone another member of the kidnap gang. McCann sits beside Stephanie. 'Are you ready to move?'

Stephanie is transformed. From being on the threshold of a total breakdown, she is now up for battle. 'Where are you taking me?' she asks, with more than a hint of impudence in her voice.

McCann grabs her arm and leads her into the kitchen. 'What did you say back there?'

'Are you hard of hearing? I said I want to know where you're taking me.' She tries to pull away from him. 'And let go of my arm.'

McCann pulls back his fist to punch Stephanie. Her eyes remain open, defiant. McCann holds back the punch, drops his arm, grins churlishly and whispers in Stephanie's ear, 'I'll kill him for you, shall I? Do you want me to put his lights out? I think you do. You've a temper, Steph. If I were you, I'd curb it before it gets you into even more trouble.'

'You can't kill him,' Stephanie retorts.

'And why not?'

'Because without him, you can't take a penny out of the bank.'

McCann sighs, his eyes looking to the ceiling and beyond for deliverance from turbulent women. 'And people think this is easy money,' he mutters. 'You're right. Sure, you're right. We can't make a withdrawal without hubby's co-operation. But you're forgetting one thing: we don't need *you* to rob the bank. I can take you out of this house and execute you up the road.' McCann spreads his hands indifferently and shrugs. 'Liam wouldn't know. He'd obey orders because he'd think you were still alive. And then, you see, if you don't do exactly as we say, we'll not only kill you, but we'll kill him *after* the robbery. Remember, he gets released from this contract only when we say so, not before.' McCann waits for his words to sink in. 'Now, big mouth, have you anything else you wish to say? Spit it out.'

Stephanie shakes her head.

'I can't hear you.'

'I'll do nothing that puts my husband's life in danger.'

'You'd better not, or you'll both be pushing up daisies.'

There's a knock on the front door, and a stick-like man enters the house. Not very creatively, the third gang member has disguised himself by wearing a grey knee-length overcoat, a New York Yankees cap and a red scarf, which covers the lower part of his face. His only other distinguishing feature is his sagging right shoulder. Stephanie instantly christens him 'Rag and Bones'. McCann and he speak in whispers. Stephanie watches the pair, consciously concealing her contempt for them. McCann hands Rag and Bones the keys to Stephanie's car and turns to her. 'You'll be in the car with him. One of my people will be following you. In the event that you hit a peeler roadblock, you'll behave normally. If the man in the second car sees anything amiss, he'll phone me, and Liam will be killed. Okay?'

'Yes.'

McCann hands Stephanie a pair of surgical gloves and tells her to put them on. He leads her to the bedroom where her husband is being held. Stephanie looks at Liam on the mattress. She can smell urine. He wants to tell her that he is sorry for all this, but his tongue won't function. Stephanie mouths, 'I love you' before McCann pushes her out. Time to get Stephanie to the safe house.

Rag and Bones sticks slits of clear tape vertically over Stephanie's open eyes so that, on the one hand, her vision will be distorted, and, on the other, no one casually glancing into the car would notice anything wrong with her appearance. This is easy money, McCann tells himself as he gets into his car. Next time, it'll be me who does the hiring and firing: it'll be me who's drawing the big wages.

Inside the car, Stephanie's fingers tap invisible keys on her leg. A hand comes over and buckles her seat belt. 'Are you comfy there?' Rag and Bones asks. 'Need your seat adjusted?'

'No,' Stephanie says. 'I'm fine.'

'Don't you go worrying yourself, missus. You're in safe hands. We won't be on the road too long.'

Stephanie can smell mint and tobacco from him. There is something else: a soapy smell, possibly aftershave. His voice sounds quite mature; she guesses he is in his late forties or early fifties.

'I'm sorry this is being visited on you and your family, missus,' Rag and Bones says. 'You mightn't believe that, but I am. Now just keep your eyes on the road straight ahead and we'll have no problems. You know there's one of our cars behind us?'

'Yes.'

'You know what'll happen to Liam if you—'

'I know. Your boss back at our house told me.'

'I'm sorry for this, missus.'

Sure you are. You'll confess this to the priest on Saturday, won't you? Pretending to have scruples! It occurs to Stephanie that Rag and Bones talks as if he is not a party to this wicked act, as if, somehow, he is a conscientious objector who has been press-ganged into partaking in this evilness. *Perhaps the idiot hasn't the sense to realise that he is as guilty as the others. To hell with him*! *Just get through this*. Stephanie wants to pull the lapels off the boiler suit around her neck, but she has been instructed to keep her hands by her sides. She cannot see anything clearly. There are lights: pastel, crimped, blue and yellow-veined, and then there is only darkness.

A telephone rings. Rag and Bones answers it. 'Hello? Okay … no trouble at all … no … bye.'

In west Belfast, Declan's glow is wilting. His heart plunges as the front door of his home closes behind him. Despite the snarling squall and slicing sleet, Declan is bathed in sweat and despair. He feels as if the life essence has been syringed out of him. It's as though he is a toy, the plaything of a bunch of cut-throat terrorists with – he has convinced himself – bucketloads of blood on their hands. In his own gloved hand, he carries a large Aston Villa holdall which contains his bank uniform. Alongside him is Billy, who puts his hand on his shoulder as if they are the best of buddies. While Billy goes down the street, Declan walks towards the tiger-kidnappers' car.

Declan is put into the back seat. An unshaven, fat-faced driver, who is wearing an ill-fitting blond wig, turns around. In his hands is a silver pistol.

'You'll be in the car for a while,' Ambrose Peoples says in a voice that is more reassuring than threatening. 'I want you to lay face down, Declan, and remain calm.'

Declan complies.

'I want you to think only of your family. Remember, only you can make yourself a casualty, so be smart and do the right thing. This is all about money. Fuck all else. It's not worth your mother's or your father's lives. Oh, and by the way, that guy who came out of the house with you—'

'Mr X.'

'That'd be him. He'll be following us.'

'Yes, he told me, sir.'

'Well, I'm telling you again – any shit and he makes the phone call to your house, and then …' Ambrose sighs. 'He's not going to have to make that call, kid, is he?'

'No, sir.'

Ambrose turns back and puts the pistol at his feet. 'You've good manners, Declan. I like that.'

'Thank you.'

Ambrose adjusts his mirror so that he can see his back-seat passenger. 'Bit of advice, son – take it or leave it – try to make this as easy as possible for yourself. Do exactly what you're told and it'll all be over before you know it.' Putting up two fingers, the amiable tiger-kidnapper says, 'There are two things you need to remember. One – the only losers in this should be the multimillionaires who own the National Bank, and, two – heroes usually die before their time.'

'Okay, sir.' Declan would like to close his eyes, to escape from this black hole, but that's not going to switch off the chattering voice in his head: *These tiger-kidnappers aren't shy about doling out advice; they must be community activists, or counsellors, or social workers in their ordinary lives. Are you a community activist, Fatso? Are you a Provo? Do you smile and dispense wisdom during the day, then terrorise innocent working families at night? Do you ever give yourself advice and, if you do, do you ever take it?*

Ambrose drives off slowly. 'What sort of music do you like, Declan?'

'Irish mostly.'

'Traditional or popular?'

'Both.'

'What about Christy Moore?'

'I like Christy, sir.'

'Christy it is then.'

Soon the car is filled with the melodic sound of 'Ride On'.

'Declan, did you know this song is actually a requiem to Shergar? Poor fella. Wins the Epsom Derby and the Irish Derby in 1981 and two short years later is kidnapped and killed by the IRA.'

A requiem to Shergar? Is this guy high? 'No, I didn't know that, sir.'

'You'd wonder why the IRA would've wanted to kidnap such a magnificent animal, wouldn't you?' Ambrose says.

'Aye, you would,' Declan says. *Do you know what makes me wonder? Whether or not you're on the same bloody planet as me? Is it beyond your grasp that Shergar was kidnapped for money – just like me? But I'm not Shergar. I'm not a rebellious stallion. I'm yes, sir, no, sir, three bags full, sir.*

'They say they killed the horse because they couldn't control it.'

'So they say.'

'You'd wonder why the IRA hadn't somebody with them who knew about horses, wouldn't you?'

'You would.'

'Are you all right there, kid?'

'Yeah.'

'Do yourself a favour: try and get a bit of kip. You'll have a long night and an even longer day tomorrow.'

TWELVE

Ructions drives up to the Big House. The front door opens and Panzer emerges. He squirms in the ferocity of the driving rain and sleet, his white open-necked shirt already sticking to his body. Ructions gets out of the black taxi.

Holding up a glass of red wine, Panzer offers a Caesar's salutation to his most prized general. The rain and sleet dilute the wine immediately. The raising of a glass is a gratuitous gesture that does not trouble Panzer: it is not a show of humility. Humility has its place, he believes: in the confessional, at an AA meeting, when pleading not guilty in court, when poor-mouthing the taxman, when meeting future parents-in-law for the first time; when, as a last resort, there is no other choice if calamity is to be avoided.

Panzer walks towards Ructions, his free hand thrust out, rain dripping off the end of his nose, eyes blinking furiously. Ructions looks down at Panzer's hand: a barbed olive branch. He takes it, more out of courtesy than respect. In a display of affection, Panzer puts his arm around Ructions' shoulder and leads him to the house. Suddenly there is a series of deep cavernous roars, followed by bolts of fork lightning. 'Quick,' Panzer says. 'Get in before we catch our death of cold.'

They step into the terracotta hall. Panzer stands on the edge of Michael the Archangel's sword, while Ructions dallies on Satan's head. 'Wait. I'll get two towels,' Panzer says, making for the bathroom.

A door opens and Finbarr walks across the hall towards the white room. Out of the corner of his eye, he clocks Ructions and flashes one of those I-got-one-over-on-you smiles at him. Ructions blanks his cousin.

Panzer returns and hands Ructions a towel. 'It's going great, isn't it?' Panzer says, his face a riot of enthusiasm. Without waiting on an answer, he walks into the white room, drying his hair as he goes along. Ructions follows him. 'I said, it's going great,' Panzer repeats.

Ructions makes no reply, an act of defiance that is not lost on Panzer.

Finbarr is seated on one of the two sofas, a bottle of beer in his hand. Panzer goes to the drinks cabinet, lifts the stopper off a crystal decanter and offers Ructions a drink.

Ructions refuses.

Panzer pours himself a fresh glass of wine. 'Sit down.'

Ructions takes a seat on the second sofa and looks into the fire. A silence descends on the room. The clock on the mantelpiece ticks loudly, relentlessly gulping time, like a glutton who doesn't know when to stop eating.

Panzer decides to get in first. 'I know you're probably wondering what Finbarr was doing at—'

'Outlet One,' Ructions butts in.

'Yes, yes. Outlet One. I sent him to—'

'Spy on me.'

'Spy on *you*?' Finbarr says.

'Shut up, Finbarr,' Panzer snaps, as he stokes the fire with the poker.

'Tell me, why would I want to spy on you?' Panzer asks.

'Funny you should ask me that because I've been asking myself the same question.'

Panzer sets the poker in the companion set, walks to the window and looks out.

Panzer doesn't want me to see his face when he gives his answer.

'I was covering your back.'

Unadulterated bollocks. Ructions' tolerance levels are breached and he points to Finbarr. 'You sent *him* to cover *my* back? Is that the best you can come up with, Panzer? Is that fuckin' it?'

Panzer had expected Ructions' attack, but he is surprised at its savagery. He turns around. 'Now, now, Ructions, there's no need—'

'There's no need for what? Did we not agree that he shouldn't know about this job? Am I wrong?' Gazing intently at Panzer, he asks again, 'Did I get that wrong?'

Panzer shoots a be-careful-with-your-words look at Ructions and plops down on a seat. He swirls his wine around in the glass and holds it up to the light of the fire before taking a sip. 'You know you didn't,' he says demurely.

'Then why did you tell—'

'He's my son.'

Ructions pulls back in mock shock. 'He's your son? That's it? That's your reason?'

'Yeah, that's it. He's my son. He'd a right to know.'

'Because he's your son?'

'Yes, fuckin' yes!'

'Who else has a right to know about this? Geek? The stable boys? The milkman? Big Tiny? Special Branch? MI5?'

'Don't be talking balls.' Panzer lowers his voice. 'And anyway, who have *you* told?'

'Not a fuckin' sinner.'

Panzer is well aware that Ructions has refrained from addressing him as 'boss'.

'That's the thing about me,' Ructions continues, 'I don't tell *anyone* I'm going to rob a bank if they don't need to know. That's what a successful bank robbery is all about—'

Panzer's face flushes. He jerks forward in his seat. 'What's this? The Gospel according to Saint Ructions? You're going to give me a sermon on how to rob banks?'

'No sermons,' Ructions says, his finger extended upwards, 'but mark this – I've a mind to pull the farmers out.'

'*You've* a mind to pull them out? *You*? Since when did *you* give the orders around here?'

'Since when did you think it's alright to take a crap on me? Since when did you think it was all right to send that …' Ructions points to Finbarr, 'child molester to spy on me?'

Finbarr jumps up, breaks his bottle of beer on the mantelpiece and waves the jagged edge in front of Ructions. 'Call me a child molester again, scumbag! Go on – call me a child molester again.'

'You're a child molester.' Ructions leaps to his feet and squares up to Finbarr.

'You want some of this?' Finbarr says, the broken bottle thrust out before him.

Ructions beckons him on with his fingers. 'Come on, paedo! Give it your best shot.'

Panzer rubs his callused hands together. *If this row goes any further, Ructions is liable to hurt Finbarr and then for sure he'll have no choice but to scuttle the robbery. No winners then. No room for manoeuvre. I've no choice.* 'Finbarr, take that bottle out of the man's face and fuck off out of here.'

Panting and foaming at the mouth, Finbarr still waves the broken bottle at Ructions. 'But Dad, he—'

'I said, leave us.'

'No. No way. He called me a—'

'Finbarr, get out!' Panzer shouts. 'Now!'

Muttering, sulking, and with a face full of fury, Finbarr leaves the room, slamming the door behind him.

Panzer beckons Ructions to sit beside him on the sofa. Ructions does so. Panzer sighs deeply, stares at the ceiling and says, 'I'm tired.' Ructions cannot help but think that he looks tired. 'Do you ever get tired?'

'Sometimes.'

'Lately, I've been tired all the time.' Panzer puts his hand on his arm. 'I want you to listen to me. Can you do that?'

Ructions nods.

'Good. Ructions, think carefully before saying something you might regret.' Panzer looks into Ructions' eyes and notes that the hot coals of rage are still smouldering. 'The two of us have staked a lot on this project and it'll cost us dearly if it collapses by default.'

Go on, old man. Get it off your chest, whatever it is, and be done with it.

Panzer bows his head. 'I'm ahh ...'

Holy shit! He's shaping up to apologise!

'I shouldn't have told Finbarr about the job, but I'd already done so before we agreed not to tell him.'

'So, he knew all along?' Ructions lowers and shakes his head. 'Why didn't you just say this when we were shooting golf balls on the mountain?'

'If I'd done that, you'd have called time on the job.'

Ructions squirms. 'I'd—'

'You'd have choked it.'

'You're right.'

Panzer opens his mouth as if gulping air, like he is about to say something that runs contrary to his nature. 'I'm sorry, Ructions. I shouldn't have deceived you.'

It is Ructions' turn to sigh. 'Okay, boss. Is that drink still on offer?'

So, I'm 'boss' again? 'Sure,' Panzer says, going over to the drinks cabinet.

'Finbarr has to stay away from me and everybody involved in the job,' Ructions says firmly.

Panzer hands Ructions his glass of wine and says, 'I can live with that.'

Ructions barely sips the wine. 'I mean it, Panzer. We can't afford L-plates. The stakes are too high.'

'I said I can live with that.'

Ructions sets down his glass and walks out to the hallway. Panzer follows him. 'You asked a question earlier on. Yeah. It's going great.'

'I thought so.'

'I should've told you earlier, boss. After this job, I'm out.'

Panzer looks puzzled. 'You don't mean that.'

'Panzer, after this, we're all out. Nothing will be the same again. It's over. Our day has come and gone – and I'm glad.'

'You don't really believe that, do you?'

'There's no place left for us to go and no banks big enough for us to rob. Now, you old fucker, I've gotta run on.'

'Old fucker, am I?' Panzer says, pretending to punch Ructions in the stomach.

Ructions opens the door, runs to his black taxi, turns around and gives Panzer a soldier's salute. Panzer returns the gesture. As Ructions drives away, it crosses his mind that Panzer never raised the question of him having called Finbarr a child molester. *You've known all along, haven't you?*

THIRTEEN

'We'll be with you shortly,' Ambrose Peoples says, closing his telephone. He and Declan Butler have been on the road for an hour now. Ambrose does not like driving with a hostage in rural areas during the hours of darkness; he will be relieved when this part of the business is over. 'Okay, Declan, here's the score. You'll be transferring to a second car soon. When you get out of this car, just keep your head down and get into the front passenger seat of the other car. Once there, look straight ahead. Declan, don't, whatever you do, look at the driver. These country fellas aren't like us city boys; they take umbrage and can be vicious.'

They pull into a lay-by and stop alongside the second car. 'Away you go. Remember what I told you and you'll come out of this in one piece. Good luck, kid.'

Here goes. Declan takes two steps and gets into the open door of the second car. Instinctively, his eyes glance sideways at the driver.

'What are you looking at?' the driver roars. 'Keep your fuckin' eyes straight ahead. And keep your hands in your pockets.'

Declan has heard the driver's accent before, but he cannot place it to a particular area. The car moves off. The small of Declan's back aches from lying down in the first car, but rubbing it is out of the question.

'Number One,' the driver says.

Declan is stumped. *Is he speaking to me?* A slight tweak of his head and the driver backhands Declan across the side of his face.

'What the fuck? Didn't I tell you to look straight ahead? Are you fuckin' hard of hearing? Are you, Butler?'

Declan gulps. 'No, sir.'

'Then why do you keep trying to look at me?'

Declan is lost for words. 'I didn't—'

'Fuck up! Fuck up, you little cunt, or I'll pull over and smash your face in with a wheel brace. Do you want me to smash your face in with a wheel brace, Butler?'

'No, sir.'

'Then do as you're fuckin' well told.'

'Yes, sir,' Declan stutters. Beads of sweat form on his forehead and his chest tightens.

The driver starts humming. The notes pull Declan back from distraction. The tune is familiar. It's 'Deborah's Theme' from his favourite movie, *Once Upon a Time in America*. He is sorry to have parted company with the other guy, whom he now regards as a sociable type of tiger-kidnapper, who'd even wished him good luck. The irony of missing your friendly tiger-kidnapper is not lost on him.

'Number One, have the sensors in the house been sorted?' the driver asks.

'Yip,' Seamus McCann answers and leans forward, his arms resting on the back of Declan's headrest. 'Hello, Declan.'

'Hello, sir,' Declan splutters.

'It's good to finally meet you. Are you going to be a good boy for me?'

'Yes, sir.'

'First class. Now just relax. We'll be there in a couple of minutes.'

Declan's curiosity is stirred – but not to the point where he intends to look behind him. He is intrigued by the mention of sensors being in the house. *What house?* It dawns on him that the kidnappers must be taking him to Liam Diver's house at Loughshore, bringing together the two men who have keys to the vault and who will be on duty the next day. *Very astute. But how do they know this amount of detail?* Like everyone else in the banking system, Declan had bought into the theory that having two separate and individual keys to open the bank's vault was an effective way of thwarting tiger-kidnappers. For starters, since one key alone cannot open the vault, it means that any potential robbers have to hold *two* families hostage in order to force *two* keyholders to hand over the money, thus doubling their chances of being caught. But even before reaching that stage, the robbers would need to know which two of the nine keyholders would be working on any particular day in order to rob the bank. *How do they know Liam and I are working tomorrow? There is only one way: they've access to the bank's weekly work rota! That has to be it.* Declan gulps for air. He feels as if he is drowning. *Oh, sweet Jesus! This is an inside job. If they know the work rota, they know everything.* Sitting upright in the car, staring straight ahead and petrified for his family and for himself, young Declan Butler's worst fears are confirmed. He is dealing with the crème de la crème of bank robbers. If he was not persuaded before, Declan is now convinced that they *will* kill his family if he does not co-operate. What was it his mother said? 'This is about money – but it's not *your* money.' When someone is desperate, desperate thoughts are entertained. *What's money? Paper – nothing but pieces of paper. Flesh and blood – that's what matters. I will survive this. As God is my judge, my family will survive this.*

Stephanie Diver is not sure if she will survive. She tries to be positive: *It's just like that lousebag back in the house said: they don't need me. Liam will make it. They have to keep him alive. They've no choice.* Stephanie can feel tears welling up in her eyes. Her body heaves.

The car turns up a country lane and jolts as it plunges into and crawls out of potholes. Finally, it stops. Rag and Bones gets out, opens Stephanie's door and takes her out of the car. After leading her into a building, he sits her down on an old leather sofa with holes in its arms. He lights a Tilley lamp.

Stephanie, who grew up on a farm, can smell mouldy hay and compost. *Cows have been here.* There is also a faint whiff of horse manure. She is in a shed of some sort. Rag and Bones, who has now put on a ski mask, pulls the clear tape from her eyes. It smarts, and she blinks incessantly. He hands Stephanie a damp cloth. 'Here, missus, rub your eyes with this.'

'Thank you,' Stephanie says, taking the cloth and applying it. Her teeth are chattering uncontrollably.

'Sit back, missus,' Rag and Bones says. 'Try and relax.'

She sits back on the old sofa and crosses her arms for heat. It looks as if she is in the corner of an old barn. In the opposite corner, on the edge of light and shadow, a section of the corrugated roof has fallen in and lies on the ground. Cobwebs dot the ribs of the roofing. Bird droppings add some decoration.

On a small table in front of Stephanie is a single page, a writing pad, an envelope and a pen. 'Copy exactly what's written on the sheet of paper,' Rag and Bones says.

Stephanie reads the page. She lifts the pen and begins writing. When she finishes, he tells her to write 'Liam' on the envelope. Rag and Bones takes the writing pad, pen and envelope, and compares the original letter to Stephanie's recently written version. Satisfied, he folds the letter, places it inside the envelope and puts it into the inside pocket of his coat. He then hands Stephanie a blanket. 'You should try to get some sleep, missus. Tomorrow's going to be a long day for you.'

Sleep is the last thing on Billy Kelly's mind as he knocks on the door of room 705 in Belfast's Europa Hotel. Ructions lets him in. They walk into the bedroom. There are a dozen mobile phones on the dressing table.

'Everybody's bedded down and things couldn't be better,' Billy says.

'Nice one, Billy,' Ructions says. 'When are you collecting the loot lorry?'

'The loot lorry?' Billy chortles. 'I like that. Tomorrow morning.'

'You're driving it yourself?'

'Yip. I'm bringing it across the border, but Big Ambrose will be doing most of the driving after that.'

'But you'll be with him?'

'Of course.'

'That's excellent because if this goes the way I think it will, you might have to do three runs.'

Billy whistles. *Three lorryloads of money? Three? I wonder how much money you'd get into one lorryload? Enough to pay us well, amigo*. 'Are you serious?'

'Yeah.'

Ructions puts on his coat and walks to the door. 'I thought that'd cheer you up.'

'Money always cheers me up – and the more money I get, the cheerier I get.'

'Don't we all?' Ructions says, his hand on the door handle.

'What's the big rush?' Billy says.

Ructions looks back. 'I've to—'

'Ructions. Hold up.'

The tone of Billy's voice startles him.

'Panzer met Tiny Murdoch in McQuillan's quarry a few nights ago.'

'What? Who told you that?'

'Floater Doyle.'

'And how does Floater know?'

'His nephew, Joseph, was there.'

'At the meeting?'

'No. Panzer and Tiny were meeting in Tiny's car, but young Joseph was hovering about in the background.'

'Holy fuck.' Ructions comes back into the room, his head tilted, an expression of scepticism on his face. He walks to the window and puts his hands behind his back. 'I know Joseph. When did he join the 'RA?'

'Last year. Tiny has taken him under his wing. He's a good kid.'

Ructions turns around. 'Do you think Panzer was telling Tiny about this job?'

Billy shrugs. 'I dunno. Nah. He wouldn't do that. What would he have to gain?'

'Billy, the question isn't what he'd have to gain; it's what he'd have to lose. People do things they don't want to do all the time. It's only a matter of perspective. These people helping us rob the bank don't want to be a party to their bank being robbed, but because we have the power to threaten a bigger interest in their lives than that of the bank, they've no choice but to help us. All it takes to make anyone do your bidding is to find their bigger interest and to own it.'

'I suppose,' Billy says. 'Still, I don't think Panzer would have told Tiny about the robbery. I mean, for fuck sake, we're talking about Panzer O'Hare here. It … it just wouldn't be him.'

Ructions stares at the floor in deep contemplation. Eventually, he nods. 'You're probably right. I ahh … I might need you after the job is finished.'

Billy has a quizzical look on his face. 'After? What does that mean?'

'I'm being cautious, that's all.'

'You suspect a double-cross, don't you?'

'I don't suspect anything, but I like to be prepared for everything.'

'And you're taking precautions.'

Ructions nods. 'If I do give you a shout, bring shooters.'

'I've got your back – as always.'

'Follow me out in five.'

Billy grabs Ructions' elbow, 'Ambrose too?'

'I'll let you know.'

'You said you'd look after me?'

Ructions had anticipated this moment. He smiles. 'Big time.'

The car carrying Declan stops outside Liam Diver's house. 'Do you know who lives here?' Seamus McCann says to Declan.

'Yes, sir.'

'Then you know what's going down?'

'Yes, sir.'

'When you get out, I want you to walk to the front door, keep your head down and your hands in your pockets.'

'Right, sir.' Declan gets out. Once he is in the hallway, a gang member turns him around, ties his hands behind his back, leads him into a bedroom and orders him to stand in a corner.

Declan hears someone leave the bedroom, but he does not know if anyone else is behind him. He shifts his weight from one foot to the other.

'Stand still,' a voice behind him demands.

'Sir, I need to go to the toilet.'

'No.'

Total collapse is at hand as Declan holds, and holds, until finally he urinates where he is standing. Tears spring from weary eyes.

'Stop your whinging,' the voice says.

'Bring him in,' McCann says, adjusting his itchy ski mask.

Declan is grabbed by the scruff of the neck, pulled into another bedroom and thrust down on a bed beside Liam Diver.

'Tell him to turn off the water tap, or he'll get hurt,' McCann says as he leaves the room, passing a guard in the hallway.

'For Jesus sake, Declan,' Liam says sternly, 'pull yourself together.'

Declan breathes deeply. Gradually the tears subside. 'They've taken over our house too, Liam,' he whispers. 'They've got my Mum and Dad—'

'They've taken Stephanie away.'

'Away where?'

'How the hell do I know?' Liam says irritably. 'I'm sorry, Declan, I just—'

McCann returns. 'Listen up, children. A man is coming to speak to you. He'll tell you what he wants you to do tomorrow. Listen carefully to him coz you're only going to get one chance at this, and the lives of your families depend on you carrying out his orders to the letter. Do you both understand? Liam?'

'I understand.'

'Declan?'

'I understand, sir.'

'That's excellent,' McCann says. 'I'm sorry about the toilet business, Declan. That shouldn't have happened. Relax, both of you. The main man will be arriving soon.'

FOURTEEN

From Ructions' car, the Diver household seems disarmingly tranquil. He closes his phone and pops a mint in his mouth before putting on his surgical gloves. With his V-for-Vendetta mask in hand, he gets out of the car and approaches the front door with his head down. As he enters the house, Ructions deftly slips the mask over his face and is greeted in the hall by Seamus McCann.

'How are they?' Ructions whispers.

'They're shaken up, but they'll survive. In here,' McCann says, indicating that Ructions should follow him into the bedroom.

Ructions puts his hand on McCann's arm and shakes his head. 'Just me.'

McCann pulls back in shock but immediately composes himself. 'I see,' he says, 'if that's the way you want it.' McCann bows deeply and sweeps his arm towards the room, indicating that Ructions should get on with it.

Ructions closes the door behind him and pulls up a chair in front of the two captives. He studies them. Both men feel uncomfortable under his V-for-Vendetta stare. It is the all-knowing, upturned smile on the mask that intimidates Declan. For Liam, the wearer of the mask seems to be saying: *You can't hide from me; I can read your mind.* Ructions puts his hand in his pocket and takes out two letters. He opens the first letter and holds it in front of Liam. 'Will you please read this?' he asks. Liam nods.

> My darling Liam,
>
> They have let me write a couple of lines to you. I do not know where I am or how long I will be here, but I am holding up and doing as well as can be expected. It must be terrible

for you, my love. I am praying every second that you are also holding up. Liam, I am convinced our captors are telling the truth when they say that nothing will happen to me as long as you do as they ask. I also believe them when they say my life is in your hands, and that they will kill me if you disobey their orders. I know you will not disobey their orders and endanger my life. I also know that our love will get us through this trauma and we will be stronger than ever.

I will love you always,

Stephanie

Liam's heart is pounding like a Lambeg drum as he wipes away a solitary tear. 'Where is she?' he asks, looking aside.

'She's safe,' Ructions says.

'Are you the boss man?'

'Yes.'

Liam turns his head so that Ructions can look into his eyes. 'Let me assure you, mister, you will have my one hundred per cent compliance.'

Compliance is such a nice word. Ructions lets Liam's words linger in the air for a few seconds before delivering his answer. 'I know.'

The softness of the voice from behind the revolting mask confounds Liam. He grasps immediately that this man has an appreciation of visual and dramatic effect; most assuredly he has a flair for the theatrical. *He is certainly the producer and director of this show. Not only that, but this is not his first production.*

Ructions shows Declan his letter. 'Will you please read this?'

'Yes, sir.'

Dear Declan,

This is probably the hardest letter I've ever had to write in my life because I know you are in great distress and under enormous pressure. But do not worry about us, son. We are being treated well. Your mummy has settled down and so has Kate. They are in bed, although I doubt if they are getting much sleep. Son, I told you before you left but I'm going to say it again, just to make sure – you do exactly as these gentlemen tell you. No ifs, no buts – whatever it is you need to do, you do it. We want you back with us. Your life is all that matters.

I have to finish now, son. Keep your spirits up. Know that you are in our thoughts and prayers. Be strong, Declan.

Love you, son,

Dad

As Ructions folds and puts the letters back in his pocket, Declan snivels. Ructions has a degree of sympathy for the young man: *Let it go, son, that's it. Get it all out of you.*

From Liam and Declan's perspective, pandemonium would seem to reign, but the reality is different. Every slap, punch, word of aggression, degradation and insult has been designed for one purpose: to regiment their responses and to bring them to a point where they behave like troopers on a parade ground, a point where they obey orders without thinking.

'Shall we start?' Ructions says. 'Are you okay, Declan?'

'Yes, yes, I'm okay. Thank you, sir.'

'Righto.' Ructions takes two mobile phones out of his pocket and hands one each to Declan and Liam. 'The only person who knows the numbers of these phones is me and I'll be phoning and texting you both at your work tomorrow. You will call me Jack.'

Both nod.

'During my calls or texts, I'll be putting a series of questions to you. Your answers will be either yes or no, for the most part. If you need to elaborate, you will make sure no one hears your conversation or sees your text. And you will smile and appear glad to hear from me. You will not lie to me. You will *not* phone out on these phones.'

Bizarrely, Liam finds something impressive about Ructions, but he can't put his finger on what it is. *You're well versed in giving orders, Jack, that's for sure. And I'd say you're used to being obeyed.*

'That's simple enough, isn't it?' Ructions says.

'Yes,' Liam says.

Declan nods.

'I think, lads, you need a glimpse – just a glimpse, mind, nothing more – into the breadth of our intelligence. You two are amongst nine keyholders at National Bank headquarters. This means that together with your little keys, you have access to all areas in the bank, in particular the vault. Declan, you weren't supposed to be working tomorrow but you changed shifts. That's bad luck for you, but good luck for us. The day after tomorrow, there will be no keyholders because a new security system will be introduced, and you, Liam, have been designated to collect all the keys. But by then it will be too late.'

Declan frowns as Ructions' words smack home. *This isn't the sort of guy who fires out words without thinking. So why did he say it was bad luck for me? Why didn't he say it was bad luck for the two of us? What does he see that I don't? Oh, sweet Jesus! How did I miss it? Because I've changed shifts, the cops will regard me as the insider. I'm screwed! I'm going to end up in jail after this. They'll throw away the fucking key.* Declan puts his hand over his mouth.

'Don't you dare vomit over me,' Ructions commands.

Declan heaves, but nothing comes. He recovers, opens his mouth and clamps it shut again. Ructions waves his hand, prompting him to speak up.

'It's just,' Declan says, 'if you don't mind me asking, how did you know I'd changed shifts?'

Ructions smiles behind the mask. He has been waiting for this question. 'The same way I'll know every move you'll make in the bank tomorrow.'

'Can I ask a question, please?' Liam asks.

'Go ahead.'

'How are you going to get the money out?'

'Oh, that's easy. You're going to bring it out for me.'

Declan is already calculating how much time he will do in prison. He presumes that the more money the villains get, the longer he will have to serve. 'Can I ask one last question, sir?' Declan says.

'Last one.'

'How much money do you expect to get?'

'All of it.'

Declan sticks his head over the side of the bed, grabs a waste basket and vomits.

When he recovers sufficiently to concentrate, Ructions says, 'Now we'll have a chat about internal security, shall we? We'll start with,' Ructions touches the nose on his mask, 'the secret telephone hotline for tiger-kidnap victims. Shhh! Outsiders aren't supposed to know about that. Then we'll move on to the nineteen staff who'll be working tomorrow. Then I'll tell you how you're going to get the money through the sterile area and into the bullion bay. You look surprised, Liam.'

'Frankly, I am, Jack.'

'Don't be,' Ructions says. 'I know everything. I know you're not going to use that hotline.'

'You have my word on that.'

'Well, that's good enough for me. Oh, by the way, when I called in to collect Stephanie's letter, she told me to tell you ... well, you don't want to know what she told me.'

'But I do. Please, what did she say?'

Ructions waves a hand as if he was expressing an afterthought. 'She said, tell my husband I love him. She's a very pretty girl.'

She's a very pretty girl? You think my wife is very pretty? Liam cringes at the power in Ructions' words. 'Yes, she is,' he says. 'Is she all right?'

'She looked mighty fine to me,' Ructions says. 'Declan?'

'I'll be phoning nobody, sir.'

Ructions did not say goodbye to Liam or Declan when he left the Diver home, and later, there are no goodbyes when, at 5.45 a.m., Seamus McCann and his men walk out the front door, leaving

Liam and Declan behind them. Before making their exit, the gang scrub all areas with disinfectant and detergent, even going so far as to mop their footsteps behind them as they leave. Ructions had long since departed.

At 7.00 a.m., Liam and Declan set out in Liam's car for work in Belfast city centre. Liam fixes his rear-view mirror and looks into it.

'Sorry for breaking down back there, Liam,' Declan says. 'It's just—'

'You don't need to explain. I was on the verge of it myself a couple of times.'

'Here, that Jack fella's tuned in, isn't he?'

'His knowledge of the bank's inner workings shocked me.'

'Me too,' Declan says. 'I know he's a tiger-kidnapper and all that, but he seemed a decent sort to me. The type of fella you'd have a pint with, ye know?'

Liam slowly turns to Declan, his face a crucible of fury. 'Tigers don't usually bare their teeth before they attack, Declan. This animal said Steph was very pretty. What did you take out of that?'

The tone of Liam's question makes Declan unsure of his ground. 'Why? What did *you* take out of it?'

'I took it as a threat. Didn't you?'

'I thought he was, you know, paying Steph a compliment.'

'Paying her a compliment? Why, in the middle of a tiger-kidnapping, would he pay my wife a compliment? Because he likes me? Because he wants to have a drink with me when this is all over? Did it ever occur to you that this is the bastard who's pulled all this crap down on us? Him. Nobody else. Not the buffoons in the house.' Liam looked in the rear-view mirror again. There are still no vehicles behind him. '*His* guys are holding *your* family, Declan. What the fuck makes you think he's a decent sort?'

Declan is embarrassed. He knows he is being chastised and it smarts. 'I don't think he's a nice guy—'

'You could've fooled me.'

'I said, he *seemed* a decent sort. I didn't say he was.'

'In this case, I don't see the difference between "seemed" and "was".'

For a moment Declan entertains the notion of returning Liam's service, of telling him he has no right to misinterpret what he says and reminding him that he's not the only one who has family members in peril. Instead, he changes tack. 'Did I tell you the fuckers in our house knew my Mum's maiden name and that she and my Dad's first house was in Beechmount Avenue? They knew my Dad was a docker before he went to work in Corry's timber yard. The head man talked to him as if he was his best mate.'

'That doesn't surprise me at all.' Liam keeps looking in his rear-view mirror. 'I believe Jack when he says he'll be watching us. Somebody in the bank – one of our friends – is a drone. He or she will be watching everything and reporting back to him. We'll not see it, but I guarantee you Jack will be on the blower to us if we as much as look like caving in.'

'You may as well know now, Liam,' Declan says, 'there's no chance of me caving in. My family's survival is more important than the bank's money.'

'I'm glad to hear you say that.'

'So am I,' Ructions mutters. Driving a quarter of a mile behind them, he has dialled into the GSM listening bug that Seamus McCann had planted under the driver's seat of Liam's car.

'There can be no sad faces or tears today, Declan,' Liam says. 'We've a bank to rob.'

Ructions grins. *Welcome to Team Ructions, Liam.*

Monday morning dawns bright and blue in Geneva. Serge pours himself a glass of pure orange juice and stares out the kitchen window. Two aeroplanes glisten in the azure sky.

His phone rings. It's an unidentified caller. *Here we go!*

'Bonjour,' Ructions says.

'I take it you haven't been to bed?' Serge says.

'Busy night, mon ami,' Ructions replies. 'How's the weather over there?'

'Chilly but bright. Blue skies. Everything as it should be.'

'Delighted to hear that. Cold and blustery here – as it should be. Good forecast for tomorrow, though.'

'Très bien. A bientôt.'

Liam Diver finds little pleasure in his predicament driving around Belfast city centre. As per Ructions' instructions, he stops to drop Declan off around the corner from the bank. Liam's phone rings just as Declan gets out. Liam answers immediately, and Declan sticks his head back into the car to listen.

Ructions drives past. 'Good. I see Dec's listening in.'

Liam looks about, but there is no sign of Ructions.

'Don't forget,' Ructions says, 'Dec goes into work first. I don't want anyone thinking you two are in cahoots.'

'Got that, Jack.'

'Declan, can you hear me?'

'Yes, Jack.'

'Just be nice and calm now. Do your job. Nothing will be happening until later.' Ructions hangs up.

Liam rests his elbows on the steering wheel, caresses his temples and looks curiously at Declan. 'How did Jack see you listening in?'

'Beats me.'

Liam begins to search the dashboard for a hidden mini-camera.

From his car, Ructions observes Declan pulling up the collar of his jacket. He walks casually, carrying his large Aston Villa holdall over his shoulder. Ructions grins. *Is Dec whistling? By God, he is. A blithe spirit merrily whistling on his way to work – on his way to making a rather large cash withdrawal. You're a good lad, young Dec.*

The master criminal is quietly elated with the way things have progressed: not a shot fired; not a hint of detection. Not only that, but Ructions is now convinced that he is not being monitored by either the IRA or the police. Phase One is over, and all is well. Phase Two is underway.

Billy Kelly drives the loot lorry, a white 7.5 tonne Renault Midlum, along the Newry bypass towards Belfast. The speedometer shows forty miles per hour. A cop stands beside a motorcycle, his speed gun pointing at the oncoming traffic. Billy sits back even further. Having passed the speed trap, he notices that the cop is not after him. Billy has a good feeling about this job.

Befuddled, sapped of energy and feeling as if his legs are encased in plaster of Paris, Declan approaches the entrance to the bank. He stops at the front door, turns around and looks in all directions. His phone rings. 'Hello?'

'What's up?' Ructions says.

Dec walks to the side of the bank. 'Nothing.'

'Are you nervous?'

'Petrified, if you must know.'

'That's not a bad thing,' Ructions says reassuringly. 'Just tell yourself you're going to work. It's no big deal.'

'I'm wrecked, sir. I feel like I'm going into prison.'

You are. You've been remanded in custody on a charge of wanting to keep your family alive. 'Listen, Dec,' Ructions says calmly. 'Take a deep breath, walk in the door and be pleasant. That's all you have to do. You'll be fine.'

'But I don't think I will be.'

I knew this wee fucker would get watery, I fucking knew it. Time for some ball-crunching. 'Listen up, fuckhead, it's not your job to think. You do exactly what you're told, when you're told, or I'll be sending you your father's head by special delivery. Have you got that?'

'Yes, sir.'

'Now pull yourself together.'

'Right, sir.'

'I'm watching you. I'm fuckin' watching you, boy.'

'I know, sir.'

'Are you up for this? You'd better be or I swear—'

'I am, sir. I'm up for it.'

'Get into that bank and do what you have to do.'

'Anything you say, sir.'

Anything I say. Dec, you'd slither under a snake's balls to save your family. There's no disgrace in that.

Declan coughs, blows his nose and marches manfully into the bank. Inside, he smiles to a female teller as he is buzzed through the security door into the staff area.

A couple of minutes later Liam arrives for work, carrying his briefcase. 'Good morning, Maria. Morning, Tom. Morning, Declan,' Liam says as he strides towards his office.

'Morning, Liam,' Declan says, grinning.

'Don't know what you're grinning about, Declan,' Liam says sharply.

Declan's heart stops. *Where the fuck is he going with this?*

'Beaten by Birmingham City, 2-1. Why can't you support a good team, Declan? Only an eejit follows Villa.'

'Hey, less of the eejit. My Dad follows Villa too, you know. We're loyal to the last.'

Of course you are, Declan. Family loyalty: that's what will get us both through this fucking nightmare.

Ructions opens the door of his apartment and flops down on the sofa. He takes out his phone and calls Liam.

'Hello?'

'It's me,' Ructions says. 'Just checking in. How's our little friend?'

'He's grand.'

'That clerk at the bottom kiosk, Roger Hull?'

'Uh-huh?'

'He's a grumpy bastard, isn't he? Not very good with customers.'

So you've been in, have you, Jack? And you know Roger's name? Aren't you the clever clogs. 'He can be abrupt.'

'It's none of my business, but if I were you, I'd find a way to get rid of him. How's my drone?'

'Drone? Did you say, drone?'

'Arrivederci.' Dog-tired, Ructions takes off his leather jacket, uses his feet to remove his shoes, shuts his eyes and dozes off.

After his call from Ructions, Liam closes his phone and looks out through his office windows at his staff. *Jack must've bugged my car*. Betty Deane walks by and smiles at him. *Is it you, Betty? Are you feeding Jack? Has he promised you a fabulous pension?* Eddie Braniff, sitting at his desk opposite Liam's office, makes a call on his mobile. *Who are you phoning, Eddie? Jack the Lad? What are you telling him?* Roger Hull turns around slowly and stares at Liam. *What are you staring at, Roger? Are you sending me a message? You were never happy here. Has Jack guaranteed you a big payday?*

Ructions' eyes spring open. *What? Where am I*? He expunges whatever air is in his lungs and runs his hands over his face. His mobile phone is ringing. 'Yeah?' he answers wearily.

'We were supposed to meet,' Panzer says.

'We were?'

'What's wrong with you? Are you all right?'

'All right? Yeah, yeah.' Ructions yawns. 'I dozed off, that's all. Give me twenty minutes, will ya? I need to freshen up.'

'Make it an hour. I've a bit of running about to do.'

'See you then.' Ructions closes his phone and his eyes. He wants to sleep, but there's a bank to be robbed.

At the Church of Our Saviour in central Belfast, the Reverend Roy Salters collects his pamphlets and Bible, says goodbye to two fellow-elders and sets out on his mission to save souls from the fires of hell. At sixty-two, the balding fire-and-brimstone preacher, with a squint in his right eye, is not sure how many souls he has saved through his missionary work, but he guesses it to be in the thousands. A former university lecturer, Roy Salters had himself been doomed to a fiery afterlife until that memorable day, 18 March 1995, when he heard the redemptive words of the Reverend John Calderwood on Belfast's Albertbridge Road. Today, he has decided to try his hand at soul-saving outside the National Bank. It is approaching Christmas; he reckons there will be a lot of lost souls tonight in the vicinity of that temple of iniquity.

Ructions pulls a floppy hat down over his face, walks into the café on the Ormeau Road, orders coffee and a cream bun and takes a seat in the bottom corner. He makes some phone calls.

Panzer comes into the café, places an order and sits across from Ructions. 'How's it going?'

'Mighty,' Ructions says.

'That good?'

'Better.'

'I spoke to Eamonn after you left the house last night,' Panzer says. 'He's all bizz.' Panzer's second cousin, Eamonn de Búrca, has a farm in County Mayo.

'I phoned him myself at six o'clock,' Ructions says.

'He said you'd called.'

'What else did he say?'

'You know our Eamonn, he doesn't say much, but he's up for it.'

'Why wouldn't he be? He's getting paid top money for doing nothing.'

A waitress leaves a cup of coffee and a plate with a cream bun on the table. Ructions nods his appreciation.

'I wouldn't say he's doing nothing now,' Panzer says.

'There's very little risk in this for him.'

'Very little isn't the same as none at all, Ructions. It's minimising the risk that matters.'

Ructions stirs his coffee, then sips. 'You're right. Still, Eamonn's getting a nice little earner here.'

'He's worth every penny of it,' Panzer says, nodding to the plate in front of Ructions. No sooner has Ructions pushed the plate over than Panzer takes a chunk out of the cream bun. 'Did I ever tell you what Eamonn got from the 'RA?' Panzer splutters.

'What was that?'

Panzer waits until he swallows the last morsel of food. 'In the 1980s, around the time the 'RA was bringing in the shiploads of gear from Libya—'

'You were holding some of that gear for them then, weren't you? For Big Tiny?'

Panzer nods. 'Anyway, Eamonn let them build this concrete underground bunker in his barn—'

'Fair play to him.'

'Just so. Then they come in the middle of the night and dump one hundred and twenty AK47s and two surface-to-air missiles in the bunker.'

'As you do.'

'Anyway, when they took it all away, the 'RA gave Eamonn a bottle of whiskey for his patriotism.' Panzer shakes his head. 'Like, a bottle of whiskey? Fuck me, Ructions, how miserable is that?'

'That's a long way from twenty-five large.' Ructions finishes his coffee. 'You're okay with this handover tonight?'

Panzer recoils. 'Work me a break, will ya?'

'It's a matter of manners, Panzer.'

'Fair enough. I'll see you then.'

'Do you want to leave first?'

'No,' Panzer says. 'You shoot on.' Panzer stirs his coffee and watches Ructions as he leaves the café.

In the small canteen of the National Bank, Declan stirs two cups of tea. He looks around. Thelma, the only other person in the canteen, gets up and leaves. Declan takes two sachets of laxatives out of his pocket, opens them, pours them into the two cups of tea and stirs again. He walks out of the canteen towards the security room.

FIFTEEN

It is six o'clock in the evening. Liam Diver and Declan Butler are in the vault of the bank. Betty Deane approaches them. 'That's me away, Mr Diver.'

'Okay, Betty. Is anyone else up top?'

'No, they've all gone.'

'Right. Well, goodnight then.'

'Goodnight.'

When Betty goes back upstairs, Liam whispers, 'This is madness, Dec. It won't work.'

'It will. It has to.'

'Who's in the control room?'

'Cecil Wilkinson and Joe Bittles.'

'Did you ... you know?'

Declan nods conspiratorially. 'I brought them a nice little cup of tea.'

Liam's mobile rings. 'Hello?'

'How's it going, Liam?' Ructions asks.

'Fine, Jack.'

'No problems?'

'None whatsoever.'

'Excellent. Here's what I want you to do—'

'Uh-huh.'

'I want you to fill Dec's Aston Villa holdall to the very top with used fifty and one-hundred-pound notes and bring the bag out to Ringland Street. There's a bus stop to the right. Go there. Someone will meet you.'

'I don't want to sound awkward, Jack, but I really think it would look less suspicious if Declan were to take out the bag. After all, it's his holdall and I'm the manager; it wouldn't look right for me to be walking out with a large bag.'

'Maybe so. It doesn't matter to me which of you shows up. You've a half an hour to get to that bus stop. Don't keep me waiting.' Ructions hangs up.

'Get your holdall,' Liam tells Declan.

In the run-down barn, Stephanie Diver's thoughts are on Liam as she rocks back and forth on the sofa. She pulls a blanket around her shoulders but it's no use; she cannot get heat into her body. Every now and then she is showered with sleet, which finds its way into the barn through the hole in the roof. She wonders if Liam has any idea what she is going through. How could he? *I will not go insane. I'll count. I'll keep my mind active. Twelve ones are twelve; twelve twos are twenty-four, twelve threes are ...*

Billy Kelly and Ambrose Peoples are in the office of a lock-up garage on the Antrim Road. Both are perfecting their disguises, with Billy fixing his wig and cap before a mirror, and Ambrose trying on a black Belfast City Council fleece. The loot lorry fills the bay of the garage. Billy phones Ructions.

'It's yourself,' Ructions says. 'How's everything?'

'Spot on.'

'You're ready?'

Billy sings, 'Bring me sunshine, in your smile.'

Ructions chortles and hangs up.

Declan hands Liam sealed plastic bags of used fifty and one-hundred-pound notes, which Liam places methodically inside the holdall. The bag is full.

'That's enough,' Liam says, zipping the bag. He looks at his watch. 'You've three minutes to be at the bus stop.'

Declan lifts the sports bag and puts it over his shoulder.

'Good luck,' Liam says, as Declan walks to the stairs. Liam stares at Declan's back. *My God! Did I just wish Declan good luck there? Is this what it's come to? I'm wishing a member of my staff good luck in handing over the bank's money to criminals?*

Declan approaches the first of the internal security doors. At the monitor, security officer Cecil Wilkinson glances up from his *Belfast Telegraph*. Declan looks up at the camera, smiling. Wilkinson buzzes Declan through. Now Declan is in no man's land, caught between the two security doors, halfway in and halfway out. He stands at the second security door, waiting. *Be calm. Nobody, except Liam, Jack and myself, know this bag is stuffed with money.* He pretends to whistle, but his mouth is so dry no sound comes out. The second security door buzzes and he walks through.

A blast of stinging December air cuts into Declan's face. The side street is empty, lifeless. He feels quite giddy. *I'm outside. Don't turn around. Keep walking towards Ringland Street. Not too fast. The bag is heavy. Wonder how much is in it? A million? That might be enough for them. No, no, it won't be. Jack said they wanted all the money in the bank. All the money! Greedy bastard.*

Ructions is on the opposite side of Ringland Street from the bus stop, looking into a shop window. He quickly glances around and spots Declan coming around the corner. 'There he is,' he says softly into his phone. 'Large as life. Be ready.' Ructions hangs up. His eyes follow Declan towards the bus stop. *Well done, young man. Sit down. Be nice and ordinary. That's a boy.*

Declan places the bag beside him on the bus-stop bench and puts his arm over it protectively. A bus pulls up and a man and woman alight. The bus takes off. Declan checks up and down the street. *Where the hell are you, Jack? You'll probably send some hapless lackey to do the collection, won't you?*

Ructions is wearing a black duffle coat with its hood up. He casts another beady eye on the street, pulls up a scarf from inside the duffle coat to cover his face and slouches across the street with his hands in his pockets. He is confident that this is not a set-up, but, still, you can't be too careful. Ructions approaches the bus stop and sits down. Without looking at Declan, he says, 'Hello, Dec.'

'Jack?'

'The same. So how much money have you brought me?'

'I don't know, Jack. We hadn't time to count it. But I'd say over a million.'

'Over a million.' *Three magic words*. 'Do you remember your First Holy Communion, Dec?'

'Vaguely.'

'Do you remember how much money you got from your family and friends?'

'A right few quid, as I recall.'

'I got nothing. My Dad took my First Holy Communion money from me and guzzled it in the nearest boozer.'

Are you looking for sympathy, Jack? 'That's pretty crappy.'

Ructions' fingers tightly gather the sides of his duffle-coat hood around his face. 'Isn't it? Anyway, listen up. We're being observed by one of my people and if I'm lifted by the cops, well, you know what the consequences will be for your family. So, nice and simple: did you or Liam alert the cops to what's going down?'

'No, Jack.'

'Are the cops or anyone else watching us now?'

'No, Jack.'

'You're certain about that?'

'Absolutely. No cops. Nobody.'

'This bag isn't bugged, is it?'

'No, Jack.'

'You know we'll be searching it for bugs, don't you?'

'Jack, it's not bugged. I wouldn't take a chance like that with my family's lives.'

'No, you wouldn't. Okay. That's what I needed to hear. Have you everything in for Christmas, Dec?'

In for Christmas? I'll be lucky if I'm not in for Christmas – in jail, that is. 'No.'

'I like Christmas, don't you?'

'Yes.'

'I'll take my Christmas present, then, shall I?' Ructions says without looking at the bag.

'Yes, Jack.'

Ructions scans the street one last time, lifts the bag, slings it over his shoulder and stands up. 'When this is all over, kid, I'm going to drop you a few quid.'

Stick it, Jack. 'You don't have to—'

'I know I don't have to, but I'm going to. But, Dec, if you do receive a brown envelope, don't hand it over to the cops. I wouldn't like that.'

'I won't.'

'You've done fine, kid. It'll all be over soon.' Ructions walks a few paces, then turns. 'Oh, I almost forgot – your mother and father send their love.'

'Thanks, Jack.'

'They're rooting for you.'

Ructions strolls off, takes his phone out of his pocket and dials. 'That went very nicely.'

'Good,' Panzer replies.

Rounding a corner, Ructions says, 'I'm coming up to you now.'

'You're sure the bag isn't bugged?'

'I wouldn't be carrying it if it was.'

Panzer is sitting in the cab of his jeep. Ructions takes a quick glance over his shoulder before removing his duffle coat and throwing it and the holdall into the back of Panzer's jeep. In a flash, he grabs hold of the brown hat that Panzer holds out the window. Panzer drives off.

Declan leaves the bus stop only when Ructions saunters around the corner with his recently acquired Aston Villa holdall. Far from being down in the dumps, Declan is pleased that the transfer has gone so smoothly. His fear had been that the police would somehow thwart the handover. That had not happened, so his family are that bit closer to safety and freedom.

In a nearby shop, Declan buys two bottles of Coke and two bags of crisps. He enters the bank the same way he had left, casually drinking his Coke and eating the crisps. Dozy Cecil Wilkinson studies the racing pages and pays little attention to Declan as he lets him through the security gates – minus the Villa sports bag.

Panzer, pensive, eyes everywhere, drives out of the city centre with its host of security cameras. Taking to the back streets, he makes his way to 'Ciggy Charlie' Callaghan's scrap and demolition yard in north Belfast.

Rumour has it that Ciggy got his name because he dabbles in the illegal cigarette importation business, but really it is because he chain-smokes. He waves Panzer over to an enclosed area of his huge yard, past two yellow forklifts and a telescopic JCB, stockpiles of wrecked cars and vans, grey palisade railings, Bangor-blue slates, scrap iron, pallets of old Belfast brick, chimneypots, and the pulpit, pews and timber from a demolished church. Panzer gets out of the jeep and shakes Ciggy's hand.

In his earlier years, Ciggy had been a cross-country runner and, when imbued with a few pints of beer, he will proudly boast that he had once run for Ireland. Now in his late sixties, with a shaved head, sagging, bloodhound cheeks and a drum-belly, he cannot run from one side of his scrapyard to the other.

Reaching into the back of his jeep, Panzer scoops up the Aston Villa holdall and follows Ciggy into his office. Ciggy wheezes as he plops down on his chair behind a large plastic-coated desk. He lights a cigarette and reaches for a receipt book. In an afterthought, he offers Panzer a cigarette, but the latter declines. As he writes out a receipt, Ciggy says, 'Panzer, I don't want to know your business, but when's the lorry coming?'

'In about an hour, maybe less. Is that all right?'

'Oh, sure,' Ciggy says, handing Panzer a receipt. 'There y'are. Thirty toilet pots and accessories sold to John O'Hare, The Garden of Eden, Hannahstown. All legal and above board.'

Try as he might, Panzer cannot help smirking. 'Toilet pots and accessories?'

'People need a sit-down when they're reading their morning paper.' Holding out a sales ledger to Panzer, Ciggy points a thin finger to a line. 'Sign here.'

Panzer signs.

'This way,' Ciggy says, 'if the law starts asking questions, I've the paperwork to say why you were here, and you've a legitimate explanation for being here.'

'And how are things with you, old friend?' Panzer asks.

'If you must know, business is awful at the minute, but it'll pick up. It always does.'

'I need to go into the back office.'

'Be my guest.'

Panzer closes the back-office door behind him, sets the holdall down on the table and runs his fingers around the rim. He knows that a 'Pieces-of-Eight' moment is almost upon him: occasions such as this are to be savoured, like a fine Bordeaux. His eyes sparkle; his tongue flicks out: he can sniff money. He takes a deep breath and feels the rise of his ribcage. Slowly he unzips the holdall. A heart-stopping moment is upon him. Panzer lifts a sealed bag of used fifty-pound notes, opens it with a penknife and fans the notes. He plunges his hand to the bottom of the bag and repeats the exercise. Pulling out a counterfeit-money pen from his shirt pocket, he runs it along a series of one hundred and some fifty-pound notes. There is no dark pencil line: the notes are genuine. *There must be at least a million quid in here, probably more.* He takes out a few notes from a bundle, zips up the holdall and clips on a small combination padlock.

Ciggy raps the door. 'Panzer, I'm heading out for ten minutes. Are you okay?'

Panzer pops his head out the door. 'I need you to do me a favour.'

'Oh?' Ciggy says, a hint of mischief in his eye. 'You saw something in the yard you'd like? The pulpit perhaps? You always fancied yourself as a preacher man.'

'And you always fancied yourself as a comedian.'

Ciggy nods knowingly. 'So, you don't want the pulpit? I see. With all due respect, Panzer, favours cost – especially the hairy ones.'

'Didn't I know that was coming? Here.' Panzer hands Ciggy a wad of money, which Ciggy counts.

'What's the favour?'

'I want to put my bag in your safe for an hour.'

Ciggy nods. 'Wait till I get the keys.'

Declan comes back from handing over the holdall to find Liam waiting for him at the interior security door. Declan hands Liam a bottle of Coke and a bag of crisps and they make small talk as they walk towards the stairs. Cecil Wilkinson glances at them in a security camera. The second security man, Joe Bittles, squirming and rubbing his stomach, accidentally bumps into Declan as he comes around a corner.

Liam says, 'What's wrong with you, Joe?'

Joe's face looks as if it has been marinated in red wine and slowly cooked over a spit. 'I've the bloody runs, Liam,' Joe says. 'Can't get off the piss-pot.'

'Could be a touch of food poisoning,' Liam suggests.

Worry descends on Declan. *Why isn't old Cecil on the piss-pot next to you?*

'Probably,' Joe says.

'Do you need to go home?'

'No. At least I don't think so.'

'Well, let me know if you do.'

'Sure.'

Cecil Wilkinson opens the door of the security office. 'Are you alright there, Joe?'

'No.' Joe hurries off.

'How's you, Dec?'

'Grand, Cecil.'

'That was a lovely cup of tea you made me earlier on.'

'It was?'

'There was a bit of body to it. What teabags did you use?'

'Just the ones in the canteen.'

'It tasted different – better than usual.'

'I'm glad you liked it.'

No sooner do Liam and Declan go towards the lifts than Liam turns back. 'Oh, I almost forgot, Cecil. It's like a rubbish dump down below.'

'I didn't notice.'

'I'm just letting you know. Myself and Declan will be finishing up later than usual this evening. We're going to be cleaning the bottom floor out and a white council lorry will be coming to pick up the rubbish. Give me a shout when it's outside, will you?'

'Sure. No problem.'

Liam and Declan walk into the vault. 'I put enough laxative in old Cecil's tea to bring down an elephant,' Declan says. 'He must have the constitution of a—'

Liam's phone rings. 'Hello, Jack.'

'Hi, Liam. That went smoothly enough. Now, part two. We talked about it last night.'

'I remember.'

'I want the trolleys in the bullion bay in forty-five minutes. And, Liam, don't keep my people waiting.'

Ructions' people, Billy Kelly and Ambrose Peoples, are waiting at a zebra crossing in the loot lorry. A police car has also stopped but is travelling in the opposite direction. Ambrose, feeling rather disconsolate, moves off slowly when the pedestrians cross the road. 'I like young Dec,' he says.

'You're feeling sorry for the lad, aren't you?' Billy says.

'Well, yes, I am.'

'Why?'

'Coz I think he'll be charged with this.'

'Can't see it myself,' Billy says, fiddling with his wig. 'This bloody thing's too big for me. When you bought these wigs, you thought one size fits all, didn't you? You thought all our heads were as big as your own.'

Ambrose is used to Billy's griping and he ignores it. 'He's from west Belfast and his family are still at home.'

'He doesn't know if they're still at home or not.'

'How's he going to convince the cops of that?'

'That's his problem. I still don't think he'll be charged.'

'He'll be charged, all right.'

'Too bad.'

Ambrose blows his horn at some schoolchildren who are lingering on the road. 'Changed times,' he says.

'Aye.'

'When we robbed the Ulster Bank in Andytown, we got eleven grand and thought it was a big pay day.'

'Aye.'

Ambrose's eyes are fixed on the road ahead as he says, 'Nowadays, bank robbers bring a big lorry to take away the money.'

'Yip.'

A fleeting glance sideward betrays Ambrose's mounting annoyance. 'You're a regular chatterbox today, aren't you?'

'I suppose so.'

'Knock it on the fuckin' head, will ya?'

'What's your point, Ambrose?' Billy says with a note of resignation in his voice. 'What's eating you?'

'I want to know …' Ambrose says, his face flushed, 'no, I'd *like* to know how much Ructions is expecting out of this.'

Billy cast a disparaging look at Ambrose. 'Who's Ructions when you're writing home? I've never heard that name before.'

Ambrose sighs. 'Okay. I meant the person who's employing us.'

'And what about him?'

'I'd like to know how much—'

'Oh, you would, would ya?'

'Is that too much to ask?'

'Yes, it is.'

Realising that there is not much meat left on the bone of the matter, Ambrose caves in. 'I was just being nosey, Billy. That's all.'

Billy lets a few seconds of silence pass before replying. 'For what it's worth, he's talking about doing three runs, if – and it's a big if – all goes well with the first two.'

'*Three*?'

Billy's phone rings. 'It's him,' Billy says, putting his finger to his lips. 'Yes?'

'Where are you?'

'At Carlisle Circus.'

'Okay. Keep coming.'

Liam and Declan are in the bank vault, filling four large trolleys with notes and covering the money with cardboard and rubbish. The intercom buzzes and Liam answers it.

'Liam?' Joe Bittles says.

'Yes, Joe?'

'That council lorry is outside.'

'Thanks, Joe. We're just loading up. We'll be up in a minute. By the way, how do you feel now?'

'Lousy. Gotta run.'

Declan walks around his two grilled trolleys, occasionally poking his fingers through the metal squares to ensure that cardboard, rather than blocks of money, is all that is visible to the naked eye. 'Finished,' he says.

Liam examines his trolleys, on top of which are old broken chairs. Both men push the trolleys out of the vault and into the large lift that will bring them to the control-room floor, which houses the interlocking security doors, the security room and the outside bullion bay. Liam closes the lift door. As the lift ascends, Declan pivots on the balls of his feet, his eyes searching the ceiling. Opening and closing his mouth, he makes popping noises.

'Will you please stop doing that?' Liam says tetchily. 'You're getting on my nerves.'

'Sorry.'

The lift stops and the two shove the trolleys to the first security door and wait. The buzzer sounds, and they proceed into the sterile area, between the two security doors. Cecil Wilkinson hits the button that opens the second security door. Liam and Declan push the trolleys, one after another, into the outside bullion bay. Only a set of steel doors separates them from the street.

SIXTEEN

Outside the front of the National Bank, the Reverend Roy Salters waves his Bible aloft and proclaims to one and all: 'The wages of sin is death!' Salters knows a sinner when he sees one. A drunken, bleached-haired, middle-aged woman with fat legs, wearing a red leather miniskirt and a white plastic coat, staggers towards him. *A loose woman for sure, if I'm not mistaken.* He wants to save her, but he is not sure if she is in a fit state to be saved. As it happens, he doubts if she would remember being saved when she sobers up.

As the lady passes, Salters shouts, 'Repent, I tell you! Repent and be saved in the blood of Our Lord Jee-sus Christ!' Salters' words are barely out of his mouth before they are carried off by a banshee wind. He takes out a handkerchief and rubs his squinting eye. It's dark, freezing, sleety, and there are not many souls about. He wonders if he should call it a day. *Would Our Lord Jesus call it a day? No. Our Lord Jesus did not feel the cold or sleet.*

Ambrose Peoples feels the cold. He is in the driver's seat of the loot lorry, which is parked outside the bullion bay. He looks in his side mirror. Hillier Street is empty. 'Now what?' he asks Billy.

'We wait.'

Roy Salters sticks his gloved hands under his armpits to keep warm. He detests sleet. Unlike snow, sleet cuts through the layers of clothing to the marrow. A car pulls in at the entrance to Hillier Street and Salters studies the driver. Even though Ructions is wearing a big hat and has a scarf across his face, Salters reckons that he has the look of one who needs saving. Salters peels off a leaflet, moseys over and taps on the window. 'Hello, sir.'

Ructions lowers the window a little and looks up Hillier Street. 'Hello, there.'

'Can I just give you a leaflet, sir?'

Ructions' head turns. 'Sure,' he says, accepting a leaflet.

'Can I ask you if you've been saved, sir?'

'Job 1:21.'

'Job 1:21?' Salters repeats. Massaging his temples, he tries to stimulate his refrigerated brain. He remembers. 'Yes. Oh, yes. "The Lord giveth and the Lord taketh away." Very profound, if I may say so, sir.'

Reverend, you've no idea how profound. There'll be serious taketh away this night.

Salters hesitates, waiting on a comment from Ructions which does not come. *The devil can quote scripture and this man did not declare himself saved.* 'Are you saved, sir? Have you bathed in the blood of Jee-sus?'

'Sure have. Now, go away,' Ructions says edgily. 'Go on.'

Salters puts up his hands and backs off. He doubts that Ructions has been saved and gives the master bank robber up for a lost soul. *Sometimes you have to give the devil his due.*

Ructions observes the door to the bullion bay opening. Then Liam and Declan push out the four trolleys. Billy and Ambrose, heavily disguised and wearing Belfast City Council jackets, get out of the loot lorry and walk behind it.

As Ambrose pushes the button that lowers the tailgate, he looks intently at Declan. 'How's it going, Dec?'

Declan knows from Ambrose's shape and voice that he is the friendly tiger-kidnapper who had driven him part of the way to Liam's house. In the nature of things, Declan should feel nothing but loathing for Ambrose, but, actually, he's glad to see him. 'I'm okay, I guess,' he says airily. 'And how are you?'

'I'm smiling at troubles, kid. Glad to see you're holding up.'

'You're almost over the line, boys,' Billy says. 'Now laugh.'

'What?' Liam asks.

'Laugh for the cameras. Both of you.'

Neither man feels remotely like laughing, but what can they do? The best either can muster is an unenthusiastic chuckle, but Ambrose gets into it, guffawing and buckling up. 'That's funny, mate,' Billy says, finding himself involuntarily laughing at Ambrose's antics.

In the security room, Cecil Wilkinson glances up at the outside camera, watches the lads making merry and quickly returns to his paper.

A few years back, local professional gambler Alan Freeland had almost reached the final table at the world poker series in Las Vegas. Since then, his fortunes at the poker table have dipped and, walking down Hillier Street, he tries to convince his wife, Jeannie, that his luck is bound to change and that he can win the forthcoming UK poker championship – if only she would ask her wealthy father to stake him.

'I told you, I won't do it,' Jeannie says adamantly. 'Now, that's the end of it.'

Dejected, feeling as if he has just been bluffed off a winning hand, Freeland pulls the lapels of his overcoat even tighter around his neck. As he and his wife stroll past the loot lorry, he notices that the two council workers seem to be wearing ill-fitting wigs and dark blue caps. Those are disguises, he thinks, and not even good ones. But the other two aren't disguised. In fact, they look like bank officials. *What's going on here?*

What's going on is that, even as Liam and Declan pretend to look unconcerned, Billy and Ambrose are undertaking the wholesale plunder of the National Bank's vaults. Keeping up the veneer of indifference, Liam folds his arms, while Declan examines the contents of his wallet. On the other hand, Billy and Ambrose push the trolleys up into the van and begin unloading the blocks of money on to wooden pallets.

Consumed by the scale of what is unfolding, Ambrose stops for a second, reaches for two rolls of industrial cling film and glances over at Billy. One word escapes from his lips: 'Jesus.'

Billy's phone rings. 'Talk to me,' Ructions says.

'It's a gift,' Billy answers. 'We're ready to go.'

'Come right ahead.'

Still outside the bank, Declan and Liam reclaim their empty trolleys. Ructions phones Liam and tells him that he wants the trolleys ready for a second run in thirty-five minutes.

'That'll be tight, Jack,' Liam says. 'It took us every available second to get those first four ready.'

'Thirty-five minutes – bigger notes only,' Ructions repeats and hangs up.

Billy hands Declan some rolls of industrial cling film and instructs him to wrap up the trolleys in it for the next withdrawal. And then, as quickly as it started, the second part of the biggest heist in Irish history is over.

As Billy and Ambrose drive off, Ructions backs up his car, lets them out into the traffic lane and wheels in behind.

Liam and Declan watch a scene which, just twenty-four hours earlier, they would have deemed inconceivable.

Alan Freeland has always had a certain amount of sympathy for those who risk their freedom to rob banks. For him, participating in a bank robbery is the ultimate punt: the all-in of all-ins. Still, he assesses that there might be a reward if he were to foil any such robbery and, for purely selfish reasons, he approaches two patrolling police officers at the front of City Hall, gives them his name and address and tells them that something is amiss in Hillier Street, that men in disguises are loading up a white lorry.

When the police officers check out the street, there is nothing to verify Freeland's account: no white lorry; no wigged men; no sign of knavery. The street is deserted. Surprisingly, the police choose not to make any further inquiries at the bank and go about their business.

As soon as Ructions is sure that neither he nor Billy and Ambrose are being followed, he phones Panzer at Ciggy Charlie's and tells him that the first load is in transit.

'The first load?' Panzer queries.

'We're going back for dessert.'

Panzer plunges headlong into laughter. 'Dessert? I *love* dessert. Fuckin' love it. Are you coming in?'

'Nah. I don't have to. But I do need a quick turnover.'

'I hear that.'

'And you, boss?'

Panzer is pleased at being given his place. 'Yeah?'

'We need to make sure the product is good.'

'I'm on it,' Panzer says, pulling a ski mask over his face.

Ructions tries to anticipate what might go wrong. *What am I missing? There's always that little detail that's been overlooked. Where are you, little detail?* Try as he may, he cannot find it.

Ambrose pulls in to Ciggy Charlie's scrapyard and Ciggy directs him to the enclosed area, where he parks beside a large truck with a sign saying PRONTO PARCEL DELIVERY on its side. Billy jumps out and lowers the tailgate.

Panzer, wearing a ski mask and driving the telescopic forklift, takes out a pallet of money and transfers it into a delivery truck. He repeats the process until all four pallets are relocated.

Ciggy Charlie looks on, a cigarette hanging out of the side of his mouth. He rubs the palms of his hands on his trousers, a telltale sign that he's on the money. Panzer had informed him that there would be a second run. *A second run? There are four pallets of money in the first run! Oh fuck, this is heavy! Every peeler in the country is going to be looking for this money. I'll have to speak to Panzer. I need more readies for the risk I'm taking.*

Panzer beckons Billy over and, leaning down from the telescopic forklift, instructs him to return to the bank for a second withdrawal. Billy grins as if they share a secret. They do. Both have known each other all their lives and Billy knows that it is Panzer's face behind the ski mask.

'What are you smirking about?' Panzer growls. 'Get on with it.'

Billy's grin vanishes and with it goes any illusions that Robin Hood is one of the good guys.

Ructions looks at his watch as Ambrose drives out of Ciggy's scrapyard. A nine-minute turnover, he notes. Not bad. A question has been nibbling at him ever since the boys left the bank. *Can a move be too easy? There must be ten, no fifteen, million in Ciggy's already, and no sirens, no distracted cops, no roadblocks, no 'RA – not even, it seems, an emergency services call to say that the biggest outlet in the National Bank chain is being systematically emptied of money. How unusual is that? Exquisitely unusual!* A euphoric mind booms: *Bring it on, bring it on. Bring it on, on, on.* Ructions adjusts his rear mirror. With no money in the loot lorry, he takes an alternative route back to the bank.

Panzer has locked up the delivery truck and brought a block of money into Ciggy's back office. He removes his ski mask, takes out some currency and checks it with the counterfeit pen. Handsome is the word that springs to his mind. Another word pops in: mortality. The Devil had once told him that it's only when you turn fifty, or have a terminal illness, that your mortality becomes an issue. Panzer wishes The Devil were here to enjoy this moment. His old man, who had once robbed the Munster and Leinster Bank on Belfast's Falls Road and made his getaway on horseback, would be proud of him. There is a knock on the door.

'Yes?'

Ciggy sticks in his head. 'Ahh, Panzer, it's me.'

'What can I do for you, Ciggy?'

'We need to talk.'

As if I don't know what's coming next. 'What about?'

'About pallets of very burny money.'

Panzer knows there is no point in trying to fob off Ciggy. He opens the door. 'Come in, come in.'

In the bank's vault, Liam walks around a trolley, sealing it with industrial cling film. He receives another phone call from Ructions.

'How's it going there?'

'Not good, Jack. Not good at all. We'll need more time if you want four trolleys.'

'We haven't got more time. How many are ready now?'

'Two.'

'Get them out now. Your rubbish van will be waiting.' Ructions hangs up as he pulls in at the end of Hillier Street.

The Reverend Roy Salters is still outside the bank and is earnestly entreating a bespectacled young man in a blue raincoat to see the light. The young man's friend's arm is rotating behind the preacher's back in a wind-up motion, but Salters doesn't need winding up; he is in full flow. Still, he glances over at Ructions' car and wonders why he's back.

Once again, Ambrose drives into Hillier Street and parks outside the bank's bullion bay. The wind and the sleet have moved on and the air is eerily motionless.

'This is ...' Ambrose's expression is one of unease. 'I don't know. Don't you think this is a bit weird?' As if to accentuate the point, his eyes shoot from one side mirror to the other. 'I mean, look at this place. We may as well be removing furniture, except we're removing lorryloads of cash, and there's not a peeler about to stop us.'

'One thing's for sure,' Billy says jovially, 'all banks should be this considerate.'

'It's almost too easy.'

'Now *you're* putting the scud on us.'

'I was only—'

'Get out and lower the tailgate. We haven't got all night to hang around here.'

No sooner has Ambrose lowered the tailgate than the bullion bay opens and Liam and Declan appear.

'Only two trolleys?' Billy asks Liam.

'That's all we'd time for,' Liam says. 'Jack knows all about it.'

'Okay. Load up,' Billy says. 'C'mon, chop, chop.'

As the loot lorry pulls out of Hillier Street, Ambrose observes the front of the bank. Four kids dressed as Goths walk by. Two bus drivers and their inspector hurry to the nearest watering hole. A businessman with a swinging umbrella ignores Salters. 'Repent, sinner,' Salters yells at the businessman, 'for the wages of sin is death.'

'I don't get any of that,' Ambrose says softly, nodding to Salters. 'I fuckin' love sinning. And the wages of sin are great.'

'What's that?' Billy asks.

'I said, I love sinning.'

Billy's eyes are everywhere. 'It has its benefits.'

Ambrose looks over his shoulder into the back of the lorry. 'How much do you think there is?'

Billy half-turns. 'What? Eight mill? Nine? About that.'

Ambrose shakes his head in amazement. 'This is one to tell your kids about – when you're ready to kick the bucket, that is.'

'We're not home yet.'

'Now who's putting the scud on us?'

SEVENTEEN

In Ciggy Charlie's scrapyard, Panzer fetches the Villa holdall and hands it to Ructions, who is in the back of the delivery truck. Ructions again hides his identity behind his V-for-Vendetta mask.

'That's your lot,' Panzer says.

'Right,' Ructions says. 'We've got the counting machines?'

'Yip.'

'And you've told Eamonn we're on the way?'

'Uh-huh.'

'You told him to have a supply of pallets in the barn?'

Panzer is beginning to feel irritated at Ructions' quizzing. 'Yes, yes.'

'Where's Finbarr?'

'He's sorting out something else for me.'

Ructions trades glances with Panzer. 'Has it anything to do with this?'

'No.'

It had better not have. Ructions looks away, then abruptly turns back. 'Let's go then. You suss out the road ahead. Any peelers – anything at all – call me.'

'I know the fuckin' drill by now, Ructions,' Panzer says cantankerously.

As Ructions begins to turn the delivery truck, Billy appears at its side. When Ructions stops, Billy reaches his hand in the truck window and, shaking Ructions' hand, says, 'Fabulous, mate. This was the best robbery I've ever been on.'

Ructions chuckles. 'It worked out rightly now, didn't it?'

'Worked out rightly? Ructions, son, I think time will reveal that to be a bit of an understatement.'

'Bill, this might be the easy part. Stay handy, y'hear?'

'Sure. If you need me, call.'

Ructions' phone rings. It is Seamus McCann. 'I've got to take this,' he tells Billy.

'Don't worry about anything,' Billy says.

Ructions talks into the phone, 'Hold on.' He looks at Billy. 'Remember what I said: Hang loose.'

'You've got it.'

Ructions takes the phone call.

'It's meself,' McCann says.

'So it is.'

In a reference to Stephanie Diver, McCann says, 'I've still got that dog.'

'Keep it in its kennel for a wee while longer. I'll get back to you soon.'

'Do,' Seamus says.

Ructions hangs up and waves to Panzer, indicating that he should drive out of Ciggy Charlie's before him.

Inside a car parked farther up a north Belfast street, Finbarr watches his father's car and a delivery truck turn right, out of Ciggy Charlie's scrapyard. He has been around long enough to know that Panzer is scouting the route ahead for Ructions. *There they are, on the final leg of the robbery of the century and I'm left out in the cold, on my own – treated like the class dunce.* A vagrant thought enters Finbarr's mind: *What would happen if my old man was to have a heart attack on the way to dumping the money? What would happen? Ructions would be the only person who'd know where the money is hidden. And then what?* 'And then he'd blow my fuckin' head off!' Finbarr says out loud. He determines to speak to his father about this anomaly – if he ever sees him again.

The loot lorry and Ructions' car are driven out of Ciggy Charlie's scrapyard by Billy and Ambrose. Finbarr ducks down as the vehicles drive past. He pops up again. *My time is coming. Go on, boys, make my millions.*

Declan gently sways on a seat inside the vault. His hands are joined and resting between his legs. Liam sits across from him, trying to read a magazine, but it is three months old and no matter how much he reads and rereads it, the words do not seem to make any sense. Liam's phone rings. Declan comes over and puts his ear to the phone. 'Hello,' Liam says.

Ructions is almost at the Irish border. 'Hello, Liam,' he says, taking a bite out of a sandwich.

'What do you want now, Jack?'

'That's what I like about you, Liam – you get to the point.' Ructions takes a drink of Coke. 'I just want to congratulate you both. Dec's listening in, isn't he?'

'Yes, Jack,' Declan says.

'How's it going, Dec?'

'I'm still here.'

'Very true,' Ructions says. 'I just want to say well done. Guys, you've both performed admirably in the circumstances.'

'We aim to please,' Liam says.

Ructions lets out a chuckle. 'Oh, that's very droll, "We aim to please." I'll keep that one for the boys, Liam, if you don't mind.'

'Not at all,' Liam says. Liam has always realised the tactical importance of keeping on the good side of Ructions and now he sees an opportunity to draw him out. 'I must congratulate *you* on a job well done, Jack.'

'Do you mean that?'

'I do.'

'Well, that's much appreciated.'

'No, really. The way I see it, you've been the maestro, and the mobile phone has been your baton.'

'I never thought of it like that before.'

'Well, there you are,' Liam says. 'The thing is, Jack, we've got to get a move on.'

'What do you mean?'

'We have to lock up and set the alarms.'

Ructions bursts out laughing again. 'Stop it, Liam! You're killing me. "We have to lock up and set the alarms." That'll keep the robbers out, won't it?'

Even Liam smiles sardonically. 'It's gratifying to hear you're in such excellent form, Jack.'

'Why wouldn't I be? Business has been good. It's going to be a very prosperous Christmas.'

'I dare say,' Liam says. 'Jack, we've done our part. We've followed your instructions to the letter and filled your lorry with millions of the bank's money. Now it's your turn to be honourable. Show some humanity, Jack. Release our loved ones now, for pity's sake.'

Ructions is approaching the border village of Blacklion in west County Cavan. 'You've had a difficult time reining in your temper, haven't you, Liam?'

'You want the truth, Jack?'

'Of course.'

'I've never been able to abide thievery, and this is thievery on a grand scale.'

'Come on, Liam, you can do better than that.'

'I don't think so.'

'Speak your mind,' Ructions says sharply.

'If that's what you want,' Liam says. 'Taking people's families away and threatening to kill them if you don't get money is a pretty cowardly occupation, Jack.'

'Suppose I was to say to you it was all a big bluff? Suppose I was to say that neither of your families was ever in any real danger of being hurt? Does that change anything?'

'Is that the case, Jack?'

'You'll never know.' Ructions contemplates pursuing this conversation and decides against it. 'Right then. When you've locked up, you both go to Dec's house. Don't go anywhere else. Don't talk to anyone. You're almost there, Liam. Don't screw up now.'

'What do we do when we get to Declan's house?'

'You'll be told.'

'How's Stephanie?'

'She's fine. You'll be with her in a couple of hours.'

'That's good to hear.'

'There's one last thing, Liam?'

'Uh-huh?'

'Don't make the phone call to the cops till half past eleven.'

'Half past eleven. Okay.'

'Other than that, all I can say is that it was a pleasure working with you both.'

'I'd like to say the same, Jack—'

'But you can't. I can understand that. You know what, Liam? Don't reproach yourself about any of this. You're a thoroughly decent man, and you did what any thoroughly decent man in your position would do.'

And you, Jack, are a thoroughly repugnant man. 'I guess you're right there.'

'Well, cheerio then. Oh, Dec?'

'Yes, Jack.'

'You played a blinder, kid.'

'Thanks. What about my family, Jack?'

Ructions has already hung up.

At Musgrave Street police headquarters, Chief Superintendent Daniel Clarke is writing a report on the Provisional IRA's involvement in illegal fuel smuggling across the border. He yawns, not bothering to cover his mouth. It has been a long shift. The report would have to wait until later. He stands up, stretches his arms and then heads into the operations room.

Five police officers are monitoring a bank of cameras that provide an overview of the major thoroughfares in Belfast city centre. Clarke stands behind his officers and skims from camera to camera. The crowds in the city centre are thinning out, with only the Christmas market in the grounds of the City Hall doing a roaring trade.

'Anything I should know about, Gerry?' Clarke asks.

'Not really, sir,' Inspector Gerry Rowlands says. 'It seems all the crims are at home counting their day's takings.'

'Let's hope they haven't much to count,' Clarke says hopefully.

A polite word here, a look of anguish there – the two bank officials' journey from the National Bank to Declan Butler's home is silent and harrowing. The paradox in their outlook is striking: Liam thinks that if Stephanie survives this experience, he is going to take her on a holiday in the sun to recuperate; Declan thinks that if he survives this experience, he is going to prison. They pull up outside the Butler household.

Declan knocks on the door and it is immediately opened. The two men walk inside. A gang member greets them in the hall and directs them to the living room.

'Dec!' Kate shouts, springing from her seat and throwing her arms around her brother.

Colette follows Kate's example, showering her son with kisses on his cheeks.

Alec waits patiently for the womenfolk to release his son. Declan is in front of him; he has survived. Alec and Declan embrace. 'You're back,' Alec says, his bottom lip trembling. 'That's brilliant, son.'

Overwhelmed, Declan gulps. On the journey up from the bank, he had tried to steel himself for this moment, but it is upon him and he has no control; the dam is breached. Like a spluttering car, Declan says, 'Dad, I'm, I'm …'

Alec puts his arms around him. 'I'm proud of you, son.'

Declan rallies and turns to Liam. 'This is Liam, my workmate.'

Liam and Alec shake hands.

'The two mobiles,' a gang member says, his hand out, fingers wriggling impatiently.

Declan and Liam return the mobile phones.

'Everybody into the kitchen. Hurry up! When we're done here, Liam, go home and wait for your wife. Speak to no one.'

No sooner are the Butler family and Liam in the kitchen than the tiger-kidnappers begin the clean-up.

Kate and Colette hold Declan's hands as they sit around the dining table. 'I don't think they're interested in anything but the money,' Alec whispers to Liam.

Liam nods politely, but Alec's words are of little relief.

'Shhh,' Declan says. 'Is that the front door closing?' He stands up and sticks his ear against the living-room door. He looks at the faces of his family before popping his head into the living room. No one is there. Declan tiptoes in and looks into the hall. 'They've gone,' he tells the others.

'Phone the police,' Alec says.

'We can't do that yet, Mr Butler,' Liam says.

'Alec, son. Call me Alec.'

'Alec, they said we've not to phone before half past eleven. They're not releasing my wife until then.'

Stephanie Diver lies in the foetal position on mossy grass. Her captors have dropped her off in a forest outside Castlewellan, County Down. She is content. It is all over. A wave of peacefulness and release sweeps her up and brings her to a plateau of extraordinary calm. *Let go. Just drift away. No! Get up!* Reaching up, she pulls the clear tape from her eyes. It hurts. She rubs her eyes, blinking repeatedly. Mizzling rain trickles down her face and waters her spirit. *Get up, dammit. Get up.* Stephanie struggles upright. The grass under her bare feet feels cold and slippery. Turning in every direction, she sees nothing but trees and darkness. She is like a blind person in a maze. *Walk, just keep walking.* She hears a car in the distance, stumbles towards it and then stops. *It might be the tiger-kidnappers. No, they'll be well gone by now.* She grabs a fallen branch and uses it to help her along. *Walk. Keep walking. No stopping. There's a light ahead.* She totters towards it and collapses. A dog appears and barks at her. A young boy emerges from the side of the house. Stephanie reaches out her hand to the boy, then blacks out.

Liam Diver is on his way home to Loughshore, County Down. He turns on the radio to listen to the news. Nothing extraordinary is happening in Northern Ireland: an arson attack on a school in the Twinbrook estate in west Belfast; a pensioner couple tied up and robbed by burglars in Holywood, outside Belfast; a forty-four-year-old man charged with attempted murder; two men kneecapped in north Belfast; a former Lord Mayor of Belfast dies. But there is not a squeak about a bank robbery in the city centre.

Worries begin to whirl about in Liam's head, like grains of sand in a desert storm. *Will they release Steph at all? What if they've raped her? What if they've murdered her?* No, *no. Why would they murder her? That makes no sense unless, unless ... she saw one of their faces. Or, unless, while raping her, one of them had ejaculated into her and left DNA. I should phone the police. I should give them a chance to find her. But what if the robbers are just about to release her and they find out I've alerted the police? What if they've a radio that's tuned into the police frequency? Am I guiltless in all this? What could I have done differently? Will Steph blame me for this world of trauma when and if she is eventually released? If she does hold me responsible, what's left? Where do I go?* The air gushes from Liam's lungs. His hands grip the steering wheel until his knuckles are white. *It's all that sewer rat Jack's fault. What was it he said? 'Don't reproach yourself about any of this.' A degenerate like that giving lectures to me on morality?*

It is half past eleven in the Butler household. Declan's face is chalk-white, his eyes bloodshot. He wrings his hands. 'It's time,' he says gloomily.

'You bear up, son,' Alec says. 'You've done nothing wrong. Now go ahead.'

Declan slowly lifts the land phone. 'It's not going to be that simple, Dad. The police won't believe me.'

'To hell with the police,' Alec says. 'You're an innocent bloody man. Now make the call.'

'Hello? My name is Declan Butler and I want to report a very, very serious robbery. I've had a horrendous ordeal.'

The delivery truck pulls into Eamonn de Búrca's farmyard in County Mayo. The farmer, his flat cap tilted, stands at the entrance to his large barn and wheels his finger, beckoning Ructions to turn the truck around and reverse into the building. Safely parked and out of sight, Ructions jumps out.

Billy Kelly phones to tell Ructions that the loot lorry and the car have been dismantled and shredded. Panzer strides into the barn, claps Eamonn on his shoulder and whispers into his ear. Eamonn leaves the barn. Both master criminals go to the back of the truck, open it up and look inside. Panzer turns to Ructions, grinning. He ceremoniously punches Ructions in the chest. For the first time since the beginning of the job, Ructions lets down his guard as he and Panzer hug and jump with joy.

'After you, my good man,' Panzer says, bowing and swinging an open hand.

'Oh, no,' Ructions says. 'That would be highly improper. After you, good sir.'

'But I insist.'

'Well, if that's the way of it.'

Ructions, then Panzer, climb into the truck. Lifting a knife, Ructions slices through the cling film that holds the money in place on the wooden pallets. Several large blocks of fifty-pound notes fall from the pallet. Opening a block, Ructions rubs the money around Panzer's face.

'We've had a good harvest,' Panzer chirps gleefully.

They sit down. Panzer takes two cigars from his coat, gives one to Ructions and lights them both.

'This is one of those moments in life that will never be repeated,' Ructions says philosophically. 'We should treasure it.'

'Oh, I will.'

EIGHTEEN

Chief Superintendent Daniel Clarke parts the venetian blinds of his office window and peeps out into the courtyard. Cradling the telephone between his shoulder and head, he rubs the lenses of his glasses with a cleaning cloth. 'And you've brought in the dog, dear?' he says. 'A good decision. It's starting to snow again.' Putting on his glasses, he walks to the mirror on the wall, inspects his teeth and makes a mental note to have them whitened in the new year. There is a sharp knock on his door. Clarke returns to his desk and sits down. 'I've got to go now, dear. I'll not be long. Bye-bye.'

Inspector Gerry Rowlands enters the office.

'What is it, Gerry?' Clarke asks wearily. It's late, nearly midnight, and he's bloody exhausted. Whatever this is, it will have to wait until tomorrow. He just wants to go home.

'It's the National Bank in High Street, sir.'

'Is it?'

'Yes, sir. It's been robbed.'

Clarke displays little emotion. 'Has it?'

'It's what they took, sir.'

'Will you get to the bloody point, man?'

'The caller—'

'Who is?'

'A Declan Butler, sir.'

'Who is?'

'A bank official, sir.'

'Continue,' Clarke says, waving his hand regally. 'Enlighten me, please.'

'Butler says he and another bank official have been tiger-kidnapped and their families held hostage for the last twenty-four hours and that the thieves have emptied the bank, sir!' Rowlands blurts out.

'What do you mean they "emptied the bank"?'

'Butler says they've practically cleaned out the bank, sir.'

'Practically cleaned the bank out? For fuck sake! Cut to the chase! What does that mean?'

'It seems they've barely left enough money to tip the cleaners. Butler said they've taken tens of millions, sir.'

Clarke looks away. He wants to laugh at the absurdity of what he has just been told, but he can't. His gaze returns to Rowlands. He stands up. 'I want the crime scenes secured immediately. I assume there are three?'

'Four, sir,' Rowlands says. 'The second bank official's wife—'

'We're not talking about Mr Butler here?'

'No, sir. A Mr Liam Diver.'

'I see.'

'Mr Diver's wife was removed from the family home in Loughshore. I've—'

Clarke's head tilts. 'Hold on, hold on. There's the bank. That's one crime scene. Then there are the two hostage houses – that gives us three. But you're telling me there's a fourth and that's because Mrs Diver was removed from the family home – which presumably means that Mr Butler's wife or kinfolk were not – otherwise we'd be talking about five crime scenes. Have I got that right?'

'Yes, sir.'

'Why was only one family unit removed?'

'I don't know, sir. I haven't spoken to Declan Butler in depth yet.'

'Where's he from?'

'West Belfast, sir.'

'A Savile Row fit, don't you think? Any form?'

'None, sir.'

'Bring him in.' Clarke takes off his glasses and folds them carefully. 'Go easy on him for now – but get him in.'

Liam Diver pulls into his driveway to find two police Land Rovers blocking the entrance to his house. A policeman trains his rifle on Liam's car, while another comes to the driver's side window. The officer asks Liam to identify himself and, upon hearing his answer, allows him to get out of the car. 'We have a report—' the officer says.

Liam shakes his head and puts up his hand. 'My wife? Stephanie. Where's Stephanie?'

'She's safe, sir,' the officer says. 'We have her. She's very shaken up, but we're looking after her.'

'Oh, thank God,' Liam says. He drops to his knees and weeps with relief and sheer exhaustion.

Panzer still cannot hide his delight. 'I'm away to have a word with Eamonn,' he says. 'I just want to make sure he knows there'll be consequences if he goes anywhere near the money.'

Ructions is in the bunker. He is still counting the blocks of money when Panzer walks back down the concrete steps of the bunker. 'Is he okay?' Ructions asks.

'He's sound.' Panzer sits on an old wooden beer case.

Ructions stacks the last block of the fifty-pound notes on a pallet. 'That's it,' he says.

'How much?' Panzer asks, his face flushed with anticipation.

Ructions presses the buttons on a calculator. 'I make it …' He continues to work the calculator. 'I make it, give or take a few grand …'

'Stop messing about. How much?'

'Thirty-six and a half million.'

Blessing himself, Panzer says, 'In nomine Patris et Filii et Spiritus Sancti.'

Ructions, his arm leaning on a pallet of money, also senses that to speak would devalue the enormity of the moment.

Eventually, Panzer finds his tongue. 'Would you …' he says softly, 'would you say that again?'

'I have thirty-six million, and five hundred and forty-five thousand pounds, in varying denominations.'

Staring ahead, his lips scarcely moving, Panzer says, 'Ructions, I was never one for confessions, but I've one to make now – I never thought you'd pull it off.' He turns towards his nephew and partner, as if awakening out of a dream. 'Don't get me wrong, I thought there was an outside chance – but only that. I never, in my heart of hearts, really believed we'd be sitting here, surrounded by thirty-six and a half million quid.'

Ructions is perplexed. 'I don't understand. Why did you plough all that money into something you didn't believe in?'

'I don't know. No, I take that back – I do know.' Panzer raises two fingers. 'Two reasons: one, I wanted to take the shot. If I hadn't taken it, I'd have gone to my grave saying, "What if?" Can you imagine that? What does it say about your life if your last thought is, "What if?" Does that make sense?'

'Perfect sense. And the second reason?'

'You. I thought, if anybody can pull this off, it would be you. I wouldn't have taken the risk with anyone else. I believed in you, son.' Panzer begins to struggle for breath.

Alarmed, Ructions goes to him. 'I ain't having you slipping out on me tonight, old-timer. Not tonight. Now, where are those bloody heart tablets?'

Panzer reaches into his jacket pocket, takes out a sleeve of tablets and pushes two through the plastic coating. 'This is our night, Ructions,' Panzer whispers. 'I've waited a lifetime for this night. Thank you, my friend.' He pops the two heart tablets into his mouth and swallows. 'It's funny, isn't it?' he says haltingly.

'What is?'

'I'm sitting here,' Panzer's hand sweeps around the bunker, 'with Blackbeard's fortune at my feet, and I'll be dead in a year. Maybe sooner.'

'Give over,' Ructions says, conjuring up a sham smile. 'You'll be robbing banks when the rest of us are stoking Oul Nick's fires.'

Panzer finds Ructions' attempt at flippancy clumsily charming – but he knows different. 'Will I?'

'Have you something to tell me?'

Panzer's cough is forced. 'I've, I've a very aggressive strain of cancer.'

'Can it be—?'

'No, it can't be treated. It's all through me.' Panzer tries to smile but grimaces instead.

'Bollocks! Fuckin', fuckin' bollocks!' Ructions yells. He walks down between the pallets of money and pivots around. 'No way. No fuckin' way. This isn't happening. This is not fuckin' happening.'

'I ought to have told you earlier.'

Ructions sits down against the wall beside Panzer, lights a cigarette, blows two rings and shakes his head. 'I should've known. Cutting back on fatty foods to lower your cholesterol, you said. I should've known—'

'It's all right, Ructions. I've come to terms with it. I don't fear death. Never did.'

'Don't say that!'

Panzer pats Ructions' cheek. 'It's okay. Look, I'm okay. I am. Now, where's that bottle of Dom Pérignon you said you'd brought?'

Ructions goes to the delivery truck and returns with the champagne and two glasses. He pops the cork and pours. Panzer stands, holds up his glass and says, 'To the greatest bank robbers since Jesse and Frank James.'

'To us,' Ructions replies solemnly.

Panzer sits down again. 'You know, you've given me cause to think after our little tiff last night.'

'What little tiff?' Ructions says lightly. 'I don't remember a little tiff.'

Panzer grins. 'You said our day had come and gone.'

'I'm sorry now I opened my big mouth.'

'Don't be. You weren't to know I'd be shipping out so soon.'

'But—'

Panzer shakes his head doggedly. 'Hey! I don't want to hear any "buts". To hell with that. Me and you – we've had good times.'

'Great times, boss.'

Panzer chuckles. 'Boss! Ha! You've been boss all along. I was always only ever a figurehead.'

'I don't think so, boss.'

'You're a good 'un, Ructions.' Panzer sips some champagne. 'So, you were saying, we've become victims of our own success?'

'That's how I see it.' Ructions waves his hand panoramically. 'Look around you. This move, it's so big, so important, it'll force technology to overtake us. The bank-robbing business is coming to an end ... well ... people will still rob banks, but it'll be done on the internet or from insider dealing on the stock market.'

Panzer clears his throat. 'So what now? Where do we go from here?'

'Nowhere. I'm out.'

'Out? What does that mean?'

'I won't be here.'

'Oh?'

This is a moment that Ructions had dreaded. 'I've had enough. I'm cashing in my chips. I'm gone after this is sorted.'

Panzer massages his chin. 'Hmm ... Gone where?'

'Don't know for sure yet, but out of Ireland.'

Panzer forces a smile. 'Can't say I blame you. Funny, I've never wanted to cash in my chips.' He hesitates. 'I'm worried about Finbarr.'

'I'm not sure you need to be,' Ructions says, his fingertips stroking his brow thoughtfully. 'He has problems – as you know.' Ructions scrutinises Panzer's face. 'But he is intelligent. He'll work out.'

'I hope so.'

A malevolent thought pops into Ructions' mind. 'He doesn't know the money's here, does he?'

'No.'

'Panzer, you've got to be straight with me on this—'

'He doesn't know about this place.'

'Would he be able to work it out?'

'No.'

Fuck it. Ask the question. 'Does anybody else know about this place?'

'Like who?'

'I don't know. Anybody.'

Panzer's eyes are now fixed on Ructions. 'Who do you think I told? The 'RA?'

'Did you?'

'Did I what?'

'Tell the 'RA?'

Panzer jumps up and pulls back his hand as if to punch Ructions. Ructions does not move a muscle. Panzer wags his finger as if chastising Ructions. 'What did you just say to me?'

'I said, did you tell the 'RA?'

Panzer walks towards the end of the bunker, spins around and, hands clasped behind his back, comes back to Ructions. He leans into Ructions' face and says in a low voice, 'Why the fuck would you ask me that? Why?'

In an equally low voice, Ructions says, 'Because you met Tiny Murdoch a few nights ago in McQuillan's quarry.'

Panzer sits down again and nods his head. 'And?'

'And I want to know why you met him.'

Panzer's finger traverses between Ructions and himself. 'You think I told him about this job?' Ructions shakes his shoulders. Panzer bursts out laughing. It takes him almost a minute before he can compose himself. Ructions smiles. 'The 'RA …' Panzer says between giggles, 'want me to front a chain of bars for them.'

'Right.'

'They were going to put two million into it.'

'You didn't agree, did you?'

'What do you fuckin' think?' Panzer says.

An arctic hush takes hold as each man delves into his own thoughts. 'I'm going over to see Serge for a few days,' Ructions says.

Panzer nods sympathetically. 'Fair enough. Anything I can help with?'

'Not really. I need to firm up the transfer of the money. I don't want any cock-ups at the final hurdle.' Both men sip their champagne. 'I know you've spoken to Eamonn,' Ructions says, 'but maybe I should have a word with him too. Just to keep him honest.'

'Nah, he's got the message,' Panzer says. 'We'll have no trouble out of him. Let's hit the road. My eyes are that heavy, they're knocking together.'

Eleanor Proctor has been dozing on the sofa. She opens her eyes. Frank is on the phone. He looks grave, but then, she thinks, doesn't he always? He sets down the phone and turns to Eleanor. 'The bank's been robbed.'

'Isn't that an occupational hazard?' Eleanor says, sitting up and smoothing down her hair.

'Don't be flippant, Eleanor,' Frank says. 'They've taken millions. Millions. The bank can't even put a figure on how much is gone. I've got to go down there.'

'Is there anything I can do?'

'No,' Frank says, as he fixes his tie.

'Any ideas who did it?'

'Too early,' Frank says. 'Perhaps the IRA. Who knows?'

I do.

As he stands at the door of his mother's home, Liam Diver feels as if he is a 6-year-old child paralysed with fear of the monsters under his bed. What scares him most is that he can only imagine the terror that Stephanie has experienced. *How will it have affected her?* Like an irate cobra, that question keeps raising its head. A police car pulls into the driveway. Liam takes a deep breath.

Stephanie is draped in a grey blanket and held up by a female police-liaison officer in civilian clothes. Liam and his mother, Ursula, go to Stephanie and put their arms around her. On seeing him, she stumbles, but he gathers her in his arms.

'It's okay, love,' he says, as he carries her indoors. 'I've got you. It's all over, Steph. You're safe now.' Despite the comforting words, Liam is momentarily stunned at Stephanie's dishevelled appearance. Her dank and tatted blonde hair is sticking to her waxy cheeks, as if superglued. But it is her eyes that cut Liam the most: sunken, colour-drained, lifeless. She leans her head into him and sobs, her body heaving uncontrollably.

By the time it takes Liam to bring Stephanie to the sofa and sit with his arm around her, he has already made up his mind that he is finished with banking. 'It's just so good to see you, love,' he says. 'I'm so sorry, so sorry. It's all over now, love.'

Stephanie's head rests on his arm, her wide-open eyes staring at the ceiling. Liam brushes the hair from her cheeks with the back of his fingers. 'My beautiful Steph,' he whispers. 'Steph?' Stephanie does not react. 'Steph?' he says anxiously, his eyes furtively noting the features of her face for indications that she had heard him. 'Are you all right, love? Speak to me, Steph. Tell me you can hear me.'

'I'll put on the kettle, shall I?' the police-liaison officer says.

Liam turns to her and indicates that he wants to speak to the officer alone. They go out of Stephanie's earshot.

'We haven't been introduced,' the police-liaison officer says. 'I'm Deirdre Fitzpatrick.'

They shake hands. 'Has she been examined by a doctor?' Liam asks.

'Oh, yes. A short while ago.'

'And what was his prognosis?'

'She has mild shock, which the doctor says is perfectly understandable. He says it shouldn't last any longer than twenty-four hours.'

'Okay.'

'He says she's dehydrated. Best to try—'

Liam puts up his hand to halt the officer. 'With respect, why isn't the doctor telling me this instead of you?'

'I suppose he had other—'

'I'm sorry but I don't want to hear supposition,' Liam says abruptly. 'I want to hear the doctor tell me about my wife's health and well-being.'

'By all means, sir. I'll make the arrangements.'

'I'd really appreciate that. In the meantime, I hope this doesn't sound rude, but I'd like some time alone with my wife.'

'Of course,' she says, her voice trailing off in a manner that leaves the impression that she has she has more to say, and she has. 'You may know that the first twenty-four hours in any investigation are the most crucial?'

'I didn't know that.'

'Well, that's the case, Mr Diver, and I ... I don't want to sound intrusive, but CID have asked me to tell you they'd like to speak with Stephanie and yourself as soon as possible.'

'Indeed.' Liam's thumb and index finger squeeze his lower lip meditatively. 'We'll speak to them when we're ready, but I don't know when that's going to be. Right now, my wife can't speak to anyone.'

'Oh yes I can,' Stephanie says.

Liam looks around. Stephanie's hand is on the arm of the sofa as she struggles to get up. Liam goes to his wife and sits her down again. 'Steph, you're not—'

'I want to speak to the police. I want to tell them what I remember.'

'Later, love. I don't think you're in a fit state—'

'No, now.' The fire has reignited in Stephanie's eyes. 'I want these bastards caught, Liam. I want to stand in a witness box, in a court of law, and I want to watch them sweat in the dock as I give my evidence.'

'Shall I get CID then?' the policewoman asks.

'Yes,' Liam says smiling. He takes her hand.

As Deirdre Fitzpatrick leaves the house, Liam follows her out. 'When will the forensic team be finished?'

'I can't really answer that. There may be vital forensic evidence in your house. I imagine the crime scene investigators will be there for some time, given the enormity of the crime.'

'One more thing. How come my wife was taken away and my co-worker's family were allowed to remain in their home?'

Deirdre smiles. 'I'm sure CID will be putting that question to your co-worker.'

'It'll be interesting to hear their answer,' Liam says.

Chief Superintendent Daniel Clarke walks around the vault of the National Bank. He does not want to be here. He does not want to be wearing a white forensic suit. He does not want to be looking at a bank vault that seems peculiarly empty. Closing his eyes, he makes a movement with his hands, as if piling large blocks of money into a trolley. He can see two men filling trolleys with money, quietly, secretively, methodically.

Inspector Gerry Rowlands enters the vault and says, 'Declan Butler has indicated that he walked past the security control room and out of the bank carrying a holdall containing an estimated one million pounds.'

'Just like that? He dandered out of the bank with a million quid and nobody batted an eyelid?'

'Apparently not, sir. He then went into Ringland Street, where he handed the holdall over to one of the robbers—'

'This was before the white lorry came to take away the first batch of money?'

'Yes, sir.'

'The dry run. In one fell swoop, the safe passage of the money out of the bank is established and the robbers know that there's no security breach.' Clarke turns around, looking at the exterior of the vault. 'You said Butler walked past the security control room. Who was manning it?'

Rowlands goes to his notes. 'A Cecil Wilkinson and a Joseph Bittles.'

'Any figures in yet?'

'They're still counting, sir, but it's in excess of thirty million pounds.'

'Do you think they're all in on it?'

'Who, sir?'

'The two security guys, along with Butler and Diver?'

'I don't know, sir. It's unlikely though, isn't it?'

'Is it?' Clarke has a vision of the four men sitting at a wooden table in the corner of a small pub, with slate tiles on the floor and oak-stained panelled walls. The bar is empty, except for the barman, who is cleaning glasses. They sup pints of beer and one of them puts a proposition to the others: let's rob our own bank.

'I think it very implausible, sir.'

'You think so, Gerry? I beg to differ. What if their relatives were in on it? What if no one has been tiger-kidnapped at all? All the relatives have to do is to stick to their stories that they were tiger-kidnapped, and they end up becoming millionaires overnight. Not only that – we'd be inclined to unquestioningly believe them, wouldn't we?'

Rowlands strokes his chin sceptically. 'It's unlikely though, isn't it?'

'Considering we're talking about enormous amounts of money, anything's likely. The bottom line is this – an individual, or several individuals who work in this bank, were and are in league with the thieves who drove away with the money.' Clarke inspects the locking mechanism on the vault door. 'I'll tell you what, Gerry,' Clarke says, 'if I'd known the security in this bank was as lax as this, I'd have been tempted to rob it myself.'

Rowlands smiles.

Clarke turns to the CCTV cameras. 'Pictures. I want you to set up a team to sift through the CCTV coverage from the entire city centre for ninety-six hours before the robbery. I want a list of prime suspects, starting with the Provos. Tiny Murdoch, I want him arrested, and his Man Friday, what's his name?'

'Colm Coleman, sir.'

'Yes, him too. And what do you call him? Panzer O'Hare's guy?'

'Ructions O'Hare.'

'Him as well. In fact, I want everyone on your list picked up. I want to know how it's possible to steal millions of pounds from a bank without crossing its front door.'

'Sir, might I suggest we put surveillance on them first for a while before lifting them? They might lead us to the money.'

Clarke thinks for a moment and nods. 'Agreed. Just for a day or two though. Get as many eyes as we can on those fuckers.'

NINETEEN

Ructions pulls up outside a Georgian house in Ballina and parks his car. The street is dark and deserted. He gets into a cream camper van with tinted windows and then doubles back.

Panzer is driving through Enniskillen towards Belfast. He is speaking on the phone. 'Will you pick up that parcel for me?'

Tiny Murdoch smiles as he leaves a Belfast city-centre hotel. 'I will, of course.'

'You know where it is?'

'Where you said it would be?'

'That's it. Did you hear the news?'

'I did,' Murdoch says, unable to keep a smirk off his face.

'Well, good luck.'

'You too,' Murdoch says, hanging up. He dry-punches the air and walks over to a phone box.

'Hello?' Colm Coleman says as he sits in his car behind a blue truck.

Murdoch looks out of the phone box and, confident he is not being followed or observed, turns back towards the phone. 'Everything okay?'

'Couldn't be better.'

'I just spoke to the Horsey-Man.'

'Uh-huh?'

'That message is ready for collecting.'

'Good. I should be there soon.'

Ructions pulls the cream camper van into Eamonn de Búrca's farmyard and gets out. He opens the barn doors and reverses in. Eamonn looks down from his bedroom window. No one told him they would be back that night. *Who's in that camper van and what are they doing? I'll dander down and see what's up.*

Ructions is loading holdalls into the back of the camper van when Eamonn walks into the barn. Eamonn has a puzzled look on his face. He strokes an old saddle, but his eyes do not leave Ructions. 'The very man,' Ructions says. 'I'll fill the holdalls and you put them in the van, Eamonn.'

'Panzer not with you?' Eamonn says as he walks towards Ructions.

'The old man's away home to his sweet dreams – the lucky bastard,' Ructions says as he walks down the steps into the bunker. He returns with holdalls and hands them to Eamonn.

'Is something wrong?' Eamonn says as he takes the holdalls. 'I didn't expect you back tonight.'

'The boss decided at the last minute we didn't want to put all our eggs in the one basket.'

Eamonn nods. 'Makes sense.'

'You know Panzer, Eamonn,' Ructions says. 'He's unpredictable. That's his strength – that's how he's survived so long.'

Eamonn puts the holdalls in the back of the camper van and returns to the entrance of the bunker. Ructions reappears with another two holdalls and hands them over to Eamonn, who says, 'He's a top man, that's for sure.'

'He's not well, you know.'

'Oh?'

Ructions stops and looks at Eamonn. 'Didn't he tell you?'

Eamonn has a baffled look on his face.

'He's got cancer.'

'Cancer?' Eamonn says. 'Jaysus!'

'I thought he told you. Eamonn, I want your word ... I didn't mention this to you—'

'No, no. You can depend on me, Ructions. I know when to keep my mouth shut.'

After another six holdalls are packed into the camper van, Ructions comes up from the bunker, closes the vehicle's doors and gets into the driver's seat. Eamonn comes around to Ructions. 'Is that you done?'

'Uh-huh.'

Eamonn looks down at his feet and says, 'Ructions, is there, y'know, is there a few extra quid in this for me? Like, I'm taking all the risk and—'

'Eamonn—'

'But—'

Ructions puts his finger to his lips. 'You *should* get more money. I'll take it up with Panzer. You know not to phone him, don't you? His phone's tapped.'

'Do you think I don't know the score?' Eamonn says, smiling. 'Course it's tapped.' Eamonn was not expecting Ructions to be sympathetic to his request for more money. He had thought that Ructions would be more difficult to deal with than Panzer. Before Ructions drives out of the barn, Eamonn makes a big deal of directing him into the farmyard. They wave each other goodbye.

It will soon be dawn. Ructions' eyes are heavy. In desperation, he opens a packet of chewing gum and lowers all the windows in the camper van. *Gotta put distance between myself and Eamonn's. Gotta sleep. Fuck sleep. Sing. Shout. Do something.*

Shane MacGowan and Kirsty McColl are belting out 'Fairytale of New York' on the radio. He joins in the chorus at the top of his voice. A large truck approaches him. He sits back in his seat. Three men are in the truck, which is being followed by a black Audi. Ructions looks straight ahead but his eyes flit towards the driver of the Audi, who is on his mobile phone and gesticulating. 'Coleman!' Ructions exclaims. He looks in his rear mirror as the truck and the Audi disappear from view. Suddenly the shutters are wide open. Ructions pulls in. He gets out of the car and starts to pace. *The fuckin' 'RA. On their way to Eamonn's to collect the money. Ah fuck me!* 'I was right,' he says aloud. 'I fuckin' knew it. Panzer, you fuckin' rat.'

Eamonn de Búrca is just dozing off when he hears the rumble of the large truck and the Audi pulling into his farmyard. *Not again. It'll be breakfast time before I get any sleep.*

Coleman gets out of the Audi and, along with one of the men from the truck, walks up to the farmhouse and knocks on the door. Meanwhile, another of Coleman's confederates opens the barn doors and walks inside. The driver of the truck reverses into the barn.

Eamonn is in his long johns. He looks out the upstairs blinds. *I don't think they're guards, but they might be. They don't look like guards. Could be Special Branch. No, they're not the Branch; they'd have kicked the door in by now. Who are they?*

Coleman beats loudly on the door again. Eamonn puts on his trousers, hooks his red braces over his shoulders and opens the door. 'Who are you?' he demands. 'What do you want?'

'We're the IRA, Eamonn. And don't worry, Panzer knows we're here.'

'What do you want?'

'The money.'

Eamonn rubs the stubble on his chin. *These boys could be anybody. Tell them nothing.* 'What money? I have no money.'

Coleman turns around, and the man beside him opens his coat to reveal a sub-machine gun. 'The money is in the bunker underneath your barn, Eamonn. How do I know that? Panzer told me. Him and Ructions put it there earlier on tonight.'

'Oh, if it's the Boys you are, it's alright then. Do what you've got to do, Commander.'

'I want you to come over and show us where the entrance to the bunker is,' Coleman says.

As they walk to the barn, Eamonn says, 'If you'd been here only a while earlier, you'd have run into Ructions. He's a good lad that Ructions.'

Coleman stops dead and grabs Eamonn by the elbow. 'What's that?'

'What's what?'

'You said I'd have run into Ructions.'

'Well, you would have.'

'After him and Panzer dropped the money?'

'Just so.'

Coleman knows the answer to his next question, but he still must ask it. 'What did he want?'

'Same as you. Money. He took away a camper van full of money.'

Coleman looks anxious. 'Show me the bunker.'

Tiny Murdoch expects to be arrested, so he is not staying in his own house. He'll get arrested when it suits *him*, not the police. He's lying on a double bed in a supporter's house watching television, but he is not watching television – his mind is in County Mayo. The house phone rings.

'We've a problem,' Colm Coleman says.

'Oh?'

'Not the Horsey-Man. The other guy, his sidekick.'

'Uh-huh?'

'He was here before me.'

'On his own?'

'Yes.'

'What's the damage?'

'He took away all the used tiles.'

'You're fuckin' joking!'

'I'm not.'

He took away all the used notes, all the untraceable notes, and left us with new notes that are probably sequenced and mightn't be worth the paper they're printed on. Why didn't I recruit this fucker years ago? 'Fuck!'

'I don't think the Horsey-Man knows anything about this.'

'Neither do I. Okay.' Murdoch puts down the phone. He gets out of bed and paces the floor. *You think it's alright to steal my money? To steal the IRA's money? We'll find you, Ructions. Who the fuck do you think you are, you sack of shit? You think you can outsmart the IRA? You think you can outrun us?* Murdoch lifts the phone.

Panzer turns in bed to get away from a dream where humans are sucked towards a gigantic magnet behind which is a character with long, unruly hair and cheeks that look as if they have been finely sliced with a cut-throat razor. Panzer is young. He feels the pull of the magnet. Then his phone rings – a distant humming sound, a summons to reality. It gets louder. Panzer turns over and lifts the phone, his eyes still closed. 'What?' he mumbles.

'It's me.'

Panzer recognises Murdoch's voice. He sits up. 'Okay.'

'I want a meet.'

'When?'

'Now. Where we met the last time.'

'Can't it wait?'

'No, it fuckin' can't. Get up there now.' The line goes dead.

Panzer's eyes are open now. He throws back the bedclothes and swings his legs out. His feet search for his slippers. *Something's wrong. What? I'll phone Ructions. But I can't phone Ructions. I can't tell him Tiny's on the warpath. The money. Something's wrong with the money. I'll phone Eamonn.*

Eamonn walks back to the farmhouse after watching the truck and the Audi pull out of his farmyard. His phone rings. Panzer's name comes up.

'Hello?' Eamonn says.

'Eamonn?'

'Am I glad to hear from you.'

'Why's that?'

'I'll tell you why … my place has been like Piccadilly Circus tonight.'

Panzer can almost feel the garrotte tightening around his throat. 'Who's been?'

'Well, first of all, there was Ructions ...'

Ructions went back to Eamonn's after we left? Without telling me? He must have found out the 'RA was going to scoop the money. But how? Hold on here ... this isn't my fault. No way! I told no one. Tiny won't think like that. He'll think Ructions and I are still working together.

'And he filled a camper van,' Eamonn says.

Panzer does not respond.

'Panzer?'

'What?'

'He filled a camper van.'

'Did the removal men come?'

'They're just away. But they're not too happy.'

I bet they're not. 'Thanks, Eamonn.' Panzer hangs up. He reaches for the glass of water on his bedside table and empties it. He coughs as much to clear his mind as his throat. Hailstones, lightning strikes, storm surges ... all seem to have been unleased in Panzer's stomach. He looks at a photo on the wall of him and Ructions, arms around each other, in a bar in Tenerife. Smiling faces, firework days. He remembers Ructions' words after the photo was taken: 'We're immortals, Panzer. We will live for ever.'

Ructions drives the camper van around the back and into the double garage of a detached house on the outskirts of Sligo town. He pulls down the garage shutter, goes around to the front of the house and opens the door. He goes straight towards the back door and unlocks it. Methodically, he brings all the holdalls into the house and puts them into a very large wardrobe in an upstairs bedroom. A king-size bed under a window beckons. He looks at his watch. Without thinking, he prises off his Chelsea boots and eases down on the bed. *A few minutes. That's all.* His phone rings. It is Panzer. He ignores the call.

It's early morning and McQuillan's quarry is deserted. Panzer and Murdoch are sitting in the IRA man's car. Another car, with two men in it, is parked at the side of the entrance to the quarry. Murdoch is agitated. 'He knew we'd be coming for the money—'

'You don't know that,' Panzer says.

'Course he fuckin' knew. Why else did he grab it?'

'He could have been planning to double-cross me all along.'

Murdoch shakes his head. 'Not a chance. Nah. I know this guy. How do I know him?' Murdoch taps his chest with his fingers. 'Coz he reminds me of me.' Murdoch nods vigorously. 'Loyalty is important to him.' Murdoch stabs Panzer's chest. 'Loyalty to you. He would never, ever, have cut you up, not in a million years.' Murdoch waves his index finger. 'Unless he thought you were going to cut him up first. I'm right, aren't I?'

Panzer nods.

'So, tell me, how did he know we'd be coming for the money?'

'I haven't a clue. He didn't hear it from me.'

'Who else, other than you, Ructions and your son knew about the job?'

'I don't know. I really don't.'

Murdoch rubs his chin thoughtfully. 'Your son told him.'

'No, he didn't. He detests Ructions. And anyway, Finbarr hasn't a clue you and I have been talking.'

'Then who?'

'I don't know.'

'What will Ructions do with the money?'

'Well, he's on the cops' radar, he knows that. And he knows the 'RA will be looking for him in Ireland—'

'Ireland? The 'RA will be looking for him in Bangla-fucking-desh if he turns up there.'

Panzer nods. *He fucked you over, didn't he, Tiny? You thought you'd it all boxed off and all you had to do was to wait and the millions would just roll in, didn't you, you greedy bastard? Chapeau, Ructions, chapeau, son.*

'You look like you're not unhappy this wanker has turned us over,' Murdoch says.

'I still think it was me he was turning over.'

Murdoch shakes his head. 'How will he shift the money? Serge Mercier?'

'Probably,' Panzer says. 'Serge was our first port of call.'

Murdoch pulls a face. 'Fuck.'

'You know Serge?' Panzer asks.

There is no disguising the disappointment in Murdoch's voice. 'Yeah.'

'Is there a problem?'

Murdoch strokes his Adam's apple. 'He doesn't like us. You're still friendly with Mercier, aren't you?'

'Sure.'

'I want you to tell him to take a call from me.'

'Sure.'

'How will he get it over to him?' Murdoch asks.

'He'll use a fishing boat.'

'What port?'

'Wexford Harbour.'

'I want the name of the boat and the captain.'

'I'd be very surprised if Ructions sticks to the original plan,' Panzer says. 'And I can't see him going back to Serge Mercier now, can you?'

'You'd better hope he does.'

In a police interrogation centre, Declan Butler, his hands on the edge of the table, balances on the back legs of a chair and gazes at the two-way mirror in an interrogation room. Chief Superintendent Clarke looks on, along with three other senior police officers.

'He looks a confident little chappie, doesn't he?' Clarke ventures. 'Not a care in the world. You'd wonder where he gets his confidence from?' Clarke turns to Inspector Gerry Rowlands. 'Has he been cautioned?'

'Yes, sir.'

'And he declined to have a solicitor present?'

'Yes, sir.'

'Hardly the actions of a guilty man,' Clarke observes as he inspects his fingernails. 'If I were the insider, I'd insist on having my brief present. Wouldn't you?'

'Perhaps he knows that, without a confession, his story would probably stand up in court,' CID officer Cyril Jones says. 'Perhaps he's had the benefit of a solicitor *before* the bank was robbed.'

'Or maybe he's had the benefit of Tiny Murdoch's experience,' the second CID man, Philip Fields, says. 'If this is an IRA job, and if he is our man, Tiny would've had him taken away and given anti-interrogation lectures.'

Clarke is unimpressed with either contribution. 'No matter who might or might not have been advising Mr Butler, they'd have told him to insist on having legal representation during interviews. That's an absolute. No, this is unusual.'

Almost as soon as he had been ferried to the Diver household, Declan had surmised that he would end up in a police cell. He realised then that his career in banking was over. Feeling sorry for himself, his mind wanders. *Can it get any worse? Can it? I mean, I've gone from having a great career, to being tiger-kidnapped, arrested and held in this shithole for supposedly helping the robbers. Helping the robbers? Has anybody ever tried to help me? Where's the justice? Surely these cops aren't stupid? Surely they've taken into account the prospect that the robbers have set me up?* Declan feels queasy. If he did not know better, he'd swear there is a school of sardines, scattering and then reuniting, inside his stomach. He can feel eyes on him, taking apart his every expression and movement. *Who's behind that mirror? You've made your minds up already that I'm guilty, haven't you?*

'Is he very self-assured or very silly?' Clarke asks. 'Let's see, gentlemen, shall we?'

CID officers Jones and Fields go into the interrogation room.

Billy Kelly is sitting inside in the warmth, looking out at the garden in his semi-detached, semi-affluent home in south Belfast. As he ponders the purchase of a polytunnel, he watches his wife, Louise, inspect a winter-beaten rose bush on the edge of the soggy lawn. The postman opens the gate and hands Louise some letters. She looks at them and waves to Billy to come out and take them. His phone rings as he approaches her. It's Ructions. Louise looks at her husband as he takes the call. She knows him; his expression tells her he's worried. He closes his phone and says to her, 'I'll be gone for a few days.'

TWENTY

Ructions is on the phone as he sits at the window of a café inside Connolly railway station in Dublin. An announcement is made over the loudspeaker that the Belfast train has arrived. Commuters stream through the passenger gate. Eleanor Proctor appears behind two nuns. She is wearing a white pinstriped coat and a yellow hat. Her only luggage is a handbag. Very classy, Ructions thinks, as he lets her pass out of the station before leaving the café to follow her. Eleanor stands outside the station, looking about her. Her phone rings.

'Hi. It's me,' Ructions says.

'I'm outside the station.'

'I know.'

'You can see me?'

'Yes. Listen, El,' Ructions says smoothly, 'I want you to walk up Talbot Street. Take your time. Look in the shop windows as you go.'

'Is this necessary, James? Really, this is too—'

'Bear with me, love. Please. We'll be together soon, I promise.'

'I—'

Ructions has already hung up.

Eleanor glances into a shop window filled with baby products. She flinches. Looking at prams and baby clothing reminds her that she has no children of her own and that her life is zipping past with the speed of a falling meteorite. She senses a presence behind her and half-turns.

'No,' Ructions says firmly. 'Keep looking in the window. Pretend we're not together.'

'Am I being followed, James?' Eleanor says nervously. 'Is that it? Why would anyone want to follow me? Am I in danger?'

'Of course not. I'm just being my usual cautious self. And you're not being followed. I've booked us a room in the Gresham Hotel. Room 414.'

'Room 414, the Gresham. Right.'

'I'll be waiting for you. I've really missed you, Eleanor.'

'And I've really missed you, James.' Eleanor searches the shop window for a reflection. 'James?' By the time she turns around, Ructions is nowhere to be seen. Two choruses battle in her mind: *414, 414. I've broken the law. 414. I've aided and abetted in a huge bank robbery. I'm a criminal. 414. Me, Eleanor Proctor, who has never had as much as a parking ticket before! 414.*

In room 414 of the Gresham Hotel, Eleanor Proctor's head rests on Ructions' bare chest. Both gasp for air. Ructions kisses the tip of Eleanor's nose. 'You just turn me on, woman. You just blow me away.'

'Talking about blowing you away.' Eleanor's head submerges beneath the sheets.

'Ah-ha,' Ructions says laughing. 'Up periscope.' He cups her chin and brings her to the surface again. 'Give the lad a chance to recuperate.'

'The lad seems pretty healthy to me,' Eleanor says. They giggle like mischievous adolescents.

'I've got to pee,' Ructions says, throwing off the bedclothes and walking to the toilet.

Eleanor lights a cigarette, opens a window and blows out the smoke. The cold December air grabs it readily. Ructions walks out of the bathroom and goes to the minibar. 'You want something? A vodka and Coke? A mineral?'

'No, thanks.'

Ructions opens a can of beer.

'So,' says Eleanor.

'So?' Ructions replies, licking the foam off the can.

'So, where's Maria these days now you've given her the heave-ho?'

Uh-huh. 'She's gone to South America. Why?'

'I was just wondering.' Eleanor tries to hide the smirk as she pummels her cigarette into an ashtray. Her demeanour changes. 'Shit. What if we get caught, James?' She sits down on the edge of the bed. Her shoulders sag a little. Suddenly, as if receiving an electric shock, she sits bolts upright and shakes her head vigorously. 'Sorry, James. I had a moment of panic there. What is it you always say? "Stay calm and in command of yourself."'

Ructions sits next to her and takes her hand in his. *I fuckin' love this woman, I really do*. He slides to the floor, kneels in front of her and cups her face with his hands. 'Aye. Calm and in command it is, sweetheart. And you can be in command of me any day.'

This provokes a giggle from Eleanor, who slides on to the floor to join him. She places her hand on his chest and pushes him with just enough force to put him on his back. Straddling him, she says, 'In case it's escaped your attention, I've broken the law for you and could quite easily end up in prison.'

'I'm sorry—'

'Shh.' Eleanor puts a censorious finger to Ructions' lips and then gently teases open his mouth. She bends her head towards him, and he feels the light caress of her hair on his chest. He draws her to him and groans as she guides him inside her.

A little while later, after pulling the duvet off the bed to cover their naked bodies on the floor, Eleanor approaches the topic neither of them want to speak of. 'It's this part of the plan that scares me the most, James. I don't want to wait a year or two to be together.'

'We'll spend the rest of our lives together when things cool down, El. You know that.'

'Will things ever cool down though? Really? I don't want to be skulking about hotel rooms for ever.'

'That won't happen.'

'It's hard enough for couples to stay together when they're not in hiding. How the hell will we survive, with you on the run in a foreign country? Hell! What if you realise you don't truly love me and I was a mere means to an end?'

'Whoa, El. Don't say that. We've talked this through again and again. You know I have to leave the country. Both the cops and the bloody 'RA will be coming after me.'

'I accept that.' Eleanor nods her head defiantly. 'What I don't accept is love on the never-never. I mean it. I've no intention of sitting back and watching you gallivant around the globe like the Playboy of the Western World while I'm stuck here waiting on your phone call. Waiting for you for an indefinite period isn't an option, James, and I won't have it. I won't fucking have it.'

Of course you won't fucking have it, Eleanor. It's not in you to allow someone else to dictate your life, but surely you have more faith in me than that? 'Where did this come from, El?' Ructions asks quietly.

Eleanor points to her heart. 'From in here.' Eleanor takes Ructions' face in her hands and gently kisses him.

'I want us to be happy, love,' Ructions says.

She kisses him again. 'So do I. But I don't want you ditching me now that the job is over.'

'Never. I love you.'

'Most love stories have sell-by dates, James. That's life. No one can ever say never.'

'Listen, if I stay in Ireland, I'm a dead man. It's as simple as that.' His face darkens. 'The IRA will come looking for me to get the money, which, by the way, they now think is *their* money. Like, we're talking twenty million quid in untraceable notes here.'

Eleanor is shocked. 'What the fuck! You've got twenty million?'

'Here's what you've got to remember, Eleanor. If the IRA find me, they'll torture me, probably kill me and bury me in some godforsaken bog to cover their tracks. So I can't be about the place, not yet anyway. But no matter what happens, I've no intention of ditching you.' Ructions kisses Eleanor on her nose, her eyes and finally on her lips. 'I love you, wee girl. Trust me, El, we'll come through this.'

What Eleanor is never going to know is less than a year ago Ructions *did* have every intention of ditching her as soon as was practicable after the bank robbery. But things changed. Secret liaisons, passion and mind-blowing sex can sometimes undermine the best of plans. He cannot recall precisely when, but their relationship morphed from a cold and calculated dalliance into a full-blown love affair. The master criminal and polished liar is discovering that relationships are governed by emotions, and emotions can sometimes be ungovernable.

'I still want to go with you. I don't care.'

Ructions kisses Eleanor's hand. 'But I care, I care about you, about us. If I disappear and then you disappear, the cops will put two and two together and convince themselves that you were in on the robbery—'

'And I – the deputy bank manager's wife – will join you on an Interpol wanted list, and they'll have a picture of me at every border crossing in the world, and we'll be fugitives for ever. I know, I know, I fucking know!' Eleanor holds out the palms of her hands as if making an appeal. 'But you and I, riding off into the sunset in a really cool vintage car ... I like that image.'

'Why not ride off into the sunset with our saddlebags full of National Bank money?'

'I can't ride horses, but I could learn. Yeah, horses would be better.'

Ructions laughs loudly. 'Next you'll have George Clooney playing me in this movie of yours.'

'You wish! More Clint Eastwood at this stage, old fella!' Eleanor retorts, dodging an elbow from Ructions.

'You got one thing right, though. We will be looking over our shoulders if you come with me. Is that really the life you want?'

'I want a life with you.'

'And I with you. That's why it has to be like this. This thing *will* calm down, El. It always does. We'll come out of this together, and we'll not be looking over our shoulders.' Ructions gets up off the ground and takes a phone out of his coat pocket. He presents it to her with a flourish. 'I want you to keep this. I'll be calling you every day on this phone while I'm away.'

Eleanor takes the phone. 'Every day?'

'Every day.'

'Not too early though. Don't wake me up at five in the morning, James.'

'I won't,' he says with a grin.

'And what if the calls stop?'

'What do you mean?'

'What if I get calls for a month or two and then they stop?'

'The calls won't stop.'

Eleanor looks to the floor.

'You've got to trust me on this. I swear, I'll not dump on you.'

'If you do—'

'If I do, what?'

'If you do ... the 'RA and the cops will be the least of your worries.'

Ructions looks at her directly. *I believe you. You're as fucking serious as a heart attack*. He goes to the minibar. 'How about a beer, love? Fancy one?'

'No. A gin and tonic. You can well afford it.'

Ructions appreciates the dig and kisses her passionately.

'Just one more thing,' Ructions says, unscrewing the cap on the miniature bottle.

Eleanor puts her hands to her ears. 'No, I don't want to hear one more thing.'

'This is important, Eleanor. Do you remember we went through the "What ifs"?'

'What if the cops arrest me?'

'That, yes. And what if the IRA arrests you,' Ructions says.

Eleanor is confused. 'It's extremely unlikely the IRA know about us, don't you think?'

'Extremely. But still, what is the golden rule?'

'Protect myself.'

'Against who?'

'Against everyone.'

'You *always, always* protect yourself. If you even get a *hint* of trouble coming, you let me know during our phone calls. Do what you've got to do to get through this, and whatever you do will be fine with me. I'll still be madly in love with you, remember that – know that.'

'Got it, James.'

TWENTY-ONE

Before Declan Butler had reached the interview room in Antrim Serious Crime Suite, police officers had discussed how he should be questioned. In the interview room, CID officers Cyril Jones and Philip Fields have spent thirty minutes making small talk with Declan, who has confirmed that his family are in shock but are coping well in the circumstances.

This lad seems to have adjusted to his own particular set of circumstances pretty well, Jones thinks. Jones is the old hand, with thinning hair, fat lips and a wino's raspberry nose. Grey curling hairs protrude from his nostrils. 'Crime can't be seen to pay, Declan – certainly not crime on this scale. You do understand that, don't you?'

Here we go, Declan thinks. 'Yes, sir.'

'Good.' Jones drops his head, sighs and then slowly returns his gaze to Declan. 'Sometimes in life we're forced to do things we don't want to do, Declan.' Declan looks stoical. 'And being forced by threat of, or actual, violence, to do something against your will is a very credible legal defence. In fact, the police are invariably sympathetic to someone who had been subjected to such tactics. Are you following me, Declan?'

'I think so.'

'It could be you were forced against your will to become the inside man in this robbery.'

'I'm—'

'Hold back,' Jones says. 'Think before you answer. Once you cross this threshold, it'll be the devil for you to get back again.'

'I've no need to think. I wasn't the insider.'

Detective Phil Fields knows that eyes are watching his performance every bit as much as they are Declan Butler's. Tall, square-chinned, with hollowed-out cheeks and intense blue eyes, the Cambridge-university graduate decides to intervene, to make his mark.

'Oh, you're the insider all right.'

Declan shakes his head.

'Who forced you to divulge security information about the bank? Was it the IRA?'

'I wasn't the insider.'

'Oh, yes, you were,' Jones says, not to outdone by Fields.

Declan is bursting to say: 'Oh, no, I wasn't,' but he restrains himself. He takes a different route. 'What you're trying to do is to coerce me into admitting a falsehood and that I won't do.'

'So, that's the way of it then?' Jones says. 'Okay. The robbers moved Liam Diver's wife out of their house, yet they let your family remain at home for the duration of the robbery. Why didn't they move your family out too?'

'I don't know.'

'Don't you think it's strange?'

'I'm not familiar with the ways of robbers, so I wouldn't know if it's strange or not.'

Behind the glass, Clarke nods in appreciation. 'A great answer. This is an intelligent lad.'

'Perhaps they knew you wouldn't grass on them,' Fields says.

'Too right I wouldn't grass on them. My family's lives are more important to me than *all* the money in the National Bank.'

Fields looks at Jones and says, '*All the money*? What money you boys left in it wouldn't get the three of us drunk!' Both officers burst out laughing.

'In case it's slipped your mind, sir, Liam didn't grass on them. He didn't phone the police either.'

'Nothing slips my mind, sonny,' Fields says, as he folds his arms, sits back and stares at Declan. Jones stands up, goes around to Declan and partially sits on the table. 'Declan,' he whispers, 'we know.' Declan looks at Jones, who nods his head calculatingly. 'We know you're our man.'

'No, sir. You've convinced yourselves I'm your man. There's a difference.'

'You're our man,' Jones says, drawing to within inches of Declan.

Declan wants to turn away, but what message would that send? That he has something to hide? He braves the reek of the smoker's breath.

'Don't take us for idiots, son,' Jones whispers in Declan's ear. 'Don't. For your own sake.'

'Remember, Declan,' Fields says, 'what you say now will be put before a judge and when you're found guilty – which you will be – the judge will take into account the fact that you didn't co-operate with the police, and he'll put you away for twenty years. That's a long time. Let's see – say, just for talk's sake, you get the twenty, and say you receive the fifty per cent remission for good behaviour: that's ten solid years in prison. How old are your Mum and Dad?'

'You keep my Mum and Dad out of this,' Declan says abrasively.

'I'm only making the point,' Fields says. 'One or both of your parents could be dead while you're banged up. You wouldn't want that, would you?'

'And even when you get out after those ten years, the word "jailbird" will be branded on your forehead,' Jones says, walking back to his side of the table. 'Nobody will employ you. You'll be subject to travel restrictions, and if we see you spending as much as a penny over what the dole gives you, we'll be all over you like a cheap suit. This is *never* going to end, Declan. You're in our sights – for life.'

'It doesn't have to be like that, Declan,' Fields says. 'We can work something out, maybe do a deal.'

'No, we can't. I haven't done anything illegal.'

'You're the IRA's man on the inside!' Fields shouts.

'No, I'm not,' Declan says in a measured but firm tone.

'Why didn't you phone the police and tell them the robbers were holding your family?' Jones asks.

'Are you for real?' Declan retorts indignantly. 'Are you? What if there'd been a shoot-out? What if one or more of my family had been shot dead? What if my family had been moved *after* I'd been taken away? How was I to know the gang was holding my family in our house the whole time?'

Behind the glass window, Clarke smiles.

'Is it a coincidence that on the day you changed your shift, the bank was robbed?' Jones asks.

'Life's a long series of coincidences.'

'Don't be a smart-ass, Butler,' Fields says. 'Answer the bloody question.'

'Yes, it is a coincidence.'

'One hell of a coincidence, don't you think?'

'I'll ask you a question.'

'No, you won't,' Fields replies.

Declan fires away regardless. 'Would I put my family through this for a few bob?'

'Come, come, Declan,' Jones says snidely. 'We're hardly talking about a few bob here.'

'How much did Tiny pay you?' Fields says. 'One? Two million?'

Jones sniggers. 'Phil, the million in the Aston Villa bag was Declan's wages.'

'What did it feel like, Declan,' Fields says, 'walking out of the bank with your own million pounds?'

Declan is undaunted. 'It felt like nothing because the money wasn't mine. It was like handing over a million pieces of paper.'

'Come off it. Tiny looked after you,' Fields says, grinning.

'Who's Tiny?' Declan asks.

'You know who Tiny is as well as I do,' Fields says.

'I don't know anybody called Tiny.'

'Why did you change your shift to work on the day the bank was robbed?' Jones asks.

'I wanted time off to go out for a Christmas drink with my friends.'

'It would've been impossible to rob the bank the next day, wouldn't it?' Fields asks.

'Don't ask me. I'm not practised in the art of robbing banks.'

Clarke taps the two-way mirror and sniggers. 'I like this little fellow. Isn't he a character? He's as guilty as Lee Harvey Oswald, but he's amusing.'

'Oh, but you are,' Jones says. 'You and Tiny couldn't have robbed the bank the next day because you'd have given over your master key and wouldn't have had any access to the vault. Is that not so?'

'Not just me. All keyholders have to hand in their master keys.'

'Yeah, but only you,' Jones laughs, pointing his finger, 'only you – amongst all the keyholders – changed your shift to the day of the robbery.'

'So what?'

'And that makes you our prime suspect.'

'Does it?'

'Why do you think the robbers picked you to walk out with the million in the Aston Villa bag?' Fields asks.

'They asked Liam first,' Declan says. 'Didn't you know that? It was his idea to send *me*.'

The grin is wiped off Clarke's face. 'He's going to be a tough nut to crack,' he says sternly. 'He's thought about this interrogation for a long time and has all the answers in his head.'

In Dublin Airport, Ructions sits in the departure lounge, listening to music on his iPod. He takes out his headphones and looks up at the 'News on the Hour' on a television screen. The opening news sequence is taken from a helicopter above the National Bank on the night of the robbery. Numerous police vehicles surrounding the bank are shown, along with officers walking about in white forensic suits.

The scene changes to outside the National Bank, where all indicators of what had once been a crime scene have been removed. A reporter looks into a camera and says, 'Less than thirty-six hours ago, this street in Belfast city centre was bustling with people going about their normal business, some heading home from work, some catching up on last-minute Christmas shopping. Others were busy too, busy carrying out the biggest robbery in British and Irish history. Estimates given on the amount of money stolen range from twenty-five to fifty-two million pounds.'

The picture changes to a news conference at police headquarters, where the Chief Constable of the Police Service of Northern Ireland, Alan Woods, sits at a table, flanked by two assistant chief constables.

The scene comes back to the reporter outside the bank. 'When I asked the chief constable earlier,' the reporter says, 'for his assessment on who he believes carried out this robbery, he said this: "In my opinion the Provisional IRA was responsible for this crime and all lines of inquiry are being undertaken in that direction".'

The reporter outside the bank looks into the camera and says, 'With unionist politicians joining the chief constable in pointing the finger of blame at the IRA, the question that now arises is – after this flagrant breach of the IRA's ceasefire, can the peace process survive? This is Roger Dunstable, for BBC News on the Hour.'

Ructions goes to the bar, buys a beer and watches the television. The barman takes the second pull on a pint of Guinness and hands it to a middle-aged man with a thin black moustache and an upturned grey hat. Slowly, reverently, the man lifts the Guinness, stares at it with the eyes of a connoisseur, takes a voluminous slug and sets the pint back down on the counter. A thin white line appears on his thin black moustache. He quickly wipes it away with a lick of his tongue.

'I'd say the boys that pulled that off done a bit of celebrating last night,' the barman observes.

'Lucky bastards,' Guinness-man says. 'Wish it'd been me.' Guinness-man turns to Ructions. 'What would you do with forty million, pal?'

Ructions smiles and shakes his head. 'I don't know. Give it to charity, I guess.'

'Give it to charity, my arse! You'd be better off giving it to me, you would. I'd buy an island in the Indian Ocean and invite you to come along whenever you wanted. You can do that, you know – buy an island. Your man bought one ... what's his name? Him, the Virgin guy?'

'Richard Branson,' Ructions says.

'The very man.'

'When I win forty million, I'll give you a shout,' Ructions says, lifting his drink and walking away.

TWENTY-TWO

Rapier-like French rain slashes across Ructions' Irish face. He pulls down his black flat hat, but it's too late: he is already soaked through. The queue to Nôtre Dame Cathedral snakes its way towards the entrance. He spots a young girl selling yellow ponchos, calls her over, buys one, and, despite the rain, sticks it inside his coat. Suddenly, he turns around. Guinness-man, from Dublin Airport departure lounge, is chatting to another man and then turns away when he realises that Ructions has spotted him. *Cops! I knew it. I knew they'd follow me instead of lifting me immediately. Good job I didn't go directly to Serge.* Ructions takes out his phone and calls Serge. 'Hi. I'm in the queue at Nôtre Dame and I've got company.'

'Can you drop them?'

'I think so.'

'How long before you go through?'

Ructions looks at the length of the queue in front of him. 'I'd say twenty minutes.'

'I'll stay here till you get back to me.' Serge hangs up.

Ructions looks behind. Guinness-man has disappeared, as has the man with whom he was speaking. *There'll be others and they'll not be so easily spotted.*

Ructions follows the queue into the cathedral. He listens to a tour guide tell visitors that Nôtre Dame was the site of a former Gallo-Roman temple to the Roman God Jupiter. He hears another tour guide say that Joan of Arc was beatified by Pope Pius X in 1909 in Nôtre Dame. Ructions pretends to have an interest in the three stained-glass windows which depict, on the north side, Old

Testament figures surrounding the Virgin Mary, and on the south, Christ surrounded by angels and saints.

A large group of Americans congregates around the altar. Ructions goes amongst them. A man and a woman look anxiously at the group of Americans and then at each other. The woman raises her hands as if to say 'Where is he?' The man shrugs. The Americans move on and the man and woman move with them, impatiently looking at the visitors' faces.

Ructions, wearing the yellow poncho he had bought earlier, saunters towards the exit.

Panzer puts turf on the fire in his study. In his head, he is sharpening knives. He reaches for his glass of cognac from the mantelpiece and turns towards a photograph of The Devil holding the reins of a horse on a street corner. A handwritten inscription at the bottom of the photograph says: 'Auld Lammas Fair, Ballycastle, 1960'. Typically, The Devil is wearing a soiled flat cap, black trousers held up by white galluses and a navy grandpa shirt. But tonight, it is his old man's cold, grey eyes that grip Panzer's attention: they are firing tracer bullets at him, excising any thoughts of romanticism, daring him to make hard choices. *I know what you'd do, Dad*. 'I said I know what you'd do, Dad,' Panzer says aloud.

As if in reply, the fire flares up. Panzer drinks some cognac.

A knock on the door heralds Finbarr's arrival. 'You sent for me, Dad?'

Panzer swivels around. 'Come in, son.'

The sun shines on the Arc de Triomphe de l'Étoile. Ructions gazes at the Tomb of the Unknown Soldier and its eternal flame. No one has followed him from Nôtre Dame; his counter-surveillance measures have worked. After walking up the spiral steel staircase to the attic, he ascends the forty-four stairs to the top. The funny thing is, no matter how many times Ructions visits the Arc de Triomphe, he still feels the compression in his throat, the gasp for air, the sense that he is walking on the waters of history. He strolls around the elevated concrete walkway, scrutinising the twelve thoroughfares that spike out from the Arc.

'It's rather splendid, don't you think?' Serge says from behind him.

'Splendid? It's more than that, it's majestic.'

'I've always been a huge admirer of Bonaparte,' Serge says. 'A friend of the Irish, if I'm not mistaken?'

'Anyone who was an enemy of the English was a friend of the Irish,' Ructions replies tartly.

They stroll on and stop to view the Eiffel Tower. 'I was glad to read in the papers that your business was successfully concluded.'

'Not as glad as I was.'

'Were there any problems?'

Ructions thinks before answering. 'No.'

'No one hurt then?'

'Oh, I didn't say that. People always get hurt.' Ructions taps his forehead. 'In here. Where nobody sees the bruises.'

'You sound melancholic, even remorseful.'

'Perhaps I am.'

Serge looks down the Champs-Élysée. 'I had a phone call from your friend Tiny today.'

Tiny Murdoch's not my friend. Is he yours? Where do your loyalties lie, Serge? With yourself, of course – with the money.

'What did he say?'

'From what I can gather, he wants to meet you to discuss your disagreement. He wants a détente.'

'That's not gonna happen.'

'He said as much.' Serge coughs politely. 'He told me to tell you he is prepared to become a fifty-fifty partner with you. Apparently, if you should accept this offer, it comes with a fully comprehensive health plan.'

'Did he say those words, "a fully comprehensive health plan"?'

Serge nods.

Ructions laughs heartily. 'That's so funny.'

Serge tries to smile but his eyes convey bewilderment. 'Why is it funny?'

'Because,' Ructions says, 'if I don't accept Tiny's fully comprehensive health plan, the IRA will put me at the top of a hit list and my health will not be guaranteed.'

'And that's funny?'

'Of course it is! Whoever threatened to murder someone by offering them a fully comprehensive health plan?'

'Would they honour any agreement?'

'I don't know. They might – at the start, but in the long term I can't see them allowing me to run around Belfast with millions stashed away, can you?'

'I very much doubt it.'

'Did Tiny offer you a deal to turn me in?' Ructions asks. 'You can say, Serge; I'd be surprised if he didn't.'

'He said he wanted to speak to me, confidentially, behind your back, but I told him I won't be doing that.' Serge grabs Ructions' arms and steers him along the walkway. He whispers in Ructions' ear. 'I don't like dealing with terrorists, mon ami. You know that. They have no fear of death and that scares me. Besides, the IRA launder their own money; they don't need the likes of me.'

Ructions nods.

'He'll come after you,' Serge says.

'I know.'

'He'll look for leverage, for your weakness.'

'I work very hard to make sure I don't have a weakness.'

In an utterly useless nod to hygiene, Ructions wipes the concrete step with a handkerchief and sits down. Serge joins him. Ructions removes a baguette from his knapsack and hands half of it to Serge.

Serge nods as he chews slowly on the baguette. He stands up and massages his knees. Ructions joins him. They walk to the top of the stairs where Ructions slips Serge a computer memory stick and says, 'I've outlined a temporary timeframe and location for the transfer. We'll pull it all together later.'

'Fine.'

'Now to the painful part,' Ructions says. 'What rate have you got me?'

'Do you remember I told you in Dublin I suspected it could be about fifty per cent, or more?'

'I hope you've got better than that.'

Serge shakes his head. 'No. That's it. My banker friends are extremely nervous regarding this transaction. I have to say, it wouldn't take much for them to walk away.'

Ructions whistles. 'Your banker friends are greedy fuckers.'

'All bankers are greedy fuckers,' Serge says. 'By the way, Panzer sent his best regards.'

'Oh?'

'Yeah. And he told me to tell you not to trust Tiny. He wished you good luck.'

Ructions smiles.

Finbarr fidgets. *Papa Panzer looks like he's in one of his dark moods. What's got him so flustered? Is he drunk? He might be. No, it's something else.*

Spread out on the desk in front of Panzer is a large stack of money, the deeds to numerous properties, three offshore bank-account books, two local bank-account books and a computer memory stick. Panzer opens the second button of his shirt and then pushes everything towards Finbarr.

Finbarr sits upright and takes a tight hold of the armrests. His eyes rummage around Panzer's face for an indication of wanton maliciousness, but he finds no emotion whatsoever. Pointing to the money and assets in front of him, Finbarr says, 'What's this all about?'

'I've transferred all the money in my offshore accounts over to you,' Panzer says calmly. 'I've also transferred the deeds to the farm and the other properties. You'll have to pay some inheritance tax on the accumulative value of the properties, but that's unavoidable.'

'What's going on, Dad?'

Panzer chuckles. 'Never mind that now.' He waves his hand at the bank books. 'Go on. I know you're bursting to see what's in them. Open them. They're yours now.'

Finbarr studies each bank book and looks up. 'I ahhh, I don't know what to say.'

'Then say nothing.'

'Can I ask why you're doing this?'

'Because I'm not going to be around much longer.'

'You've lost me,' Finbarr says, startled. 'What do you mean you're not going to be around much longer? Are you going away somewhere? Somewhere hot, away from this rain and sleet?'

Panzer feels an avalanche of humour rolling his way. 'Am I going anywhere hot?' he chortles. 'Oh, that's good! I fuckin' hope not.' He looks at The Devil's photograph. 'He's a funny wee lad, Dad – like his mother.'

Christ Almighty! *My old man's flipped. He's talking to photos now.*

'Where was I?' Panzer says, beaming. 'Yes, somewhere hot. Actually, I'd like to think I'm going somewhere cool.'

'I don't understand.'

'I'll make it simple for you, son: I'm dying.'

'You're dying?' Finbarr says feebly.

'I can see you're taking this hard,' Panzer says, smirking.

Finbarr's Adam's apple bobs. He puts his hand on his forehead. *What do I do now? Cry? I should cry – shed a few tears for my dear papa.*

As if reading his son's thoughts, Panzer laughs. 'Watch you don't pretend to be sorry.'

'I am sorry, but I don't know how to cry.'

Panzer goes to the drinks cabinet and pours a drink for Finbarr. Carrying the glass and the bottle over to the desk with him, he says, 'Get that into you.'

Finbarr downs the cognac in one gulp and puts the glass on the desk. Panzer pours his son another drink and sits behind his desk again. 'We've a lot of business to get through.'

'Is there a timeline, Dad?'

Panzer shrugs. 'You want to know when I'm gonna die? Soon.'

'Why didn't you tell me this earlier?'

Panzer spreads his two hands as if appealing to a jury. 'What was the point? What would you have done? Moped around and treated me like a geriatric? To hell with that! These things happen, Finbarr. Everybody dies sometime.'

'All the same—'

'Finbarr, let's not have a stewards' enquiry into this.'

'Still—'

'*I said* let it go.' Finbarr shrugs and Panzer lifts the bank books. 'There's just over one million quid in these accounts and it's yours. You can do whatever you want with it. After tonight, it's no longer my concern. I'm going to sell the Garden of Eden.'

'But I thought—'

'That the house was always to stay in the family?' Panzer grips the side of the desk. 'So did I. That's no longer feasible.'

'Don't sell it, Dad.'

'And don't you be an asshole, Finbarr! You've left me no choice.'

'Me? I don't understand.'

'The 'RA know you're a paedophile—'

'I'm not!'

Panzer points an accusing finger. 'Finbarr—'

'But—'

'Why the fuck do you think they didn't put a bullet in the back of your head on that country road, eh?' Finbarr looks bewildered. 'Because I stepped in and saved you. I gave them the National Bank robbery. And I'd have given them Ructions, too, only he bailed out with most of the cash.'

'But—'

'Shut up!' Panzer shouts as he jumps up and comes around the table to his son, his hands clenched. His manner instantly changes. 'The 'RA know you're a paedophile, they know you're fuckin' weak ... and their greed won't be satisfied till they've drained you dry. To begin with, they'll take the farm off you, but they'll do it legitimately; they'll offer you buttons for it and you'll have no choice but to take their offer. Then they'll go after the few quid I'm leaving you! I'm fucked if I'm going to allow that.' Panzer stares at Finbarr, who diverts his eyes. 'You have to get out of the country. For good.'

'But where will I go?'

'Go wherever the fuck you want,' Panzer snaps. 'Christ almighty! Have I to take you by the hand and plant you in a house abroad? When this is all over, you'll have over two million quid in your tail.' Panzer walks slowly back to his desk and slumps down in his chair.

Suddenly, without any effort, Finbarr's eyes fill up. 'I don't want you to die, Dad.'

'It's okay. It's the way of it. Just go now, son. We'll talk later.'

TWENTY-THREE

As they stroll along the Andersonstown Road in west Belfast, Tiny Murdoch and Colm Coleman cover their mouths with their hands in case they are being lip-read by undercover members of the security forces.

Coleman stops and turns towards Murdoch. 'God's truth, if I didn't know that boy Ructions pulled it off, I'd have said you organised it.'

They walk into a wallpaper shop, nod to the shop owner and retreat into a corner. Three police jeeps pull up outside the shop. The shop owner comes over to the two men. 'The cops are outside, Tiny,' he whispers out of the side of his mouth. 'I think they're coming in.'

Murdoch leaves Coleman, walks into another aisle, lifts a roll of wallpaper and brings it to the counter. 'I need nine rolls of this,' Murdoch says, 'and three packets of paste.'

'Doing a bit of wallpapering then, Tiny?' a voice says. Murdoch turns around. 'Let me see your wallet,' a police officer says, his hand outstretched.

'You've no right—'

'Robert Henry Murdoch, I am arresting you on suspicion of robbing the National Bank in Belfast on the eighteenth of December 2004. You do not have to say anything but …'

Murdoch puts his hand to his mouth, smothering a yawn.

'Have you anything you wish to say?' the officer asks when he finishes the caution.

'I want to see my solicitor.'

'Hand me your wallet.'

Murdoch hands over his wallet. The police officer takes out five twenties and three tenners and puts them in a plastic evidence bag.

'You're very melodramatic,' Murdoch says.

'And you're very arrested,' the officer says. Another officer leads Coleman out of the shop. 'And so's your shoeshine boy.'

Frank Proctor has never been beyond the front desk of a police station before, and now he is in a sparse room with bland, white walls, sitting across the table from two bland detectives. Frank is nervous. He wipes his glasses with a blue cleaning cloth. He wishes he had shaved before coming to the station.

'You all right, Frank?' Chief Superintendent Daniel Clarke says. 'You look … distressed, if you don't mind me saying so.'

'I've never been interrogated by the police before.'

'It's not an interrogation, Frank,' Inspector Gerry Rowlands says, 'and you're not a suspect, but I'm making you aware that this interview is being video-recorded.' Rowlands points to a camera on the wall. 'You should see this as more a process of elimination.'

Frank takes no comfort from Rowlands' statement that every word he is going to say will be dissected later.

'I'm not going to beat about the bush,' Clarke says. 'You had access to the rotas.'

'No, I had more than that. I made out the rotas.'

'So you did,' Clarke says. 'And you downloaded them on to your home computer?'

'I made them out on my home computer. I've been doing that every week for the last two years.'

'And you sent them to … whom?'

'Liam and Declan.'

'For the camera,' Clarke says, 'Mr Proctor has acknowledged that he sent the rota to Mr Liam Diver and Mr Declan Butler. Is that right, Frank?'

'Yes.'

'Did you send them to anyone else?'

'No.'

'You're sure about that?'

'Absolutely certain.'

'Who, besides yourself, uses your computer?'

'My wife, but she wouldn't have access to bank files.'

'How do you know that?' Rowlands says.

Frank looks perplexed. 'She doesn't have the computer passwords to get into the bank files.'

'You don't know that,' Rowlands says.

'Don't be ridiculous,' Frank says. 'She doesn't know the passwords.'

Rowlands and Clarke glance at each other. Frank spots the look of consternation on Rowlands' face and puts up his hands. 'I'm sorry, officer, I didn't mean to be rude.'

'So you've never gone for a piss and left the bank files open on your computer?' Rowlands asks.

'Perhaps,' Frank says.

'Or left the computer on when a friend came to the front door?'

'It's possible.'

'So, it not beyond the realms of possibility that your wife could have accessed the files when you were out of the room?'

'It's possible, but it didn't happen.'

'Do you ever drink alcohol when you're working on the bank's files?' Clarke asks.

'Sometimes.'

'What's your tipple?' Rowland asks.

'Smirnoff.'

'I like a wee Bushmills myself when I'm on the home computer,' Clarke says reassuringly. 'I wouldn't sweat that one, Frank.'

Frank is sweating it; instead of the intended smile, his lips twitch.

'Do you ever get drunk when you're working on the bank's files?' Rowlands asks.

'I don't like getting drunk.'

'That's not what I asked you,' Rowlands says. 'Have you ever been drunk while working on the bank's files?'

'I don't remember.'

'You don't remember being drunk?' Clarke asks. 'Is that because you've been so drunk, so often, you simply can't remember?'

'Everybody gets drunk sometimes.'

'Are you an alcoholic, Frank?' Rowlands asks.

'Don't be absurd.'

'But you're often drunk at the computer?'

'No, I'm not.'

'How often do you change the passwords?' Clarke asks.

Frank shakes his head. 'Once a year.'

'When was the last time you changed them?'

'I can't remember.'

'Is that because you were so drunk you can't remember?' Rowlands asks.

'No. I genuinely can't remember off-hand.'

'Could your wife have accessed the computer when you were drunk? Say when you passed out?'

'I've never passed out.'

'So you turn off the computer every time you leave your seat, do you?'

'Of course not.' Frank wrings his hands. 'Look, please ... you've got to believe me. My wife isn't involved in this.'

'The problem for us, Frank, is that you don't know that,' Clarke says. 'She could have had access to the bank files, couldn't she?'

'You! You're a ...' Frank is on his feet and leaning over the table, his index finger wagging accusingly in Clarke's face. 'How dare you!'

'Sit down, Frank,' Clarke says.

'Eleanor's no fucking bank robber! Holy Christ! Have you any idea what you're saying?'

'Sit down, I say!' Clarke shouts.

Frank sits down but he still leans forward and points his finger. 'My wife is a lady. Why on earth would she want to rob the bloody bank? Why? You tell me.' Frank leans back. 'I've never heard anything so preposterous in my life.'

'We're not saying she robbed the bank,' Clarke says. 'All we're saying is, she might have had access to the bank's files.'

'She hadn't.'

Declan Butler enters the interview room, followed by a detective. Chief Superintendent Daniel Clarke sits at the table. Clarke stands up, introduces himself and shakes Declan's hand.

'How are you getting on, son?' Clarke asks in a fatherly tone. 'Any complaints?'

'No, sir.'

'You know you're entitled to have a solicitor present during these interviews, don't you?'

'I don't need one. I happen to be innocent.'

'Innocent people have ended up in prison before, Declan.'

'I know that. My father is a friend of Gerry Conlon, the Guildford Four guy.'

'Is that so?'

'Can I ask a question?'

'Of course.'

'How long do you intend to hold me?'

'We can hold you for seven days, if needs be.' Clarke stands up and says, 'Follow me, please.'

They walk out of the room, down a corridor and out into a small rectangular yard. Declan fills his lungs with fresh air as Clarke takes him into a corner and offers him a cigarette, which Declan declines. Clarke lights up. 'I've brought you out here because I don't want this conversation recorded.'

'How do I know you're not recording this on your cell phone? For all I know, you could be wearing a recording device.'

'As it happens I'm not, but it doesn't matter one way or the other. You don't have to say anything you think may incriminate you. Is that fair enough?'

Declan nods and looks down at his shoes.

'I want to help you,' Clarke says. 'You probably don't believe that, but it's true.'

'If you really wanted to help me, you'd release me.'

'I can't do that.'

'Then *how* can you help me?'

'You mightn't realise it, son, but you've got a lot going for you.'

'I have?'

'Oh, sure. You've an impeccable record, for a start. Not a hint of criminality.'

'Why would there be? I'm not a criminal.'

'They called Robespierre "The Incorruptible" – and then they chopped off his head.'

'Sorry?' Declan says. 'I don't get the analogy.'

'The point is – everybody is corruptible.'

'I'm not.'

Clarke opts to ignore Declan's declaration of incorruptibility. 'You come from a highly respected, law-abiding family, and that's good.' Clarke waits for Declan's response. When nothing emerges, he continues. 'Now,' Clarke lowers his voice, 'if I can tell the judge you collaborated with the IRA under duress, and that you fully cooperated with police inquiries, you'll walk out of court. I can guarantee that.'

'Am I being charged then?'

'Declan, listen to me. I'm offering you a deal, a package – a pathway to freedom. You can have a new life in any country of the world that takes your fancy—'

'I—'

'Let me finish,' Clarke says, putting up a stalling hand. 'Hear me out.'

Declan nods.

'You're being offered immunity from prosecution, relocation to a country of your choice, and one hundred thousand pounds cash to get you started. It's a new life, Declan, a golden opportunity. Don't rush in with a rejection before you think it over.' Clarke searches Declan's face for a sign that he appreciates the enormity of the offer. There is none. Instead, Declan gives a rather spartan, defiant grin. 'You don't seem very impressed?'

Declan shrugs indifferently.

'I see. Well, it's up to yourself. The alternative is years in prison, years of counting down the days to your release date.'

'Am I being charged then?'

'You will be.'

Declan gulps. 'But that's not right. I'm innocent.'

Clarke drops his cigarette on the ground and unceremoniously squashes it with his foot. 'What's not right is stealing thirty-six million pounds – and you're not innocent—'

'I'm—'

'Don't waste your protestations on me. Seriously, son, I've heard it all before. Thirty years I've been in the force and I've interviewed all the major terrorists and gangsters. You get to know the innocent from the guilty – and you're guilty.'

'But—'

'Declan, hold on. I said I was here to help you, and I am. I don't want to see a young lad like yourself going to jail and throwing away his life.'

'No jury will convict me.'

'Ah, Declan, Declan,' Clarke says, shaking his head in wonderment. 'What makes you think you'll have a jury? Son, you're going to be tried in a Diplock court. Didn't Tiny tell you that before he put you in the frame?'

'No jury?'

'No jury.'

'What does a Diplock court mean?'

'It means there'll be just a judge sitting alone, looking at the evidence, looking to convict – not because you're a nationalist or a Catholic – but because the evidence points to you being the *only* person who could have made this robbery happen. You, Declan,' Clarke waves his finger, 'nobody else. And the judge will throw the book at you for putting the court to the trouble of running what will be a very expensive trial.'

Declan swallows hard.

Clarke lights another cigarette. 'The offer hasn't moved anywhere. Just answer a few basic questions and this will all go away.' Clarke waits and waits. 'All I want you to do is to answer yes or no,' he says desperately. 'That's not too difficult, is it?'

'No, it's not, but you're expecting me to tell you who robbed the bank. Can't you get it into your head? I can't tell you because I don't know. I just don't know.'

A uniformed officer opens the yard door. 'Sir, the chief constable is on the phone.'

'Tell him I'll be a minute.'

The officer closes the door.

'Do you know why the chief constable is phoning me, Declan?'

'No.'

'He wants to know if you're going to work with us. If you are, he has people to talk to and arrangements to put in place.' Clarke decides that he has no option but to press on. 'Are you in the IRA?'

'No.'

'Did the IRA carry out this robbery?'

'I wouldn't know about that. I wasn't involved.'

'Why did you change shifts?'

'Because I wanted to go out for a Christmas drink with my friends.'

'I see. Well,' Clarke says despairingly, 'I tried. Remember *that* when the judge is sentencing you. Let's go back.' He gestures for Declan to lead the way, but before they walk into the building, Clarke takes his arm, stopping him. 'I'm not closing the door on your co-operation. I want you to think about the serious situation in which you find yourself. If you want to talk to me, I'll make myself available.'

'You said I'm entitled to a solicitor,' Declan says. 'I think I'd like to talk to one now.'

TWENTY-FOUR

A hush settles on The Grave Diggers Inn when Tiny Murdoch and Colm Coleman appear in the front doorway. Murdoch coldly surveys individuals whose kneecaps he had ordered shot for carrying out armed robberies and burglaries, while Coleman looks around apprehensively at individuals and former friends with whom he had carried out armed robberies – men who now walk with limps. Blank faces stare back at them, faces that give nothing away. Murdoch weighs up the situation; it is not a crowd with whom he is entirely comfortable, but he is not in the least intimidated. Coleman, on the other hand, just wants to turn away.

Someone shouts, 'Up the 'RA.' Someone else cries out, 'Brilliant job, Tiny!' Another wag yells, 'Any chance of a few million, Tiny?' The bar erupts. Murdoch enters. Coleman hesitates. Murdoch pulls Coleman in by the lapel of his jacket. Revolutionary backs are slapped, rebel hands are shaken and comradely eyes are winked. Everybody has breastfed on the media speculation; everybody likes the idea that a bank has taken a hammering. What's not to celebrate?

Celebrated more than esteemed, Murdoch and Coleman eventually end up at Paul O'Flaherty's table. As they sit down, O'Flaherty, a teetotaller and a member of the IRA Army Council, grasps his straw, leans down and sips an orange mineral. An almost undetectable nod of O'Flaherty's diminutive head beckons Murdoch closer. With his head still bowed, O'Flaherty quietly says, 'I ordered you to get to the bottom of this robbery. Have you done so?'

'I know who ripped us off, Paul.'

'Who?'

'His name is James O'Hare.'

'Panzer's nephew?'

Murdoch nods.

'Get him,' O'Flaherty says. 'Get our money but don't use our people if things get out of hand. We don't want to upset the Army Council. Look towards Dublin for assistance.'

A pensioner comes over to Murdoch and wobbles precariously in front of him. It is a situation that Murdoch has encountered before, and he slips his uncle some money. A waiter arrives and asks him what his company are drinking. When Murdoch asks for the identity of the buyer, the waiter points to a man whose punishment beating with baseball bats he had ordered two years before. All is forgiven, it seems. Murdoch can live with that. He waves and the man waves back. Murdoch looks at the table and orders the drinks.

His arm is being tugged and he turns around. 'Keep the movement out of it, y'hear?' O'Flaherty says again.

'Got it, Paul.'

A well-dressed young man approaches Murdoch and says something in his ear. Murdoch barely blinks. He nods to Coleman. Murdoch says farewell to O'Flaherty and, along with Coleman, leaves the bar. They get into their car and drive across the road into Milltown Cemetery.

They pull up at a small car park at the bottom of the cemetery, where a grey Renault is parked. Coleman turns on a tape recorder in his car, gets out, approaches the Renault and peers in. He wags a finger to those inside. Finbarr emerges. Coleman puts up the palm of his hand to Geek to indicate that he has to stay where he is. Standing at the side of a grave, Coleman tells Finbarr to remove his coat and shoes, and to open his shirt. Finbarr complies.

'Look, Mr Coleman, I'm clean. There's no way I'd come near you with a bug.'

'Okay,' Coleman says. 'Into the back seat.'

Finbarr gets into the back seat of Coleman's car and Coleman gets in behind the steering wheel.

Murdoch, now in the back seat, stares at Finbarr.

'Mr—'

'Shh,' Murdoch says. He continues to stare at Finbarr. Eventually he says, 'I'm told you've something to tell me.'

'I have. I've information I think will be very useful to you.'

Murdoch lifts the *Irish News* and peruses it. He turns several pages before saying, 'Well?'

'First of all, can I have it in writing that it's safe for me to live in Northern Ireland?'

Murdoch laughs. 'Who are you?'

'I'm Finbarr O'Hare.'

'Never heard of you.'

'I'm Panzer O'Hare's son.'

'Panzer O'Hare ... he's the guy who fixes dog races, isn't he?'

Finbarr is confused. He did not think it would be like this. He has information and he expected Murdoch to welcome what he has to say with open arms. 'My father doesn't fix races,' he says timidly.

'It doesn't matter to me what he does for a living,' Murdoch says. 'What does interest me is why you think it wouldn't be safe for you to live in Northern Ireland? And what's your safety got to do with me?'

'Can I be frank?' Finbarr says.

Murdoch's expression hovers between bemusement and anger. 'Frank? You can be John, Paul, George or Ringo for all I care.'

Finbarr ignores Murdoch's attempt at humour. 'Can I have an assurance that the IRA won't murder me?'

'I hope you're not asking me to speak for the IRA because I'm not in the IRA. Are you asking me to speak for the IRA?'

'No, no, I'm not.'

'I'm glad we've got that sorted,' Murdoch says. 'But I'm intrigued. What makes you think you're under threat?'

'I just think I am.'

'I see. Maybe I can help you.' Murdoch gets out of the car and nods to Finbarr to follow him. They walk up through the graves.

Murdoch says, 'I suppose it's my civic duty to help keep you safe, if I can – but because I'm *not* in the IRA. You understand that?'

'Yes.'

They stop at the grave of members of the McCoole family.

'Brian McCoole,' Murdoch muses. 'We knew him as "Finn McCoole".' Murdoch bends down to read the gravestone. 'That's him, all right. He was a teacher in St Thomas' – a right bastard.' They walk on. Murdoch stops and looks to the Black Mountains that tower over Belfast. 'Hmm ... it seems to me you think your life is in danger. Is that right?'

How many times are we going to go around this maypole? 'That's right, sir,' Finbarr says.

'Perhaps it is,' Murdoch says. 'I've no idea one way or the other but what I can do is to pass on what you tell me to a priest I know, and he might be able to talk to some republican people, who might be minded to let you live.' Murdoch spins around to face Finbarr. 'Yes, I think that's the way forward.'

Finbarr's mouth is slightly ajar, and his wide eyes betray his bewilderment. It is entirely possible he has just received a death threat, but he cannot be certain. 'Thanks.'

'No problem, son,' Murdoch says in a confessional tone. 'Now, let's hear what you've got to say.'

'Sir, I hope you don't take this the wrong way, but I'm still not sure the IRA won't murder me.'

Murdoch's manner changes dramatically. 'Neither am I. Now fuck off.'

'I don't—'

'I told you to fuck off, didn't I?'

'But you said—'

'I said I'd try to help you, but you don't seem to want my help. So fuck off.'

Finbarr puts up his hands in surrender. 'I apologise. I'm sorry.'

Murdoch sighs deeply. 'You try to help some people and they think they can piss all over you.' He raises an index finger. 'One last chance. That's it. Just one.'

Finbarr cannot get the words out quickly enough. 'I was in the house the other day and the phone rang. It was a friend of my Dad's.'

'What this friend's name?'

'Squire ... Squire Delaney. He owns a speedboat in Carlingford.'

'A lot of people own speedboats,' Murdoch says.

'A lot of people aren't bosom pals with Ructions O'Hare,' Finbarr says.

'Ructions O'Hare, Ructions O'Hare ... that name sounds familiar.' Murdoch rubs his chin. 'This Squire Delaney owns a speedboat, you say?'

Finbarr nods.

'That's interesting,' Murdoch says. 'Feel free to tell me why you've brought me this information, lad – and don't hold back.'

Eleanor Proctor is in the same interrogation room her husband had occupied. Across from her is Chief Superintendent Daniel Clarke. Eleanor lifts another mugshot from the bunch on the table and puts it down again. She lifts Tiny Murdoch's photo and puts it down. She lifts Ructions' photo and puts it down, but the well-seasoned Clarke discerns a tiny spark of recognition.

'Do you know him?' he asks, pushing Ructions' face back towards her. 'Take your time.'

Eleanor shakes her head slowly. 'No,' she says, 'No, I've never seen this man before.' Eleanor pushes away the mugshot and lifts another one.

Clarke picks up the photo of Ructions and studies it. He repeatedly stares at Eleanor, then at the mugshot. She knows that the police officer is gazing suspiciously at her, but she ignores him.

'James "Ructions" O'Hare,' Clarke says. 'Does that name mean anything to you?'

'No.'

'Are you sure, Mrs Proctor?' Clarke pulls his chair around so that he can get close to her. He takes her hand. 'I'm a friend, Eleanor. You should know that. But believe me, if I find out – and I will – that you or your husband helped O'Hare or anyone else to rob that bank, either or both of you will be going down for a very long time. Do you understand that?'

Eleanor nods.

'So, I'm giving you this opportunity to tell me if this man pressurised you in any way to assist him to rob the National Bank. We can help you. If you're involved in any way with O'Hare, we can help you.'

Eleanor takes away her hand. There is rebellion in her eyes and Clarke can see it. 'I don't know him, officer.'

Clarke nods. He begins gathering up his files. 'We'll leave it there for now, shall we, Mrs Proctor? And thank you for your co-operation. You've been most helpful.'

Tiny Murdoch is sprawled on top of a bed in his underpants, a television remote control in his hand. He had enjoyed his short sojourn in police custody and the look on their faces when his brief presented them with video evidence of him attending his nephew's nativity play on the evening of the robbery. And Coleman was mighty glad in the end-up that he'd dragged him along too. Tiny looks at the plate of crispy shredded chicken in honey-chilli sauce beside him on the bed. He takes a piece and chews it slowly. On the television screen is footage of Eleanor and Ructions in the gym car park, taken by the bald man in the yellow Volkswagen van. 'Mr James O'Hare is getting out of his own car and is walking towards the car of Mrs Eleanor Proctor,' the bald man says. Murdoch replays the tape. When it's over, he taps his chin thoughtfully with the remote control. He lifts his phone and dials a number. Before the person can answer, he ends the call. He deliberates further and dials the same number again.

Panzer is sitting in front of the fire. Murdoch's name comes up on his phone. He hesitates before answering it. 'Hello?'

'Usual meeting place, thirty minutes.'

Murdoch is at McQuillan's quarry before Panzer drives in. Both men are unaccompanied. Panzer gets into Murdoch's car. Murdoch pats him down for recording devices. This time there is no small talk.

'I'm very annoyed at you,' Murdoch says.

You're easily annoyed, bucko. 'I'm listening.'

'You're listening? That's very kind of you,' Murdoch says sarcastically.

'I didn't mean—'

'Eleanor Proctor.'

'Who?'

Murdoch shakes his head in mock disgust. 'Maybe Finbarr knows her. I'll get the boys to ask him.'

'Oh, Eleanor. Yes. I remember now.'

'Thought you would. I'd like to talk to her. Would you be so kind as to tell me where I might find her?'

'I know where she lives, if that's what you mean.'

'*I* know where she lives, but she hasn't been where she lives for the past few days. So where might she be living now?'

Panzer is perplexed. He throws up his hands. 'How do I know, Tiny? I only knew her through Ructions and I've never even met her.'

'You wouldn't be covering for her, would you?'

'No way.'

'You fuckin' better not be, Panzer.'

Detective Cyril Jones takes a mugshot from Declan. 'Declan, you disappoint me. What about him?' Jones passes a mugshot of Colm Coleman across the table to Declan and says, 'Do you know this man?'

Declan shakes his head.

'And this one?'

Declan lifts Tiny Murdoch's photo, studies it and sets it down again. 'No.'

'You must know him,' Jones says.

'I don't.'

'You live in west Belfast and you don't know Tiny Murdoch?'

'My client has already answered your question,' Declan's solicitor, Anthony Price, says.

A mugshot of Ructions is put before Declan. Declan studies the mugshot. Jones notes Declan's hesitation. 'Do you know this man?'

'No.'

'You paused before answering.'

'I don't know him.'

'Look again,' Jones says. 'James "Ructions" O'Hare. Does that name mean anything to you?'

Declan looks at Ructions' eyes. *Jack? Those eyes look like Jack's. Maybe I'm wrong.* 'No,' Declan says. 'The name doesn't ring a bell.'

'But you recognise him?'

'Listen, officer,' Declan says, as he leans back in his seat, linking his fingers behind his head. 'For the umpteenth time, I couldn't pick anybody out. They were wearing masks and disguises. So you tell me how in the name of God am I supposed to identify someone when I didn't see his face?'

'The problem you have, Declan, is that we think you do know what they look like,' the detective counters. 'In fact, we think you're one of them.'

'So you keep saying.'

'So *you* keep denying.'

'And so I will continue to keep denying.'

It is two o'clock in the morning. A stuttering wind is blowing stonewashed clouds across a waxing moon. Billy Kelly and Ambrose, driving a refrigerated lorry with a sign saying 'Salway's Fish', pull up at the side of Ructions' safe house on the outskirts of Sligo town. They get out and are silently greeted with handshakes from Ructions. Billy opens the back of the lorry, which already holds stacked, plastic containers of frozen fish. Ambrose and Billy bring empty containers into the kitchen where, along with Ructions, they half-fill them with blocks of money. The containers are brought out to the lorry, covered with frozen fish and stacked neatly in the back.

The long-line fishing boat, *Le Neptune*, slips out of the port of Saint-Nazaire on the French Atlantic coast. A fully clothed Serge Mercier lies on a cot, his fingers gripping a mug of tea that rises and falls on his heaving chest. Above him, in the cockpit, is the boat's owner: his nephew, Antoine. Serge shivers, pulls up the fur collar of his overcoat, looks into the side mirror of a cupboard and reverts to melancholy to ward off the nocturnal chills. *Time is like an F5 tornado: it destroys everything in its path. After this transaction, I'm retiring; no more derring-do, no more buccaneering for me. Ça suffit!*

Serge puts the mug to his mouth, but the tea is cold. He drinks it anyway. The money launderer is confident that his involvement in the collection of the bank money will not be a particularly hazardous undertaking, having reasoned that if the police were to put in an appearance at the handover point, or thereafter, they would have to catch him in possession of the money to get a conviction. To offset that improbability, Antoine has rigged the boat with four small incendiary charges, which he would set off by remote control from the safety of the rescue dingy. The equation, as Serge sees it, is simple: no evidence equals no guilt.

As Ambrose drives the fish lorry through Cavan town, Ructions' phone rings. It is Serge. To an eavesdropper, it would appear that the pair are engaged in small talk, but when Ructions asks Serge what the weather is like, the Frenchman replies that it is 'first-rate', thus indicating that he is on course for their rendezvous on the high seas.

While Ructions speaks to Serge, Ambrose notices strobe lights in his rear mirror. Ructions finishes his conversation with Serge and looks behind. The sickening screech of a siren is getting louder by the second. Tension grips his chest.

'What d'ya reckon?' Billy says, trying to hide the anxiety in his voice.

Ructions reaches for the handgun in the waistband of his trousers. 'I'll handle it.'

'Killing peelers isn't part of the deal, Ructions,' Ambrose says. 'Fuckin' sure it's not. I didn't—'

'Shut up, Ambrose,' Billy says. 'It won't come to that.'

Ambrose keeps looking in his rear mirror. The flashing lights are approaching rapidly. 'That's a fire engine,' Ambrose says, clearly relieved. He pulls over to the side of the road and lets the fire engine zoom past.

Tiny Murdoch reaches over to the bedside cabinet and looks at his watch. He cannot get Ructions O'Hare out of his mind. *Where are you now, Ructions lad? What are you up to? What's your plan? Are you tucked up somewhere in a warm bed with Eleanor Proctor, dreaming of swimming in a pool of National Bank money? Or, are you out? Out where? Out plotting? Outmanoeuvring? Outfoxing? Outdoing? I think you're out, boyo.* Murdoch's mouth is dry. He licks his lips nervously. *Have I thought of everything? Could I have done anything else? Can that little shithead Finbarr be trusted?* The words of Paul O'Flaherty find their voice in his head too: 'Get our money, but don't use our people if things get out of hand.' *Are things going to get out of hand, Ructions?* The tumult in his stomach tells him they might.

Panzer zips up his coat as he looks out from an upstairs window. He feels a mixture of elation and sadness. *The last chapter of the Book of Panzer has been written. All that's left is the epilogue. Who will write it? Finbarr? Ructions? Can't see it. Tiny Murdoch? No. Maybe it won't be written. Maybe it's better that way.*

TWENTY-FIVE

It's 8.30 a.m. at Carlingford harbour and a honeycomb-and-purple sky creeps in over the Cooley Mountains. The harbour is 300 metres at its widest and 100 metres at its mouth. A variety of small boats are anchored offshore. Directly overlooking the north quay of the harbour is the impressive ruins of King John's castle, which dominates the lough and the harbour.

Ructions, Billy and Ambrose are parked on the southern side of the harbour. All but the cabin of the fish lorry is shielded from prying eyes by a billboard on the northern side. Ructions watches across to the northern side of the harbour through infra-red binoculars.

'Doesn't look to me like anything's happening,' Billy says.

'He'll be here,' Ructions says, as he turns on the radio.

> And here is the BBC News. A bank worker was granted bail yesterday after being charged in connection with the £36 million National Bank robbery that was carried out earlier this month. Mr Anthony Price, solicitor for twenty-five-year-old Declan Butler, of Riverdale Close in west Belfast, told the court that Mr Butler had strenuously denied the accusation while in police custody and said that the evidence against his client was entirely circumstantial. Detective Inspector Gerry Rowlands objected to bail, saying that there was a risk of Mr Butler fleeing the jurisdiction. Judge Duncan MacIntyre granted Mr Butler bail on condition that he report to police three times a week.

Ructions turns off the radio.

'Sounds like wee Dec didn't break,' Billy says.

'Why would he?' Ructions says. 'He didn't do anything.'

'He wouldn't be the first innocent man to admit to the cops that he was guilty,' Billy says.

'He should beat the rap,' Ructions says. He feels sorry for Declan Butler but not sorry enough to admit to the police that he is the mastermind behind the crime and that Declan is blameless. He is perplexed – who could have foreseen things turning out like this?

Ructions is scanning his environs with the binoculars. Squire Delaney's thirty-foot speedboat enters the mouth of the harbour, followed by the sound of squawking seagulls. Ructions opens a bottle of water, takes a sip and nudges Ambrose with his elbow. Ambrose's hand dislodges from under his chin and his head flops onto his chest.

'Ahh!' Ambrose groans. 'Who the—?' He springs up. 'What did you do that for?'

'It's time.'

Ambrose shudders and says, 'I'm fuckin' foundered.' He rubs his hands together to generate heat and strains his eyes to see what is happening at the north pier. 'I can't make out a bloody thing. What am I looking at?'

Squire's speedboat approaches the north pier. 'The transport,' Billy says.

Ructions has one more look through the binoculars. He scans the walls of King John's castle and then looks out to sea. Nothing is amiss. 'Let's head over.' Just then, four young men, wearing Christmas party hats, stagger towards a Toyota car at the entrance to the pier. One fiddles with keys. This diverts Billy's and Ructions' attention and they watch with interest as the Toyota is driven out of the harbour area. Ructions nibbles his thumbnail. *Nah, they're not a threat. Let's have one last gander through the bins – just to be sure.* Ructions lifts the binoculars. *No Irish naval gunboats on the horizon; no cops anywhere; it can't get any better.*

Ructions peers up at the walls of King John's castle as Ambrose approaches the north pier in the fish lorry. 'Go right down to the speedboat,' Ructions orders Ambrose. The fish lorry pulls up. 'Wait here.' Ructions walks over to the edge of the pier and speaks to Squire Delaney, who is in the speedboat. He returns to the fish lorry. 'Nice and slowly now, let's get the fish on board.'

Billy gets into the back of the lorry and begins to drag the plastic containers to the back entrance. Ambrose climbs down into the speedboat and Ructions and Billy begin handing the plastic containers down to him and Squire.

Billy is about to lower the last container to Delaney when Ructions grabs his arm. 'Not that one. That's for you and Ambrose. I said I'd look after you.'

Billy nods. 'Fair play to you, Ructions.'

They hug. 'You've been a good friend in hard times,' Ructions says.

'You sound as if you'll not be back in Ireland,' Billy says, as Ambrose climbs ashore.

'I won't be, if I can help it. I might—'

'I'm hit!' Ambrose shouts. Ructions and Billy freeze, then immediately grab Ambrose by his coat collar and pull him over to the front of the lorry.

'I didn't hear a shot,' Ructions says. 'Did you?'

'No,' Billy says, 'whoever's up there must be using a silencer.'

'What's happening?' Squire Delaney shouts.

'Keep your head down!' Ructions shouts, 'and throw me up your first-aid kit!'

A barrage of shots silently peppers the back of the lorry. The first aid kit lands beside Billy.

'That's a sub-machine gun with a silencer,' Billy says as he rips open Ambrose's shirt and inspects the wound. 'He's been hit in the shoulder,' Billy says. He tears off Ambrose's shirt and holds a dressing to the wound.

Ambrose cries out in pain. 'Ahh! Take it easy, will ya? That's fuckin' painful! Why does shit always happen to me? This is the second time I've being shot. How come you never get shot?'

'I think they're up on the ramparts,' Ructions says apprehensively. He looks around him. 'We can't stay here or Ambrose *will* bleed to death.' Ructions sticks out his hand and fires three shots at the castle. An instant volley of sub-machine gun shots pelts the ground at the side of the lorry. 'They've us nailed down,' Billy says.

Ructions pulls off the wing mirror and warily holds it up to give himself a view of the castle ramparts. He can see no movement. 'Squire, bring the boat as close to the pier as you can.'

'What are you gonna do?' Billy asks.

'I'm gonna get into the lorry and reverse it at speed till it's past the castle. That'll draw their fire and you both escape in the speed boat.'

'Are you fuckin' mad?' Ambrose says. 'You'll be riddled to death!'

'Squire, as soon as they're on board, get offside pronto.'

'Is it a dead hero you want to be?' Billy says to Ructions.

'Okay then,' Ructions says, 'what's your plan?'

'I haven't got a plan,' Billy says, 'but neither have you. Fuckin' wannabee superhero!'

'I'll keep my head down.'

Ambrose winces. 'Ahh! Take it easy, will ya?'

'I don't think I've ever met a bigger whinger in my whole life than you,' Billy says to Ambrose.

'Me? A whinger? You'd know about whinging, wouldn't you? You'd—'

'Billy, I want you to fire a few shots at the castle walls from that side.' Ructions points to the passenger side of the fish lorry. 'That'll give me a chance to get into the front.'

'Are you deaf? What did I fuckin' say, eh? No more heroes anymore.'

'It's our only chance!'

'Bollocks!'

On the castle ramparts, taking aim at the fish lorry, is Benzo Mullins. Beside him is Twenty Bellies McClure, clutching a sub-machine gun with a silencer.

A dark figure, gasping for air, climbs up the last rung of the ladder on to the rampart. Benzo springs around. Panzer, dressed in a black suit and a trilby, has his arm extended as he fires at Benzo and then Twenty Bellies. Both fall. His arm still extended, Panzer approaches and delivers the *coup de grâce* by shooting both men in the head. He looks over the rampart and waves his hands.

Ructions can see someone in his mirror. 'That looks like … that's Panzer,' he mutters. 'It's the boss!' he exclaims, standing up.

'Couldn't be,' Billy says.

Panzer grips his chest and collapses to his knees, his eyes bulging, the gun wheeling around and out of his index finger.

Ructions and Billy run towards the castle and ascend to the rampart. Panzer is leaning backwards on his knees, his head on his chest. Gently, Ructions lays him down straight. He rummages frantically through Panzer's coat pockets.

Panzer's breathing is very shallow. He puts up a hand to stop Ructions. 'Too late for tablets,' he says softly. 'Don't, son.' He shakes his head, 'Don't.'

Ructions gulps. He gathers Panzer up in the crook of his arm and tenderly strokes his cheek. 'Boss …'

Panzer smiles. 'Ructions … I'm sorry.'

'I know that.'

'They were going … to kill Finbarr.'

'Don't talk, boss.'

'I couldn't …' Panzer lets out a deep breath.

'I know.'

Panzer grips Ructions' arm. 'He's looking for … Eleanor,' Panzer murmurs.

Ructions gasps. 'Who's looking for Eleanor? Boss, who's looking for Eleanor?'

'Tiny …' Panzer's eyes glaze over and his mouth remains open. He passes away.

Ructions hugs Panzer and silently weeps.

Billy takes Ructions' arm. 'You've got to let him go, Ructions.'

Ructions holds on to Panzer.

'Ructions, the cops will be here any minute now.'

Ructions tenderly lays Panzer's head down on the rampart.

Colm Coleman and two IRA men sit in a camper van outside the harbour. Two police cars, followed by two ambulances, drive past, their sirens sounding. Coleman makes a phone call to Murdoch. 'There's no sign of our two friends coming out but the quare fellas and two ambulances are away in. I think it's gone.'

'Keep me posted,' Murdoch says, hanging up.

'Pick up, Eleanor. Pick up, will ya?' Ructions gets an answering machine. 'For fuck sake!' He hangs up and leans back in the seating area of Squire Delaney's speedboat as it bounces off the waves.

It's time for the unthinkable, time to turn informer. Ructions makes a phone call. The phone rings and rings. 'Pick up,' Ructions utters.

'Police Exchange?'

'I'd like to speak to Chief Superintendent Daniel Clarke, please.' Ructions waits as he put through.

Clarke is looking at his computer. His phone rings. 'Clarke.' A pause. 'Hello?'

'Mister Clarke ... it's about Eleanor Proctor.'

'Uh-huh?'

'You need to protect her.'

'I'm sorry, can I have your name?'

'My name isn't important. You need to protect Eleanor Proctor right away.'

'From whom?'

'From the IRA. From Tiny Murdoch. They're planning to abduct her.'

'How do I know this is a genuine call?'

'I'm Jack.'

'Jack who?'

'You know who I am.'

'I'm afraid I don't.'

'Then ask Liam Diver or Declan Butler. Ask them about the drone I used to monitor their every movement during the National Bank robbery.' Ructions hangs up. He opens the porthole and throws the pay-as-you-go phone into the sea.

Clarke looks at his phone. *Jack? That was the name of the man who controlled the robbery. His name was never released to the press. That was fuckin' Jack! But who the fuck is Jack?* He lifts mugshots from his in-tray and sets them down on his desk one-by-one. *It wasn't you, Tiny, you're hardly going to inform on yourself.* He puts Tiny's mugshot back in the in-tray. *Nor you, Coleman.* Six mugshots are left, and they are neatly laid out in two rows on the desk in front of him. Included are Panzer's and Ructions'. *It's one of you six. But which of you cares enough about Eleanor Proctor to tell me she needs protection from the IRA? How important are you, Eleanor? Important enough for Jack to stick his neck out. Is Jack your lover? You supplied him with the rotas, didn't you?*

Approximately three miles out to sea, the plastic containers are transferred from Squire Delaney's speedboat to *Le Neptune* and Squire returns to Carlingford harbour. Afterwards, Ructions lies on a cot in Serge's fishing boat. He is whacked. He looks out through the porthole. A sailing ship dots the horizon. *Panzer. Eleanor. It's not supposed to be like this.*

TWENTY-SIX

A helicopter hovers in the sky over east Belfast. Inside, a crew member looks at an infra-red screen. 'Subject is approaching the Newtownards Road. Over.'

Chief Superintendent Daniel Clarke has set up a mobile headquarters inside a large removals van. Sitting on a small swivel chair, he drinks tea from a beaker.

'Don't lose her. Over,' Detective Cyril Jones says.

'Roger that,' the helicopter crew member says.

Jones, who is sitting beside Clarke, says, 'Penny, have you still eyes-on? Over.'

'That's a roger. Subject is on the Newtownards Road. Over.'

Clarke turns to the police Special Branch officer who is sprawled out on a chair and texting on his phone. 'Where are they?'

Without looking up from his phone, the Special Branch officer says, 'They'll be there.'

'You're sure of that?'

'They'll be there.'

'They'll be there, what?'

The Special Branch officer looks up. 'They'll be there, sir.'

Clarke has little time for Special Branch, but he has to admit that, having infiltrated the IRA, they are usually right in predicting IRA activity.

The drains have been flooded with rain water. A fast-running torrent gushes down from the main road. The heavy showers have eased off, but Eleanor still keeps up her see-through umbrella. She is almost at her friend Stacy's home when the phone that Ructions had given her in the Gresham Hotel rings.

'It's me,' Ructions says.

'James! Are you okay?'

'Where are you?' Ructions asks urgently.

'On the Newtownards Road. I'm just going to Stacy's.'

'Don't. Eleanor, don't do that.'

'Why not? What's wrong?'

'I want you to go to a nearby hotel – now – and stay there till I get back to you. And don't use your own car. Get a taxi. And don't tell anyone where you are, not your husband, nobody. And when you get to the hotel, don't leave your room. And don't answer the door to anyone.'

'James, you're frightening me. What's—'

'Listen to me.'

'But—'

'Eleanor! Remember the "what ifs"?'

'I remember.'

'Bottom line – we agreed that you protect yourself at all costs, even if it means giving me up? Right?'

'Right. But James ...' Eleanor steps in to a side street. A London-type black taxi pulls up beside her, forcing her to stop. The back door of the taxi opens, and two men jump out, seize Eleanor by the arms and drag her inside.

Across the road, plain-clothes police officer Penny Harbinson draws her pistol and runs towards the taxi, which speeds away. 'Subject has been abducted,' Harbinson shouts in a high-pitched voice. 'Repeat, subject has been abducted.' Harbinson's eyes follow the taxi. 'Target vehicle: black taxi, license number Zeta, Alpha, Delta, 2735, heading towards Lower Newtownards Road. Repeat – black taxi, licence number Zeta, Alpha, Delta, 2735, heading towards Lower Newtownards Road. Over.'

One of the men clasps the back of Eleanor's hair and pushes her face to the floor. 'Keep your fuckin' head down!'

Eleanor can taste the DNA of Belfast's hard streets, the coarse grime from the soles of a thousand passengers. She spits and tries to turn her head to the side to breathe, but her head is lifted and bashed against the floor.

'Didn't I tell you to keep your head down?' a deep voice booms.

Blood oozes from her nose. Someone's shoe is on the small of her back.

'Who was that back there?' the second abductor says, unable to disguise the panic in his voice.

'I didn't see anybody,' the first abductor says.

'I did. A woman with a gun,' the driver says.

'She might be a peeler,' the second abductor says. 'Oh, fuck! Bet she was a peeler! It's a fuckin' set-up! We've been set up! Let me out!'

'Shut up!' the driver shouts. 'I'm trying to drive here!'

'Throw her out!' the first abductor says.

'Oh, sufferin' Jesus,' the driver says in a pathetic voice. 'That car behind us ... are those peelers? They look like peelers.'

The first abductor looks behind. 'They're peelers.' He lifts Eleanor up and sits her in a seat. 'Missus, we weren't going to hurt you. It was mistaken identity. Gary here thought you were his old girlfriend, you know? The one who was going to squeal to his wife about him having an affair.'

'And I just wanted to frighten you, or sorry, her off,' Gary says. 'Sorry, love. Mistaken identity.'

The helicopter crew member who is monitoring the infra-red screen says, 'Target is approaching the Short Strand.'

'Go, go, go!' Clarke shouts into his microphone.

There is a detonation of revved engines and sirens. A searchlight beams down from the helicopter onto the taxi. The police car behind the taxi comes alongside and another police car takes its place behind. Three police jeeps pull out of a side street and block the road. The taxi stops.

'Nobody move,' the driver says in complete shock as they are encased in police presence. 'Easy does it.'

Police officers, pointing rifles, surround the taxi.

'I'm only the taxi driver, officer,' the driver shouts. 'I don't know these people.'

'You dirty bastard,' the first abductor says.

'Driver, throw the keys out the window and get out of the vehicle with your hands up.'

The driver complies.

'Now lie on the ground with your arms outstretched in front of you,' an officer says through a megaphone.

With the kidnappers handcuffed on the ground, Clarke goes to the back of the taxi, where Eleanor is shivering uncontrollably. 'It's alright, Eleanor,' Clarke says. 'You're safe now.' Clarke helps Eleanor out of the taxi and puts his coat around her. He looks at her bleeding nose and addresses his driver, 'Andy, bring the first-aid kit, a blanket and some water.' Clarke leads Eleanor to the back of a police car and sets her down. He leans in. 'Are you all right?'

Eleanor's eyes look straight ahead. She shudders.

'You've had a particularly nasty experience, Eleanor.'

Andy comes to the car with the first-aid kit and a blanket, which Clarke puts around her. He holds a dressing to Eleanor's nose. 'She'll have to go to hospital to be checked out,' Clarke says to Andy. 'We'll take her in my car.'

'Right, sir.' Andy drives while Clarke sits in the back with Eleanor. He takes away the dressing from her nose. 'It seems to have stopped bleeding,' he says.

'Thanks. Who were those men?' Eleanor asks.

'They're IRA.'

'IRA? What do the IRA want with me?'

'You're the wife of the deputy manager of the National Bank that was robbed. They were going to hold you hostage.'

'But why? What's any of this got to do with me?'

'That's the million-dollar question, Eleanor,' Clarke says. 'Look, you're in serious trouble. The IRA don't give up easily. They'll be back looking for you, and, believe me, they will find you.'

Eleanor's nose starts bleeding again. Clarke applies the dressing once more.

Eleanor pushes his hand away. 'This is bloody crazy.' Her eyes rest on Clarke. 'Why on earth would the IRA want to find me? Why would they try to kidnap me in the first place?'

'I got a phone call from a male saying that your life was in danger and that the police needed to protect you,' Clarke says. 'That's why we were on hand to arrest your kidnappers and free you. The caller, whoever he is, probably saved your life.'

'You said he?'

'Yes. He didn't give his name, but he was very concerned for your safety. Have you any idea who he might be?'

Eleanor fidgets. 'Have you a cigarette?'

'Andy?' Andy passes in a cigarette packet and Eleanor takes one but keeps it between her fingers rather than lighting it. 'What am I going to do?'

'I can help you,' Clarke says.

'How?'

'I can declare you an assisting offender and take you into protective custody. I can take you outside of Northern Ireland. I can give you an immunity deal that will ensure that you will not be prosecuted for any involvement you may have had in the robbery. I can promise that you'll be resettled wherever you want in the world, and I can guarantee you an attractive financial package to get you started in your new life. I can do all that, Eleanor, but you've got to honest with me. You've got to tell me everything and you'll have to testify in court.'

'And you'll protect me from the IRA?'

'Yes.'

'You promise?'

'I give you my word.'

Eleanor lights the cigarette and blows the smoke out the window. *'Protect yourself at all costs,' Ructions had said. What choice do I have? None.* She turns her face abruptly towards Clarke. 'I know the identity of the male who phoned you. It was James O'Hare.'

'That'd be James "Ructions" O'Hare?'

'Yes. Ructions. He robbed the National Bank.' Eleanor turns her head towards the window. Tears come. *It wasn't supposed to be like this. Why is it like this, James?*

It is a week since the National Bank money had been transferred to *Le Neptune* at sea. Ructions and Serge are sitting outside a café in central Paris. The presence of a large overhead electric heater takes the edge off a diamond-cutting night chill.

Ructions is reading *The Irish Times*. 'Listen to this,' he says. '"Police in the Republic believe the two males shot dead in Carlingford village, County Louth, were involved in a drug deal that turned sour. A third man, Johnny 'Panzer' O'Hare, died of a heart attack at the scene. Mr O'Hare was a leading Belfast crime figure."'

'Poor Panzer,' Serge says. 'He didn't deserve an end like that.'

'He'd have preferred to go that way rather than waste away to cancer,' Ructions says, setting down the newspaper. 'You were saying?'

'How do you know it's the police and not the IRA who have arrested Eleanor?'

'There's a report in another paper that three men from Catholic areas were to be charged with the abduction of a woman on the Lower Newtownards Road. Eleanor was on the Newtownards Road when I last called her, and her phone went dead. The woman is Eleanor; the men are IRA. The cops have her.'

'Better them than the IRA,' Serge says.

'For sure.'

'So what happens now?'

Ructions smiles forlornly. 'I thought I'd get longer than this.' He takes out his phone and dials a number. The phone rings.

'Hello?' a deep voice says. 'Hello?' the voice says again.

Ructions' finger moves to the 'off' button, but he hesitates. He puts the phone back to his ear. 'Who's this?' he asks timidly.

'This is Chief Superintendent Daniel Clarke. Who's this?'

'Where's Eleanor?'

'Is that you, Ructions? It is you, isn't it? Don't hang up,' Clarke says hurriedly.

'Hello, Clarkey.'

Don't fuck this up. 'Thanks for letting me know about the IRA's attempt to abduct Eleanor Proctor,' Clarke says. 'I really appreciate it.'

'I don't know what you're talking about.' Ructions ends the call. *Eleanor has given Clarke the phone I gave her, which means she's told him everything. It's time, Ructions.*

TWENTY-SEVEN

Three days after speaking to Clarke on the telephone, Ructions pulls up in the cul-de-sac outside Grosvenor Road police station. His solicitor, Kevin R. Summers – a tall, bespectacled man with a worried face – emerges from his car and approaches Ructions. Ructions gets out of his car and they shake hands.

'This is a formality,' Summers says. 'You'll be charged and questioned. Are you okay with that?'

'I'm innocent,' Ructions says. They go into the police station.

As Ructions walks into the reception, he is approached by Clarke and Cyril Jones. Jones holds out a set of handcuffs. Ructions offers his hands and is cuffed. 'James Peter O'Hare,' Jones says, 'I am arresting you on suspicion of robbing the National Bank on …'

'How's it going, Ructions?' Clarke says after the charge has been read out.

Ructions shrugs. 'Okay.'

'Can I get you anything? Tea? Coffee? Are you hungry?'

'I'd an Indian and a bottle of Dom Pérignon before I came in.'

'Alone?'

'What?'

'Did you eat alone?'

'I never eat alone,' Ructions says.

'Who was with you?'

'A couple of friends of mine, if you must know: Jesus and Lucifer. The craic was great. They were quarrelling. Couldn't shut them up.'

Clarke smiles. 'I'm sure. I've never understood the big deal with Dom Pérignon,' he says, as he leads Ructions and Summers into the inner sanctum of the police station. They wait for an elevator. 'What were Jesus and Lucifer quarrelling about?' Clarke asks.

'The usual.'

Clarke has the look of a man who is trying to figure out why he lost all his money to a three-card trickster. 'I get it. It's a metaphor. Good versus evil, and all that?'

'Maybe.'

'Who won the argument?'

'Lucifer always wins, Clarkey.'

They get into the elevator.

'Was it worth it, Ructions?'

'Was what worth it?'

'The National Bank robbery. Three people dead, one of them Panzer; Eleanor's life destroyed; bank officials' lives ruined. Was it worth it?'

'After taking my solicitor's advice, I wish to answer no comment.'

Ructions' transfer by police car to the Antrim Serious Crime Suite is uneventful. He refuses to engage in small talk with Clarke and Detective Jones, who are escorting him.

'What I can't get my head around,' Clarke says, 'is why you came back. Off the record, Ructions, why did you come back?'

It is not long after being signed into the custody suite that the first interview begins. Ructions finds it a monotonous affair. Clarke takes the lead. He outlines events leading up to and during the robbery. He puts it to Ructions that this is his opportunity to come clean on his role in the robbery, saying that if he does not, it would look very bad in court because the police have a strong case against him in the form of a witness.

It has been a long interrogation session. The questioning focused on Ructions' movements at the time of the National Bank robbery, the nature of his relationship with Panzer, and the fact that he has only £5,000 in his bank account. Did he know Declan Butler? Did he know Liam and Stephanie Diver? Was he ever at Loughshore, County Down? Did he ever conduct a business transaction in the National Bank? Who helped him rob the bank? What was it like holding all that money? How did he launder it? Was the IRA involved? Did he know Tiny Murdoch?

Ructions yawns. 'No comment,' he says repeatedly in a voice that is barely audible.

'Do you know a woman called Eleanor Proctor?' Clarke asks.

'No comment.'

'She knows you.'

'No comment.'

'She knows you very well,' Clarke says. 'She says she gave you the bank's staff rotas before the robbery took place.'

'No comment.'

'She says you made it clear to her that you intended to rob the National Bank of Ireland and, indeed, you did rob the National Bank of Ireland.'

'No comment.'

'She was your lover, wasn't she?' Jones says.

'No comment.'

'Let me qualify that,' Jones says. 'Eleanor Proctor was *one* of your lovers, wasn't she?'

'No comment.'

'Ms Maria McArdle. Remember her? She's currently working as a translator in Buenos Aires. Well, she has provided us with written testimony that you were supposed to have joined her a few months after she left for South America. She wasn't aware you had a bank to rob first, of course. It is our belief you were planning to join Maria after you'd laundered the money in Europe. That was the plan, wasn't it? String Eleanor along, rob the bank with her help, funnel the money from Europe to South America and then join Maria? You used Eleanor, didn't you?' Clarke says. 'You used this vulnerable woman to rob the National Bank, didn't you?'

'No comment.'

It is early morning. Tiny Murdoch comments that the Garden of Eden sign would have to be pulled down as Colm Coleman and he drive under it. They get out of their car and approach the Big House. The door opens and Finbarr comes out. Murdoch ignores Finbarr and spirals slowly around, taking in his new acquisition. He nods approvingly. 'This'll do nicely,' he says. 'Oh, yeah, this'll do very nicely.'

'What was that, Mr Murdoch?' Finbarr says.

'I said it was very decent of you to give me first refusal on the property,' Murdoch says.

Finbarr manages a weak smile. *As if you gave me a choice. You bullied me into it. I could've got twice the money you offered me for it.*

Geek O'Reilly and another employee canter into the yard on horseback. Geek stares down coldly at Murdoch. Both men remember a night in 1998, when a breeze block was thrown through the front windscreen of Murdoch's car while it was parked outside his front door. Murdoch later found out that Geek was the culprit. After Geek was picked up by the IRA, he was taken into a dark room and made to sit on the floor in a corner. When Colm Coleman asked him why he had thrown the breeze block, Geek said it was because he had heard that Murdoch had given the order to burn down his portable taxi depot because it was in competition with his. Murdoch, who was in a room across the landing, listened carefully as Coleman repeated what Geek had told him. The IRA leader had taken pity on Geek that night and rather than have his kneecaps blown off with a sawn-off shotgun, which was his first option, he only ordered that his leg be broken by having a breeze block repeatedly thrown on it. A breeze block attack for a breeze block attack – Murdoch had thought that an appropriate punishment.

Finbarr holds up a set of keys. 'Here they are. The keys to the Garden of Eden.'

Murdoch pulls out a set of keys from his pocket and holds them up. 'I already have my own.' He reaches over and takes Finbarr's keys. 'But I'll have yours too. You'll not be needing them anymore. Colm, get Iggy up tomorrow to change all the locks.'

Coleman nods.

'Would you like me to show you around?' Finbarr says.

'Aye, that'll be useful.'

They go into the hall of the Big House. Murdoch had been in the house before, but now he sees it through new eyes. 'This Holy-Joe stuff,' Murdoch says, nodding to the terracotta floor, 'what's it all about? Who are these people?'

'Him with the sword ... that's Michael the Archangel and the guy he has his foot on is Satan.'

'Fuck that shit. They'll have to go,' Murdoch says. 'I don't hold with religion. Each to his own, I say. What do *you* say, Reverend Coleman?'

'I'm with you on that one, Reverend Murdoch.'

Finbarr takes the two IRA men to the stables.

'How many horses does it hold?' Murdoch asks.

'Twenty,' Finbarr replies.

'Not enough. I'll have to double it in size, maybe triple it if I want my stud farm to pay.'

'So you're opening a stud farm then?' Finbarr says.

Murdoch turns to Finbarr. 'You still here?'

'I thought—'

Murdoch puts his arm around Finbarr's shoulder, takes him over to the corner and murmurs into his ear. 'They say the Mediterranean climate is conducive to a long life. Have you heard that?'

Finbarr blinks incessantly. 'Yes, yes, I have.'

'You should go to the Med and live long.'

Finbarr opens his mouth, but Murdoch closes it by tapping under his chin with his index finger. 'Enjoy a long life, Finbarr.'

TWENTY-EIGHT

Ructions is escorted by a police officer into a white room in which seven other persons of roughly the same age and height as himself are lined up with their backs to the wall.

'Have you any objections to anyone in this parade line-up?' the police officer asks.

Ructions walks along the line, looking at each man. Eventually, he shakes his head and chooses to stand between the last two people in the line-up. He stares into a two-way mirror. *Are you watching me now, El? Are you going to pick me out, love? You are, aren't you? Sure you are.*

Detectives Fields and Jones escort Eleanor Proctor into a room adjacent to where those in the line-up are standing. Also in the room is Kevin R. Summers, Ructions' solicitor.

'Eleanor, I've explained to you what this is about,' Fields says. 'What I want you to do is to take your time, look through the window at the men in the room beyond and tell me if you recognise the man to whom you gave the National Bank rotas. Can you do that?'

Eleanor nods. She goes to the window and peers into the room. Her eyes pass from one man to the other until finally they come to rest at Ructions. 'That's him,' Eleanor says.

'Which one?' Fields asks.

'Number seven.'

'I want you to look at all the suspects again. Take your time.'

Eleanor's eyes once again stop at Ructions. 'It's number seven.'

Fields turns to Summers. 'Do you accept that Ms Proctor has picked out your client, James O'Hare, aka "Ructions" O'Hare?'

'I do. I wish to confer with my client right away.'

'Of course.'

Jones walks out of the room, performs a karate routine and lets out a massive, 'Yes!' Clarke comes through the door and Jones grabs his hand. 'We have him,' Jones says. 'He didn't provide an alibi when questioned and she's picked him out. When a jury hears how he groomed her, they'll convict. We have him.'

Clarke has a puzzled look on his face.

'I think a celebration is in order,' Jones says. 'A few pints down in the Red Bull?'

'Not for me,' Clarke says, frowning.

The joviality ebbs from Jones' face. 'What's up, boss? You look like you think he's going to walk.'

'It's too easy, Cyril.'

'It's an open and shut case,' Jones says. 'He's fucked.'

'Why did he come back?' Clarke asks, his mind swarming with questions. 'To volunteer for a twenty stretch? Why didn't he buy himself an alibi?'

'Maybe he thought we'd nothing much on him,' Jones says. 'Maybe he decided to take his chances in court. He wouldn't be the first to go down that road.'

'Most of those boys who gave themselves up had spent all their money and were living on handouts,' Clarke says, the puzzled expression still etched on his face. 'Our man's not there – his piggybank isn't empty.'

The corridor door opens, and Ructions is led out by an officer. He shows no emotion as he passes Clarke and Jones.

Fields escorts Eleanor out of the room and into the corridor. She smiles timidly at Clarke, who says, 'Thanks, Eleanor.'

She stops and wrings her hands. 'He looked so powerless in there.'

'He's not powerless, Eleanor.' Clarke stares straight into her face. 'I want you to be honest with me, Eleanor – have you still feelings for him?'

'No, not at all.'

'You're sure?'

'Yes, I'm sure.'

'He used you, Eleanor.' Clarke wags his finger authoritatively. 'He had his real girlfriend, Maria McArdle, waiting for him in South America. Never forget that.' He is determined to come in hard, to banish any lingering illusions Eleanor may be harbouring. 'He used you and then threw you away like you were a wet towel.'

Eleanor whimpers, 'I feel like such a fool.'

'Don't beat yourself up,' Clarke says. 'You wouldn't be the first lady to be used and abused by criminals. I'm not saying it happens every day, but it does happen.'

'But,' she spreads her hands, 'this is *me*. Falling for a gangster. It's … I don't know. It's like I've been sucked into a Quentin Tarantino movie, you know? Where everything is exaggerated and nothing seems real. Does that make sense?'

'Of course it does,' Clarke says. 'You were only ever a means to an end for him.'

'I know that now. I just feel like an idiot, you know, like a cheap trollop. It'll come out in court, won't it? All the sordid details. Won't it?'

'Cyril, can you excuse us?' Clarke says.

'Sure, boss.' Jones leaves them.

'Eleanor,' Clarke says, 'I can't predict what'll come out in court, but I'll try my best to protect you.'

'Can I talk to him? Can I? Just for ten minutes? To give him a piece of my mind?'

Clarke shakes his head. 'Oh, no. Can't do that, Eleanor. Sorry. It might destroy the entire fabric of our case.'

'I see,' Eleanor says, her disappointment evident. 'You're a good man, Mr Clarke.'

'Let's get a cup of tea,' Clarke says. As they walk up the corridor, Clarke stops and turns to Eleanor. 'You won't let me down, will you, Eleanor?'

'No, Mr Clarke, I won't let you down.'

Ructions holds his plastic mug under the tea urn and pulls the lever down. The tea flows. Once his mug is full, he walks to a table at the back of the recreation room. Several other remand prisoners nod to him and he returns their friendly gesture. One prisoner wishes him good luck and shakes his hand. He has been on remand in prison for seven months. Amongst his fellow-inmates, he is regarded as the real deal: the man who fucked the system, good and proper. Inmates whisper amongst themselves: 'They've never found his money'– 'It's all invested in stocks and bonds'– 'He bought property on three continents'.

Ructions sits down beside 'Spotter' Walle: a thick-set, black-haired man with a crumpled roll-up hanging out of the side of his mouth. Spotter is one of those guys who has to shave twice a day, who, given a few hours' growth, looks as if he has been on the booze for a fortnight. He had been on the booze for four days when he caught his wife and her lover in bed and stabbed the lover fifty-two times. Ructions likes Spotter. He believed him when he said he still adored his former wife, but Ructions did not detect any remorse on Spotter's part for the death of the interloper.

'Trial starts tomorrow then?'

'Yeah,' Ructions says.

'How long will it run?'

'A couple of weeks, at least.'

'What do you think you'll get?'

Ructions shrugs. 'They're gonna hit me hard.'

Spotter fishes a flake of tobacco out of his mouth with his fingers, flicks it away and sets his roll-up on an ashtray. His mouth opens and closes like a goldfish in a bowl. 'You'd, ahh, you'd better believe it.'

'I'm reckoning on twenty,' Ructions says.

'Personally, I think you'll come in at twenty-five, maybe thirty.'

'I can see you think of time in multiples of five,' Ructions says. 'That's handy.'

'Then again,' Spotter says, 'you might come in at twenty. Judges are funny bastards.'

Tiny Murdoch and Colm Coleman walk out of the corner shop with ice-cream cones in their hands. 'How does anybody live here?' Murdoch says, licking his ice-cream. 'Look at it. Not a sinner about. I reckon you could go for weeks in this place without seeing a living soul.'

They get into their car and drive out of Manorhamilton, County Leitrim. Murdoch is aggrieved that he must make this journey. 'I tell ya, Colm, this dickhead O'Flaherty has got to go. Court-martialling me! Me! Who the fuck does he think he is?'

'It's fucking crazy, Tiny,' Coleman says.

A small Seat car with an elderly man and woman trundles along at twenty miles an hour. 'Ahh, for fuck sake,' Murdoch exclaims. He beeps his horn repeatedly. 'Pull the fuck over!'

The old couple ignore Murdoch's bad manners and drive even slower. He keeps beeping his horn until the elderly man pulls in to a lay-by. Murdoch puts his foot down on the pedal.

Coleman has a curious expression on his face. 'What do you mean "O'Flaherty has got to go", Tiny? Go where?'

'You know,' Murdoch says.

'You've got me, Tiny,' Coleman says. 'Go where?'

'We need to get rid of him. He still thinks this is 1972.'

'You're not thinking of stiffing him, are you?'

'Course not. Well, not unless I have to. Where the fuck is this place?'

They come around a bend and are confronted by a herd of cattle being driven by a man and a boy into a nearby field. Murdoch hits the brakes and gets out of the car. 'Get those cattle off the fucking road,' he shouts.

The man holding a stick is unruffled. He looks at Murdoch and continues to shunt his herd. Murdoch gets back into the car. 'You spoke to the solicitor, didn't you?'

'Sure. No problem.'

'He'll be there?'

'Oh yeah. Flynn's rarin' to go,' Coleman says.

'So am I.'

The National Bank trial has entered its second week. Amongst the officials of the bank, police officers and members of the public who had given evidence during the first week had been Declan Butler.

'And the man to whom you handed over the Aston Villa holdall containing an estimated one million pounds,' Crown Prosecutor Olivia Moore QC had asked. 'Did you recognise him?'

'No, ma'am,' Declan had answered. 'His face was covered with a scarf.'

'Did he threaten you?'

'No, ma'am.'

'But still you handed over the holdall containing the bank's money?'

'Yes, ma'am. I had to.'

'Why had you to?'

'Because his gang were holding my family under threat of execution.'

'Can you furnish the court with a reason why the tiger-kidnappers did not remove your family from your family home?'

'No, ma'am.'

'But you would agree, wouldn't you, that they ran an unnecessary risk of detection in not removing your family?'

'I can't rightly answer that, ma'am.'

'Why not?'

'Because I can't get into the minds of the tiger-kidnappers and I've no idea what contingency plans they might have had in place.'

'Had you escaped from your captors, would you have informed the police that your family were being held?'

Declan hesitates. 'I doubt it.'

'You doubt it?'

'Yes. My family would have been under even greater stress and in even greater danger had the police appeared at our door.'

'Oh, come come, Mr Butler. You're not seriously asking the court to believe you think police intervention would have exacerbated the situation?'

'That's exactly what I'm saying.'

During further cross-examination, Declan made it clear that he took the Aston Villa holdall out to Ructions only because Liam Diver, his boss, had suggested it.

Stephanie Diver had been no less forthright than Declan. Dressed in a black trouser suit and white blouse, she had dabbed her eyes with a handkerchief during much of her testimony.

'And you were convinced that the gunman would have shot your husband to death?' Olivia Moore had asked.

'Oh, absolutely. I'll never forget his words: "I'll kill him for you, shall I? Do you want me to put his lights out?"'

'So, had you answered that question in the affirmative, your husband would have been murdered?'

'At the time I believed so.'

Murdoch and Coleman drive up a hedged, two-tracked lane with tall grass growing in the middle. They pull into a small cobblestone forecourt in front of a blistered cottage that looks as if it might have been whitewashed in the 1950s. The cottage sports two eight-paned windows, a half-door and a black-slated roof with a chimney pot at each end. Smoke is coming out of one of the chimney pots. Two crows dally on the roof. Running at a forty-five degree angle to the cottage is a barn, covered over with rusty, corrugated sheeting. Outside the barn door is a tractor and at the side a dilapidated 1958 Hillman Minx. A robin redbreast makes a perfect landing on top of the car's bonnet and just as quickly takes off again. Murdoch taps the steering wheel.

'Are you all right, boss?' Coleman says.

Murdoch lets out one of those heavy sighs. 'Let's get this over with.'

As soon as Murdoch steps into the cottage, he is grabbed by his arms by two men. Another man stands in front of him. 'Oglach

Robert Henry Murdoch, I am arresting you in the name of the Irish Republican Army.'

Murdoch shows no emotion as he is led into a room where the curtains are drawn and the floor is covered with well-trodden, yellow oilcloth. A turf fire burns in the hearth. On the wall are photos of President John F. Kennedy, his brother Bobby, and one of IRA leaders Michael Collins, Éamon de Valera and Laurence O'Neill at a Gaelic Athletic Association match in Dublin's Croke Park, in 1919. There is an old bookshelf stacked with dusty books in the corner.

Three judges sit behind a teak table. Paul O'Flaherty, the President of the Court, wears a black blazer, a grey woollen shirt with a button collar and a green tie. He is reading from a sheet and does not look up when Murdoch is brought into the room.

Tiny Murdoch sits to the right of the judges. Beside him is his counsel, Kevin Flynn, a leading Belfast Republican and a solicitor by profession.

Ructions had taken copious notes during that first week. Now, midway through the second week of the trial, he walks into the dock of Belfast's High Court carrying a briefcase. A prison officer takes off his handcuffs and orders him to sit down. Dressed in a smart suit and tie, Ructions looks around the court. Seated in the front row is Chief Superintendent Daniel Clarke, flanked by Detectives Jones and Fields on one side and Inspector Gerry Rowland on the other. Clarke nods to Ructions, who nods back. Behind the police officers are Billy Kelly and his wife and at the end of the row is Frank Proctor.

The judge enters the courtroom. All stand.

O'Flaherty reads from the sheet of paper: 'Oglach Robert Henry Murdoch, you have been given due notice of the intention and purpose of this court martial. It is being convened because allegations have been made that you stole funds from the Irish Republican Army, that you subverted the lawful authority of the

Irish Republican Army, and that you brought the name of the Irish Republican Army into disrepute. You have legal representation—'

'If it pleases the court, Mister President, I represent Volunteer Murdoch in this matter,' Flynn says.

Murdoch jumps to his feet. 'I protest at this court martial.' Murdoch points his finger and looking intently at O'Flaherty. 'Paul, this is ridiculous. This is me!'

O'Flaherty comes around the table and stands beside Murdoch. 'Oglach Murdoch, aire!'

Murdoch springs to attention.

'Never,' O'Flaherty says with all the gravity he can muster, 'never let me hear you call an IRA court martial ridiculous again. Do you hear me, Oglach Murdoch?'

'Yes, O.C.'

'Sit down.'

Murdoch sits down.

The IRA prosecutor stands up. 'I call Geek O'Reilly.'

TWENTY-NINE

'I call Mrs Eleanor Proctor to the stand,' Olivia Moore QC says. Ructions stares at Eleanor but she keeps her eyes fixed on the Crown prosecutor.

'You are the wife of Frank Proctor, the deputy manager of the National Bank, are you not?'

'Yes, I am.'

'And is it your understanding that it was part of your husband's job to organise staff rotas at the National Bank's central Belfast branch?'

'That is my understanding.'

'I'll come back to that,' Olivia Moore says. 'Mrs Proctor, I want to take you back to the thirty-first of May 2003. Did you attend a Bruce Springsteen concert in Dublin's RDS on that date?'

'I did.'

'And did you meet a man there?'

'I did.'

'Can you tell the court in what circumstances you met this man?'

'A youth snatched my bag and the man retrieved it for me.'

'That was very gallant of him.'

'Yes, it was.'

'And did you subsequently have an affair with this man?'

'I did.'

Geek O'Reilly walks into the room. O'Flaherty looks over his glasses at Murdoch, who catches his gaze. A light switches on in Murdoch's brain. *O'Flaherty's brought O'Reilly into this? He's done his homework.*

Flynn whispers to Murdoch, 'Who's this? What's he gonna say?'

Murdoch looks out the window.

'And is this man in court?' Moore asks.

'He is,' Eleanor says.

'Can you point him out?'

Eleanor looks to Ructions and points to him. 'That's him.'

'May it please the court, the witness has pointed to the accused, James O'Hare,' Moore says.

Clarke makes fists of delight.

Ructions buries his head in his hands.

'So, Mr O'Reilly,' the IRA prosecutor asks, 'in 1998 a portacabin, owned by you and from which you conducted a taxi business, was burned down. Is that right?'

'That's correct.'

'Who burned it?'

'The IRA.'

'How do you know it was the IRA?'

'Because a member of the IRA came to me before it was burned and ordered me to close the business.'

'But you didn't close down?'

'No. Why should I? I'd as much right to earn a living as Tiny Murdoch.'

'Indeed. How did you know that the man who ordered you to close down was in the IRA?'

'Because he said he was.'

'He used those words "the IRA"?'

'Oh, yes.'

'Do you know this person who claimed to be in the IRA?'

'No.'

'And then, what happened?'

'I refused to close up and he,' Geek points to Murdoch, 'got the IRA to burn down my portacabin because me and him were competing for the same punters.'

'And that was the end of the matter?'

'Jesus, no. He got the IRA to drop breeze blocks on my leg. They broke it.'

'Who got the IRA to break your leg?'

Once more Geek points to Murdoch. 'Him. Tiny Murdoch.'

'Did the people who broke your leg say they were from the IRA?'

'Yes.'

Olivia Moore QC pulls her gown around her right shoulder. 'And you're sure that the person with whom you had an affair was the accused, James O'Hare?'

'I am.'

'How often did you and the accused meet during those two years?'

'I can't rightly say.'

'Ten, twenty, one hundred times?'

'Usually four or five times a month. It wasn't always easy to make the arrangements; he seemed to be out of the country a lot.'

'I see,' Moore says. Turning her face away from the bench, Moore fiddles with her wig. Clearly, she has a decision to make. She turns back to Eleanor Proctor. 'Would it be true to say that the accused, James O'Hare, and yourself were in love?'

'I was in love with him.'

'But was he in love with you?'

'I thought so.'

'Would it be fair to say that he led you to believe he was?'

'Yes.'

'And was it a torrid love affair?'

'Pardon?'

'Did James O'Hare and you have sex whenever you met?'

'If possible.'

Kevin Flynn has been looking forward to questioning Geek O'Reilly. 'Mr O'Reilly, do you like Mr Murdoch?'

'No.'

'I suppose that's understandable given that you believe he destroyed your business and ordered that you be punished by the IRA. You said the IRA ordered you to close down your business?'

'That's right.'

'Did the man say which IRA he represented?'

Geek looks perplexed. 'I don't get that question.'

'Did he say if he was in the Provisional IRA, the Official IRA, the Continuity IRA, the Real IRA? Did he identify which IRA he was in?'

'No.'

'And the people who broke your leg ... did they say which IRA they represented?'

'No.'

'So, they could have been from any one of them and not necessarily the Provisional IRA?'

'I suppose so.'

Flynn turns towards the IRA judges. 'Members of the court, I must protest at this man giving evidence. He manifestly does not know who burned down his portacabin or who was responsible for breaking his leg. Clearly his evidence is worthless and should be struck out.'

The IRA prosecutor replies, 'I agree with Mr Flynn that Mr O'Reilly's evidence would be worthless, if it were to sit in isolation, but it doesn't. I propose to call a witness to substantiate what Mr O'Reilly has said.'

'Did the accused make it known to you that he was a career criminal?' Olivia Moore QC asks.

Alan Hill SC, Ructions' counsel, springs to his feet. 'I object, Your Honour. My client has never been found guilty of any crime and my learned friend is not only making presumptions, she is leading the witness.'

'I'll withdraw the question,' Moore says. She taps her hand with a pen and looks meditatively to the ceiling, before bringing her gaze back to Eleanor. 'Mrs Proctor, what did you think the accused did for a living?'

'At the start he told me he was an antiques dealer.'

'At the start of the relationship?'

'Yes. But as time went on, I began to have doubts.'

'Why?'

'He started asking questions about my husband's bank.'

'And that raised suspicions in your mind?'

'Yes, it did.'

'What type of suspicions?'

'Well, the main suspicion was that he might have an ulterior motive for continuing with our liaison.'

'What type of questions was he asking?'

'Nothing that you could put your finger on at the start, but he was interested in when and where Frank worked and what his job description was.'

'And did he persist in this line of questioning as time went on?'

'Yes. He seemed obsessed with Frank and the bank.'

'Obsessed? Hmm ... I want to bring you to the period immediately preceding the National Bank robbery,' Moore says.

Like bare electric cables brought down in a storm, Eleanor can feel the raw nerve ends spark in her stomach. She reaches for a glass of water.

'Are you, all right, Mrs Proctor?' Moore asks.

Eleanor shakes her head. 'I feel a bit queasy.'

'Can we have a short adjournment, Your Honour?' Moore asks.

Ructions is in a consultation room with his barristers. 'What do you think?' he asks.

'Mrs Proctor's evidence was predictable,' Alan Hill says, 'but that doesn't make it any less potent. The facts at present are: she said you and she had been in a long-term relationship; she was able to pick you out, and, she alleges that you expressed an inordinate amount of interest in the National Bank. All that, in itself, would probably not be enough to convict, but it is damning as far as the jury is concerned. Will Mrs Proctor say she gave you the rotas?'

'I dare say she will.'

'That's not good,' Hill says, shaking his head, 'not good at all.' He looks through his briefcase and produces a large notebook. 'If Mrs Proctor sticks to her guns in regard to the rotas, we could be in real trouble.' Hill and Ructions stare at each other. 'There are times during the course of a trial,' Hill says, 'when we must be realistic, and, realistically, I can't see anything good coming out of Mrs Proctor saying she gave you the rotas – especially since you have made it clear you don't intend to take the witness stand to rebut her testimony.' Hill is clearly uneasy. 'What I'm about to say will not sit well with you, James, but I think, in light of the evidence Mrs Proctor has already given, and considering what you believe she will say, I think it would be prudent to consider changing your plea to guilty.' Hill studies Ructions' face for a reaction, but there is none. 'I can have a quiet word with the prosecution. I think, rather than expose Mrs Proctor to further cross-examination, the Public Prosecution Service might be up for giving you a reduced sentence were you to change your plea to guilty.'

Ructions resolutely shakes his head. 'Nope. No deal,' he says. 'Hit her with everything you've got.'

Finbarr O'Hare has been sworn in to give evidence at the court martial.

'So Mr Murdoch made you an offer?' Kevin Flynn asks. 'An offer you thought to be below the market value of your property?'

'Way below it,' Finbarr O'Hare says. 'Less than half its value.'

'But that's the way the property business operates, isn't it?' Flynn says. 'You put your price on the property, and I offer what I think is a reasonable price. I don't have to accept your valuation and you don't have to accept my offer.'

'But I did have to accept his offer,' Finbarr replies.

'You're telling the court that you accepted his offer, which you didn't think was reasonable?'

'That's exactly what I'm saying.'

'Why did you do that?'

'Because I thought it was an offer I couldn't refuse.'

'An offer you couldn't refuse? Did Mr Murdoch threaten you into accepting the offer?'

'Not in so many words.'

'In how many words did Mr Murdoch threaten you?'

'None.'

'Perhaps I misunderstand what you're saying – Mr Murdoch did not threaten you?'

'No, he didn't.'

'So someone made you an offer and you took it of your own free will? That's the reality, isn't it?' Flynn says.

'I suppose so,' Finbarr replies.

Flynn sits down.

The IRA prosecutor stands up again. 'Mr O'Hare, can you tell the court what you meant when you said, "Not in so many words"?'

'It was the way he made the offer. He told me if I wanted to live abroad, I'd be wise to sell the property to him.'

'How did you interpret that as a threat?'

Finbarr stares at Murdoch. 'I thought he was really saying that if I didn't sell the farm to him at his knock-down price, I mightn't be alive to go abroad.'

'Mrs Proctor,' Olivia Moore QC says, leaning back against the wooden partition, 'did you pass the National Bank staff rotas over to James O'Hare in the week before the National Bank robbery?'

'I did.'

The gravity of Eleanor's words reaches Ructions' legal team like an airborne virus. Clarke leans forward so that he can hear every word. Billy Kelly's wife whispers something in her husband's ear. Kelly nods.

Moore looks through some papers before returning to Eleanor. 'And did these rotas pertain to the staff shifts on the eighteenth of December 2004, the day of the National Bank robbery?'

'Yes, they did.'

'How do you know they did?'

'Because I examined them before I handed them over to him.'

'Why did you do that?'

'Because James ... sorry, Mr O'Hare, was interested in the shifts on that particular week.'

'And did Mr O'Hare tell you why he was interested in the staff shifts on that particular week?'

'Yes, he did. He said he wanted to rob the bank.'

'The National Bank?'

'Yes.'

'He told you he wanted the staff rotas so that he could rob the National Bank?'

'Yes, he did.'

'Did he tell you how he was going to rob it?'

'No.'

'Did you ask him?'

'I didn't want to know anything about it.'

Clarke sits back in his seat, folds his arms and crosses his legs. *It doesn't get any better than this*. He looks at Ructions, who, feeling the strength of the stare, turns his head towards Clarke. Clarke smiles. Ructions does not return the smile.

'Call Colm Coleman,' the IRA prosecutor says.

Murdoch gulps. He feels as if a nail bomb has just exploded in his stomach.

O'Flaherty witnesses the change in Murdoch's countenance. 'Are you all right, Oglach Murdoch? Do you need a break?'

Murdoch shakes his head. 'I'm ... I'm fine. I'm okay.'

THIRTY

Alan Hill SC has been questioning Eleanor for over an hour. Sometimes his line of questioning has been mundane and at other times it has been very condemnatory.

'Did you often break into your husband's files on his computer?'

'No.'

'Did you know his password?'

'No.'

'But you were able to access his computer?'

'Yes.'

'How?'

'When he had a drink on him, he sometimes forgot to turn off the computer.'

'And on a particular night you say you sneaked in and retrieved the rotas?'

'Yes.'

'Mrs Proctor, when it boils right down to it, we've only your word that you did sneak in, haven't we? You could be making this all up, couldn't you?'

'I'm not.'

'So you say, but I'm right, aren't I? We have only your word for it that your husband was so drunk he forgot to turn off his computer and, consequently, you recovered the staff rotas?'

'I don't accept that. The police told me they discovered the rotas had been accessed when they examined the computer.'

'I'm aware of Chief Superintendent Clarke's testimony to this court and I don't dispute that *someone* accessed your husband's files. My problem is this: your husband testified that he couldn't remember whether or not *he* had accessed the rotas.'

'He didn't.'

'But you don't know that,' Hill says curtly. 'Were you standing over him every minute when he was on the computer?'

'No, I wasn't.'

'So he could have accessed the rotas. I come back to my point: we have only your word for it that you accessed the rotas on your husband's computer?'

'You can come back to your point all day long, sir,' Eleanor says defiantly, 'but the facts won't change. I did access my husband's computer, I did access the staff rotas and I did give them over to James O'Hare.'

The relationship with her husband Frank was raised. 'Were you angry with your husband for having an affair with another woman, a younger woman?' Hill asks.

'Yes.'

'When did that affair end?'

'About ten years ago.'

'Ten years ago. Have you had sex with your husband since then?'

Moore objects but the judge deems the line of questioning relevant.

'Have you had sex with your husband since you found out he was having an affair?'

'No.'

'Why not?'

'I couldn't bare him to touch me.'

'I see. You felt betrayed by your husband's infidelity?'

'I did.'

'And you were very angry?'

'Yes.'

'So much so that you wanted revenge? Is revenge the reason why you were open to having an affair with the accused?'

'No.'

'But your husband humiliated you, did he not?'

'Yes, he did. But that was a long time ago. We became friends again.' Eleanor's voice drops to mere whisper. 'It suited us both that way.'

Colm Coleman sits within feet of Tiny Murdoch, but he does not look him in the eye.

'Let us be clear about this, Oglach Coleman,' the IRA prosecutor says. 'Oglach Murdoch ordered you to arrange the burning of O'Reilly's portacabin in 1998?'

'Yes.'

'And you understood this to be an IRA operation?'

'I did.'

'Did it cross your mind that this operation had more to do with Oglach Murdoch lining his own pockets than with advancing the aims and objectives of the IRA?'

'It did not. I was given an order and I carried it out.'

'I'd like to come to another matter. Do you know Finbarr O'Hare?'

'Yes. He's a known paedophile from Belfast.'

'Did you arrange to have Finbarr O'Hare arrested?'

'Yes.'

'Who gave you the order to arrest O'Hare?'

'Oglach Murdoch.'

'Are you aware that that order did not come from the Army Council, that it came solely from Oglach Murdoch?'

'I wasn't when I carried it out.'

'Why do you think Oglach Murdoch had Finbarr O'Hare arrested?'

'He'd found out that O'Hare was a paedophile and he hates paedophiles. Also, he saw an opportunity to put pressure on Panzer O'Hare.'

'Panzer O'Hare is Finbarr O'Hare's father?'

'Yes.'

'But why would Oglach Murdoch want to put pressure on Panzer O'Hare?'

'He was always going on about what he would do if he owned Panzer's farm and how he would open a stud farm there. I think he saw an opportunity and had Finbarr arrested in order to get Panzer to hand over the farm to him at a knock-down price.'

'So he used the IRA to enrich himself?'

'Yes.'

Alan Hill scratches his temple. He waits before asking a question. 'Did you know that while the accused was going out with you, he was living with another woman, a younger woman, a Ms Maria McArdle?'

'Yes.'

'And you were comfortable with that arrangement?'

'No, I wasn't.'

'But you were prepared to tolerate it?'

'I was not,' Eleanor declares. 'I told him in no uncertain terms to finish with her.'

'And did he?'

'He told me he had finished with her.'

'When was this? Before or after the bank robbery?'

'Before.'

'And you believed him?'

'Yes. He told me she had moved to South America after he'd broken up with her.'

'Do you still believe him?'

'Pardon?'

'Do you still believe he has broken up with Ms McArdle?'

'No.'

'So you think they're still together?'

'Yes.'

'Indeed.' Hill lifts some loose pages, peruses them and then looks at Eleanor. 'It was happening all over again, wasn't it?'

'I'm sorry?'

'I said it was happening all over again. For a second time, someone you loved was betraying you. While the accused was stringing you along for access to rotas, he was planning a life with

Maria McArdle – his one, true love – in South America. But you weren't going to sit back and take it this time. No man – never mind James O'Hare – was going to get away with humiliating you. You'd been used and abused by one man too many. Isn't it the case that you were going to strike back, to get revenge?'

'He's a bastard,' Eleanor says under her breath.

'I beg your pardon? Mrs Proctor? What did you just say?'

'Nothing.'

'No, you did say something. What did you say?'

Eleanor's head turns towards Ructions. 'I said he's a bastard.' She raises her voice. 'He's a bastard.'

'You hate James O'Hare, don't you?'

'Yes.'

'I put it to you, Mrs Proctor,' Hill says, 'that you were a woman scorned, a woman who had been doubly shamed, by your husband and then by James O'Hare. I put it to you, Mrs Proctor, that you invented this ridiculous story about giving my client the staff rotas to get revenge on a man whom you considered to be a love rat: a man whose only crime was that he promised you the world and delivered only heartache. You wanted revenge, didn't you?'

'No, I did not want revenge.'

'You did not give him the rotas, Mrs Proctor.'

'I did.'

'You wanted revenge, didn't you, Mrs Proctor?'

Eleanor raises her head. 'Yes! Yes, I did! He's a two-timing bastard!'

'And you didn't give him the rotas, did you?'

Eleanor looks dazed.

'You didn't give him the rotas, did you, Mrs Proctor?'

Eleanor's head drops. She maintains a sniffled silence.

'Will you please answer the question, Mrs Proctor,' Hill insists. 'Did you give Mr O'Hare the rotas?'

Eleanor still stays silent.

Hill says, 'Mrs Proctor, have you heard of the term perjury? That is a criminal offence which occurs when you lie in court.'

Eleanor is unmoved.

Hill looks to the bench. 'Your honour ...'

'Mrs Proctor,' the judge says, 'you will answer counsel's question.'

'No,' Eleanor says in a voice that is barely audible. 'No. I didn't give him the rotas. I never saw the rotas.'

'And so that we may be absolutely clear – as far as you're concerned, Mr O'Hare is innocent of the charge of robbing the Northern Bank?'

'No! No! No! I know he robbed it! He did it. He's a thief! He's—'

'But you didn't give him the rotas.'

'You're twisting my–'

'That will be all, Mrs Proctor.'

Eleanor Proctor leaves the witness box.

'Your Honour,' Hill says, turning towards the bench, 'in light of Mrs Proctor's evidence, I move that all charges against my client be dismissed.'

Ructions yelps and jumps up. Clarke covers his face with his hands. Billy Kelly punches the air.

There is silence in the IRA court as an audio is played: 'I tell ya, Colm, this dickhead O'Flaherty has got to go. Court-martialling me! Me! Who the fuck does he think he is?'

Coleman's voice is heard to say: 'It's fucking crazy, Tiny.'

Murdoch looks at O'Flaherty. He detects a glint in his eye, or is that a smirk at the end of his lips?

The recording is fast-forwarded. Coleman's voice is once again heard: 'What do you mean "O'Flaherty has got to go", Tiny? Go where?'

'You know.'

'You've got me, boss. Go where?'

'We need to get rid of him. He's still thinks this is 1972.'

'You're not thinking of stiffing him, are you?'

'Course not. Well, not unless I have to.'

Murdoch leaps to his feet and puts his two hands around Coleman's throat. 'You treacherous little scumbag!' Murdoch yells.

Three IRA men try to pull Murdoch's arms away from Coleman's throat, but Murdoch holds on. Coleman's face is getting redder and his lips are turning blue.

'Die, you fucker, you ...' Murdoch hisses, saliva bubbling on his lips.

Paul O'Flaherty calmly opens a drawer and takes out an expandable baton. He flicks it open, walks around the table and smacks Murdoch over the back of his head. Murdoch still holds on. O'Flaherty pulls back slowly above his head and again brings it down hard on his head. Murdoch's hands slacken, and he collapses on top of Coleman.

It is almost three o'clock in the afternoon when a delighted Ructions and his legal team stream out of court. Apart from those involved in the National Bank robbery trial, the foyer is empty. Ructions shakes hands with his defence team. Billy Kelly and his wife come over and Ructions throws his arms around his friend. Kevin R. Summers chats with Alan Hill SC.

From another exit, Chief Superintendent Clarke and his subordinates emerge. Amongst Clarke's entourage is Eleanor Proctor. She has a tissue in her hand and has obviously been crying. Clarke sits her down on a seat. 'I'm sorry, Mr Clarke,' Eleanor says. 'I wanted him put away. He robbed that bank. I know it.'

'Don't worry about it. These things happen.'

'Will I be charged with perjury, Mr Clarke?'

'I very much doubt it. A file will have to be sent to the PPS, but I can't see them acting on it. It's not in the public interest.'

Tiny Murdoch is handcuffed. Two IRA men put him into the back seat of a jeep and stand guard at the doors. Paul O'Flaherty comes over and waves the guards away. He leans into the jeep. 'You're lucky I'm a forgiving man, Tiny. You got off lightly.'

'I forfeit my businesses, and I'm getting whacked in the two kneecaps. You call that getting off lightly, Paul?'

'If it hadn't been for me, you'd be getting one in the back of the head. And you're only getting flesh wounds.'

'Why did you do it, Paul? I thought you were my friend.'

O'Flaherty holds up two fingers. 'Two reasons: you were using the name of the IRA to feather your own nest.'

'I'm hardly the first and I won't be the last to do that. And the second reason?'

'Panzer O'Hare.'

'What about him?'

'Panzer was my friend. I knew him long before I knew you. Not only that, but I used to billet in his farmhouse in the seventies when I was on the run. And he held gear for us, not just when the Libyan shipments came in, but on many other occasions. He came to me and spilled his heart out.'

'I don't know what you're talking about,' Murdoch says.

'Oh, I think you do. You're a disgrace to republicanism, Tiny, and you should count yourself lucky you're walking out of this alive.' O'Flaherty turns and walks away.

Finbarr O'Hare walks out of the house, escorted by a burly IRA man.

'Hey! Paul,' Murdoch says.

O'Flaherty turns around.

'You're going to shoot *me* and you're letting that paedophile walk?'

O'Flaherty looks at Finbarr with disdain. 'He's not going to be walking for a long time. He's going with you.'

'You're not having him shot alongside me? Paul, don't do that to me. Blow my knees off, blow my fuckin' head off if you want, but don't have me shot beside a paedo. Not that.'

O'Flaherty walks away.

Colm Coleman appears at the entrance to the cottage with a phone to his ear. He walks towards the jeep that holds his former boss. 'There's a fella here wants to talk to you.' Coleman puts the phone to Murdoch's ear.

Murdoch is puzzled. 'What the fuck's this?'

A soft voice says, 'You're up to your neck in the brown stuff now, Tiny.'

'Who's this?'

'You know me as "the Horsey-Man's sidekick".'

'What the fuck! I thought you were—'

'Going down for the robbery?' Ructions says, glancing towards Clarke, who is taking a great interest in him as he makes his call. 'Not a chance. I've just been acquitted. Aren't you going to congratulate me?'

'So you and Coleman—'

Ructions walks into a corner. 'CC and me go way back, Tiny. We were apprentice bank robbers. We did jobs together. I know his whole family. I used to go out with his sister, Isobel. Didn't you know that?'

'No, I didn't. Was he in your pocket all along?'

'Not at all. He was your man till you tried to have me whacked at Carlingford. That was a bad mistake.'

'Was the turncoat easily paid?'

'Sure what's a few quid when you've tens of millions?'

'You won't have tens of millions for long.'

'And who's gonna take it off me? You? You're about to be kneecapped, pal, and I'm about to go on a year-long world cruise.'

'It's not over, asshole. I'll—'

'You'll take the bullets and you'll grin and bear it.'

'Oh, I'll grin and bear it, don't you worry about me, dickhead.'

'I won't. You know you made the capital mistake, don't you?'

'And you'd know about capital mistakes, would you?'

'I know enough not to let greed cloud my judgement.'

'You? You're going to lecture me about greed? The only difference between you and me, *pal*, is that you got lucky — this time.'

'Luck's got fuck all to do with it. The difference between you and me is this: I'd the wit to pay the ferryman. You hadn't. You could've dropped CC a few quid, but no, you wanted all the loot for yourself.'

Coleman takes the phone away from Murdoch's ear.

Murdoch points a finger at Coleman. 'You're fucked, Coleman. You take it from me – you are totally fucked.'

'Are you threatening an IRA volunteer, Tiny?'

'Threatening you?' Murdoch finds it impossible to hold back his loathing for his former comrade. 'I'm going to bury you alive in a coffin before this is over. And I'm gonna empty a sackful of starvin' rats into that coffin, just to keep you company.'

Coleman takes an audio tape out of his pocket and holds it up. He rewinds the tape and pushes the play button. Tiny's voice is clear: 'Threatening you? I'm gonna bury you alive in a coffin before ...'

Coleman dramatically thrusts the audio recorder in Murdoch's face. 'Is there anything else you want to say, Mr Murdoch?' Coleman speaks into the audio recorder. 'Mr Murdoch has nothing else to say.' Coleman puts the recorder in his pocket and says, 'That's twice your big mouth has got you into trouble.'

Ructions chuckles as he hangs up on Tiny Murdoch. Suddenly he spots Mickey McArdle about to exit the courthouse. He catches the older man's eye and mouths a thank you. McArdle tips his flat cap in acknowledgement and slips out the door. Ructions remembers shooting golf balls with Panzer up the Black Mountain and suddenly misses him. He would have enjoyed today. *You were right, Panzer. The McArdles are good stock. Old Mickey came through, and Maria ... she was brilliant. I'll see them both right for this.* He looks over at Eleanor, who is now standing alone. He smiles at her. She returns the smile. Clarke catches this subtle exchange out of the corner of his eye, and his eyebrows almost meet. He turns, head cocked. His stare darts between the two and finally rests on Ructions. Ructions nods to him, an acknowledgement that defies the spoken word. Clarke's expression remains stoic. He walks over to Ructions and puts his hand on his shoulder.

'You must think you're really clever, you fuckin' reprobate. You planned the whole thing – right down to Eleanor's confession.'

'I don't know what you're talking about, Mr Clarke.'

'Come on now, Ructions, you know exactly what I'm talking about,' Clarke snarls. Suddenly he smiles, turns towards Eleanor and beckons her over.

Eleanor approaches somewhat cautiously.

'I'm surprised at you, Mrs Proctor,' Clarke says. His smile disappears as quickly as it had appeared.

'Why, Mr Clarke?' Eleanor is startled by his change in demeanour.

'You've made a fool of me.'

'I ... I don't understand.'

'Oh, I think you do. I don't think I can reopen this case at present or have you charged with perjury, but I won't forget this.'

Eleanor bows her head. 'Mr Clarke, it's not what you think.'

'It's exactly what I think.'

Ructions puts his lips to Clarke's ear and says, 'Do you remember what I told you when I first presented myself in Grosvenor Road to be arrested?'

'Remind me,' Clarke says.

'I said I'd been having dinner with two old friends?'

It is coming back to Clarke. 'You said: "Lucifer always wins".'

'Correct.'

Ructions and Eleanor walk towards the exit.

'You played a blinder, El,' Ructions says proudly.

'Didn't I just,' Eleanor replies.

'Hey, Ructions!' Clarke shouts.

Ructions looks over his shoulder.

'It's not over.'

'Funny, you're the second person to say that to me today. Don't know why.' Ructions smiles and waves a jaunty goodbye.

EPILOGUE

It is two years to the day after the National Bank robbery, and a thick layer of snow covers Belfast. In the Butler household, Alec places another two pieces of turf on the fire. Declan leaves his father and the heat to answer a knock on the front door. When he opens it, an immaculately dressed man stands before him. Declan's mouth opens. 'You!' he exclaims.

'Hello, Dec,' Ructions says.

Declan puts up his arms defensively and steps back inside the hall. 'Jack. No, Ructions. Which is it?'

'Both.'

'I'll phone the cops.'

'No, you won't,' Ructions says sternly. 'The cops tried to stitch you up. You'll not help them. Besides, how helpful do you think you'd be? You never saw my face.'

How do I handle this? Suddenly, from a spring that he did not know existed, Declan draws the courage to grab Ructions by the lapels of his black Armani overcoat. 'You ... you lowlife shit-shoveller,' Declan says, pulling back his fist to punch Ructions.

Ructions tilts his head upwards. 'Go on, son. I'll not stop you. A dig on the chin is the least I deserve from you. Get on with it.'

Declan hesitates and releases his grip on Ructions. 'You're not worth breaking a knuckle on, you dirty bastard.' Declan hears a noise and looks behind him. 'Here's my Dad. Say nothing.'

Alec pops his head out the living-room door and looks at the visitor and his son with a mixture of curiosity and uncertainty. He can't see clearly who it is but senses something is off. 'Is everything all right, son?' he says. 'Who's that?'

'Oh, it's only Phil, Dad. Old mate from the bank. I'll be in in a minute.'

'Is that so?' Alec says. 'Do you want to come in for a cup of tea?'

'No thanks, Mr Butler. I was just saying to Dec, we'd some good times in the bank. I really enjoyed my time there.'

'So did Declan until ...' Alec hesitates. 'Well, good luck, Phil.' He closes the living-room door.

'Before I forget, Dec, congratulations on beating the charge. Getting a separate trial from me was important. Your lawyers did well there.'

'You can stick your congratulations up your arse,' Declan says. 'You put that man and my family through hell. Do you know something? My father's a good man; he's a hundred times the man you'll ever be.'

'I don't dispute that,' Ructions says. 'For what it's worth, I'm sorry.'

'Are you? Are you really sorry? If you were ...' Declan searches for the right words. 'If you'd been cleaned out by the police – if all your money was confiscated, would you do it all again?'

Ructions has to stop and think before answering. He plunges his hands into the pockets of his overcoat and nods. 'Yes, yes, I think I would.'

'So you're not sorry – not really. You're only saying you're sorry because it's the right thing to say right now. Isn't that it?' Declan points down the driveway. 'You know what? Fuck off. Go on, get away to fuck from this door.'

Ructions just stares at Declan. 'I made you a promise,' he says flatly.

'You what? A promise? What the fuck are you on about *Jack*?'

'I've come to give you back your Aston Villa holdall.'

'That's it?' *The cheek of this prick – coming back to my house, standing there with that stupid holdall.* 'Can you give me back my life? Can you stop the whispering, and the finger-pointing, and the sniggering whenever I go the doctor's or the dentist's or out for a pint? Can you tell everybody I wasn't the inside man, because they all think I was?'

Ructions holds up the holdall.

Declan looks at it as if it contains nuclear waste.

'Go on, take your bag,' Ructions urges. 'It's yours.'

Declan does not move.

Ructions sets the bag inside the door and says, 'You came through, Dec. You did okay. Merry Christmas.' He turns and walks away.

Declan watches as Ructions trudges through the snow towards the front gate. It's snowing heavily now. Declan closes the door and brings the holdall into the living room.

Alec glances warily at Declan. His eyes travel to the holdall. Instinctively, he hauls himself up on his chair. 'Holy Jesus and His Blessed Mother! It's the Aston Villa—'

'Dad—'

'Then your man was—'

'Jack.' The father and son exchange glances as Declan sets the bag down on the sofa. 'Maybe we should phone the police, Dad.'

'Maybe we should look in the bag first,' Alec replies.

Declan nods.

Alec tentatively unzips the holdall, puts in his hand and takes out bundles of fifty-pound notes. He breaks the paper seals, fans the money in his hands and mutters, 'Holy Christ … there must be … there must be a million quid in here.'

Wide-eyed and mouth agape, Declan can barely find his voice. 'Yes.' He shakes his head incredulously. 'Yes! Dad, I'd bet my life on it. There's exactly a million quid in that bag. Not a penny more, not a penny less.' Alec empties the holdall onto the sofa. Bundles of money spill to the floor. Declan can't help but smile as he remembers Ructions' words in Ringland Street: 'When this is all over, kid, I'm going to drop you a few quid.' *So you did, Jack. You kept your word.*

Declan looks at his father. 'What should we do, Dad? Should we call the police?'

Both men turn and look at the phone on the sideboard. 'Let's not rush into anything, son.'

ACKNOWLEDGMENTS

I had almost finished *Northern Heist* in 2012, but it still wasn't right, so I shelved it to begin work on another book, *In the Name of the Son: The Gerry Conlon Story*, which was published in October 2017. Not long afterwards, at the prompting of my daughter, Berni, I rewrote and finished the first draft of *Northern Heist*. I can't thank Berni enough for her encouragement.

I would like to thank the Northern Ireland Arts Council for the help they gave me in writing this book.

I am indebted to David Torrens of No Alibis bookshop, Eoin McNamee and Malachi O'Doherty.

A big thanks to Conor Graham of Merrion Press, who saw the value in the book. I would also like to thank his staff, especially Fiona Dunne.

I would like to express my appreciation to a wonderful editor, Maria McGuinness.

I am much obliged to Peter O'Connell Media for the sterling work they carried out in publicising this book.

To my literary agent, Jonathan Williams, I convey my deepest gratefulness.

I would like to thank my friend, Dennis Johnson, and all the team at Melville House for their hard work in publishing this book. Decent, honorable people.

My family, as ever, were unreservedly supportive. To my wife Bernadette, daughters Stephanie and Berni, and son Conchúr, I send my love and warmest gratitude.

The next RUCTIONS O'HARE novel by

RICHARD O'RAWE

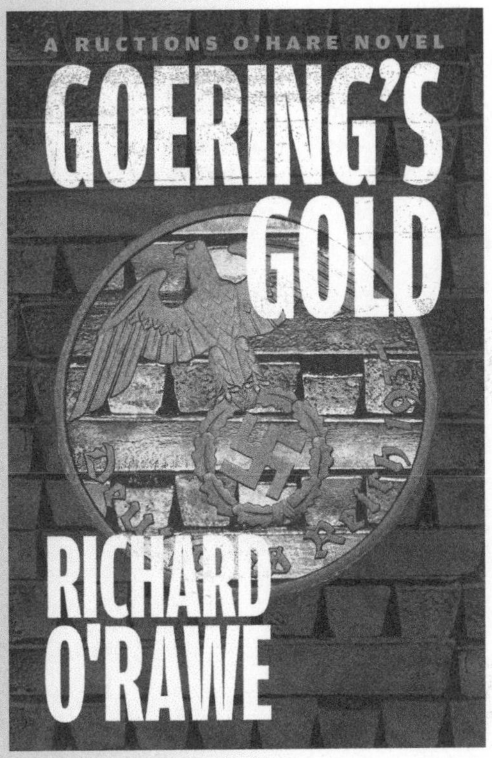

Ructions O'Hare learns that — as real-life historians speculate actually occured — Nazi leader Hermann Goering hid a huge stash of plundered gold bullion in Ireland during World War II. However Ructions will have to once again outwit the IRA, and a band of neo-Nazi killers, to find it. As the *Wall Street Journal* said of *Northern Heist, Goering's Gold* is "full of double- and triple-crosses," as well as "stopwatch tension."

COMING MAY 2022